The Power of Love

The Three

R.J. Kinnaird

ISBN: 978-1-7394634-6-5

For more info on The Power of Love Series®

thepowerofloveseries.com

First edition: August 2024

First Print: August 2024

Edited by Imogen Howson

Cover by Ardel Media

To Imogen,

As the writing journey of an ordinary man extended beyond his dreams, you took faith in it, enhanced it, lifted it to heights of an impossible reach.
There, where lay a raw mix of talent and failure, you patiently observed the potential of a quiet voice and made sure it would be heard.
Thank you.

To the ones who believed in The Power of Love Series,
To the ones who felt close to Daniel, Anita, and Noah,
To those who not only wanted to see more LGBTQIA+ representation in books but believed in a gay relationship at the center of the entire saga, I say thank you.

May the Power of Love be with you,
ALWAYS

CONTENTS

Chapter One
The Beginning

∞

Since the very moment I came into existence, I felt the magnitude of my energy—the unreachable limits of our mother's magic. I knew how strong we were together and how much power we truly held once again, when Soul, Health, and Time came back to life. And yet, a simple Human being haunted my heart as if it were the only thing that mattered. If I had possessed my brother's magic, I would have known how a soul could enchant a God, magnetize his will. Instead, I faced the discovery alone, against the odds, risking the fate of the entire universe. One soul, Daniel's soul, drove me insane. His heart, his dreams, his connections with the ones he loved whispered of an unbreakable bond. There, at the turning of the tide, at the tipping point between existence and demise, his soul saved me, saved us all.

Throughout centuries and millennia, my true nature and existence had been forgotten. My being, my pure essence, had been overwritten by Human history, replaced by their traditions, myths, and legends. What I once was, transformed into fairy tales, religions, and fantasy. The prolonged absence of my magic, along with the disappearance of my Awoken Ones, aided in the process of eradication, extinguishing every spark of truth from their minds and hearts.

Cherish, the Awoken of Memory and Preservation, had long since departed, and in the last thirteen thousand years, every piece of history had been lost. I failed to return so many times that Humans learned to rely on their own creations, slowly falling under the malevolent influence of the many Harpies roaming the Earth. Death, the king of all evil, had turned mankind's almost immortal destiny into a fleeting moment in the eternal sequence of life. With him, his army ravaged the world, initiating wars, pain, and sorrow across the planet.

Little did the Humans know their story had been rewritten hundreds of time, their history buried and lost under layers of soil. Their once-lush cities had been turned to dust, their stunning achievement brought forth by me and the Awokens became the foundation of new generations who had no memory of what it had been, who kept rising to a life weaker and emptier than the previous ones. Every living creature and every matter created by the one God who had rebelled against the never-ending nothingness were forced into a constant reboot, during which the forces of evil grew stronger each time.

My story, everyone's story, truly began when Creation, the one who was born out of cosmic power, the one who had woken up to consciousness, came to be. Like a spark of energy in the depth of pure emptiness, she pierced the very fabric of the universe. In a single flicker of power she became the pure essence of defiance. To Nothing's everlasting dominion, she became a challenge, a subverting force to his silent ruling.

In the beginning, before time could even be, the two entities lived in a delicate balance, an intricate duality of light and darkness, night and day, life and death. They lived untouched, they dismissed one another's presence until the moment I came to be.

Compelled to be more, to exist in many forms, Creation brought to life a few worlds, Earth, Varayal, Talush, and Runae. They were formed at the four corners of the universe, while she sat at its centre, a point of magical gravitation for everything and everyone who defied the darkness of Nothing. The long, silent emptiness was no more. Creation's act of making soon would become an act of war, as she usurped Nothing's rightful place as sovereign, harnessing the immense power of being and making.

The worlds, creatures, and everything she had crafted became a source of pride, a cherished treasure, taking a form of its own, unleashing a spell of pure attraction towards its own maker. As Creation observed the beauty of her own cosmos, she became aware of a new surging power within herself. She fell in love with the very life she had brought forth. The intensity of that newfound power sought its own existence, detaching from her and coming into its own realization. It was then that a new God was formed. In that very moment, I came to exist.

Creation had finally found a companion, a son to cherish, someone who could bear the vastness of this new power on her behalf. I was crowned as the God of Love, the one who could embody the powerful emotions of my mother, the personification of why she had dared to challenge the dark enemy. My sole existence gave more than meaning; it transformed Creation's work into a weapon.

Nothing, the untouched, the timeless king of silence and emptiness, awoke to a new revelation. The balance of the universe had been disrupted; Creation had cheated in a game that he had conceded for too long. With two equally powerful Gods now standing against him, the gentle breeze of defiance had transformed into a storm. In Nothing's eyes, my own manifestation was an act of war.

However, if this deception was already known, the King of Emptiness was blind to a greater threat taking shape. If worlds and their inhabitants could be loved and cherished, then more was yet to come. In our deep desire to make our creations immortal, my mother and I gave rise to a third God. Health appeared to grant the people of every planet the strength of their makers. Their flesh and bones were made strong, their bodies perfected, physically equipped to face an eternal life. Soon after, Soul came to be. His duty was to bestow upon life the gift of consciousness. Every living being could finally possess a will of their own, the ability to think, to dream, to create. Lastly, Time was born. Suddenly, there was a past to be remembered, a present to be nurtured, and a future to be preserved.

The pantheon of Gods and our powers spread across the vast unknown universe, encroaching upon Nothing's dominion, usurping his lands. His tranquil, silent throne was now under an unacceptable menace. If we had continued our ceaseless creation, his true existence would be relegated to a forgotten memory. Wrathful and resolute in restoring the rightful balance, the obscure master marshalled his forces for battle. As everything we had done encroached upon his doorstep, he had no other choice but to annihilate our very existence. There wasn't going to be room for division or duality between what had been and what was going to be. Nothing reclaimed his absolute control. Whatever had caused Creation and her children to exist was inconsequential. The King of Emptiness would be radical and final. Every single act of existence had to be extinguished.

Around the time Humans referred to as fifteen thousand B.C., a gathering of Gods, a ritual we had maintained for millennia, commenced on Earth. For the hundred and first time, we convened again, exchanging stories, consulting on recent developments. Health and Soul engaged in a spirited conversation, while Time silently observed the discourse.

'I understand Talush is situated close to the enemy, but we cannot leave our worlds unprotected.' Time finally spoke, gazing from a large opening in an enormous room. In front of him the distant horizon opened up wide; his eyes pointed to the sun as it gently caressed the sea's soft skin. His radiant figure challenged the grandeur of the celestial star, casting a trail of sparkling lights upon the tranquil waters. 'We all have our own evil growing within our very homes.'

'If we remain divided, we will surely lose,' Soul countered.

'We must unite once and for all. Together!' Health pushed against our brother's resistance. 'One by one, he will claim us all.'

'And what will happen when we mobilize together while his armies of scavengers raid our worlds? We may be challenging him, but he already has his pawns in place everywhere. Murmurs stir in the shadows of the Cloudy Mountains, and I keep failing to see how to prevent them from spreading across the lands. Runae is currently holding its ground against the forces of evil, and it will continue to do so as long as I remain vigilant by its side.' Time refused to yield.

'I must agree,' I chimed in, taking the others by surprise. They had gathered within my own house, my planet, as guests in my home, but I had kept quiet, my worries taking control of my mind. I gazed down from the towering heights of the secret meeting place, my eyes fixed on the Humans far below. 'This world is falling under the tightening grip of the one we dare not speak of. I cannot see him, but I can witness his influence more frequently now. I have come to realize that I cannot control it as a singular being. I need to do more. I need to be more.'

'What do you mean?' Soul drew nearer, placing his hands on my shoulders, sensing a burgeoning power.

'I believe I have discovered a way to be present in all places at once, to be everywhere that matters. I can manifest myself out of my own essence, much like our own mother. I can generate new embodiments of myself,' I explained, turning around to meet Health's gaze.

'This is incredible! You can actually give birth to new lives within yourself?' Health marvelled at the possibility.

'This is madness!' Soul thundered. 'This is too great a risk. If you are truly considering dividing your essence among others, you are not creating, you are unmaking!'

'I don't fully understand what all of you are discussing,' Time interjected as he joined us in the open space. The brilliance of our light far surpassed that of the sun.

'Love is attempting to forge more Gods by partitioning his power among many.' Soul's expression carried the weight of a deep concern. His crystal face turned hazy, as if the light of the sun had been lost behind heavy clouds. 'This is not the power of Creation; it is the antithesis. You are diminishing yourself into smaller replicas, each possessing less power.'

'If Love believes this is necessary to protect this world, so be it,' Time proclaimed. He had suddenly found in my words a way to justify his stance. If I chose to remain and defend Earth, it aligned perfectly with Time's desired outcome. Secretly, he too had embraced the idea of bestowing his power upon those who would aid him in his quest. Somewhere within Runae, a spark of Creation's power awaited discovery in the depths of the large Mog, waiting to be unearthed, brought into the light, and transformed into Flares. If he succeeded, his people would possess the power of their own God.

'Whatever this magic will do, it will require Mother's approval,' Soul had just used his last resource to close the argument once and for all.

We had to wait no longer to know if my idea was birthed by madness, to know if we had to protect our planets or merge our efforts to save Talush; the answers came to us fast. In the opening between time and space, a long, flickering line appeared in the air, top to bottom, like a cut through matter and reality. Creation walked into our level of existence, bringing the pure power of a fortifying smile. With her rounded face and large eyes, she infused the gathering with an edifying force. As she moved in between us, silence followed. We all waited for her to speak, and just beside her, respect walked around the room.

'You all are right…' she started; her voice was soft, almost musical, '…and you all are wrong. We need to accept the idea that we won't be avoiding this battle any longer, and we need to accept we have enemies within our ranks, among our loved ones.' And she briefly smiled at me.

'So, what do we do, Mother?' Health asked.

'We stand at our positions, ready to fight. I will face the evil myself if he moves any closer. As Love said, there is a way to do more and to be more…' At that remark, Soul turned his gaze away from mine. As he embodied the power of one mind, one spirit, he struggled to accept the idea of partitioning our essence among many. 'Each one of you will find your own way to do so, ' Creation continued. 'In the meantime, I'll be the one leading the fight, pushing Nothing back to his empty dominion.'

'He is very close to Talush.' My sister was worried still. 'Little we'll have to wait before he strikes.'

'This is what he wants us to believe,' Creation replied. 'He is close to your world indeed, but in the dark of his eternal mind, he is also plotting and conspiring across the four corners of the universe. He is already setting the field for his next moves. If he strikes Talush, it won't be long before he moves against Varayal, Runae and Earth. Some he might even try at once, I'm afraid.'

'We need to strengthen our position, Mother,' I let out.

'And you will. All of you. Make sure your homes are filled with the very nature of your powers. Make sure those worlds will fight with us, if and when the time comes.'

It wasn't long before we had come to an agreement. Eventually, under the leadership of our trusted maker, my brothers and my sister left, back to their strongholds. In the silence of a warm afternoon, with a dying sun sealing the secrecy of an upcoming revelation, our mother delayed her parting and gave me a new, different lead.

'It's time for me to leave and keep a close watch on your sister's lands. I didn't want to worry her more than she already is, but she's right—Nothing is getting closer to Talush. However, before I do that, there's something I need to tell you…'

'What is it?' My attention was fully on her.

'You have been with me longer than the others. You have been by my side in the making of many things, including your brothers and sister. And even then, you have never walked the skies with pride or arrogance. You have been existing as a giver, a maker of your own. You were right in saying there is more you can do; there is more you can be...but it's not what you think it is, not just that, at least.'

'Why do I have the feeling you're about to create something again?' I was dancing around my words, almost mirroring the way we were circling the tower.

'There is a way of holding on to your powers and on to your very existence through something permanent. Something that cannot be fully destroyed. It's made of matter like everything we have made. It can be turned to dust, burnt, consumed by dark magic, but it cannot be put out. Like the very dying flames under hot ashes, your fire can be reignited again, in case any of you should succumb to the evil.'

'Through transformation, every part of us can move from being one thing and being something new, but never entirely dissolved,' I recited, recalling old memories. 'I do remember, Mother. Nothing can be truly destroyed, only changed.'

'This is the power that will stand against Him.' Creation came close and held my hands. Her eyes flickered. 'This magic can be used to tame his evil will, if I find a way to master a spell powerful enough to contain my own energy…'

'So, you mean our core being held in custody by some form of amulet, something that will channel our coming back from death?' I was reaching the solution fast.

'Yes. But those would be just a way through. The hard part is to find a way to make this magic spell permanent. Making you immortal through something that will absorb your energy to then release it again.'

'In other words, instead of matter being transformed into something else entirely, following the law of making, our energy would be transferred to those objects. Then, it would release it back to us to reform the very being that we once were?' I knew the laws of existence well. Whatever new magic my mother was about to unfold, it was risky.

'I think I know, deep down, a way to make it possible. But before that, I need you to help me in creating those artefacts.' And Creation released the grip on my hands, moving away.

'There is something else, isn't there?' I asked, following her out onto the open terrace. The cold night had approached fast.

'I might need more from you than we both realize now. But, as your brother would say, there is no need to put tomorrow's worries on today's burden.'

And with those words, our mother vanished in the same soft, warm way she had walked in, her brief smile leaving the scene. In the silence of the high tower, I was left alone, my mind puzzled, my heart beating fast.

If a few millennia had passed, for the five of us time had come in an instant. Through the unfolding of our present and future, the moment when our fate was going to be bound to our artefacts had come. Not long before the dark king would place his hands on Talush, our mother and I made our next move. In the depths of the universe, in a place the Humans of the future would call the Andromeda Galaxy, we set our eyes on a precise spot. A gigantic cluster of dense matter flashed in the silent space. Its power containing the one of Creation, it was going to fuel the force that would forge the secret weapons.

'It took me a long time to finally come to master it, but we are ready now.' Creation had just appeared like a shining dot in the dark space. Beside her, I followed suit, silent. 'It does require two things. The power of a cosmic explosion to forge them and a spell of sacrifice to seal them.'

'To sacrifice what?' I was afraid I already knew the answer.

'To infuse your essence in them and make it possible for you to come back, a piece of me has to be given. A trigger, a spark of making to initiate the regeneration of a God. But you know that already…' And my mother smiled. 'You have done the same with your Awoken Ones. They indeed have a piece of you.'

'It didn't feel like a sacrifice…' I replied, challenged.

'It never does, when we believe it's the right and only thing to do. Now, we move to our final, vital step. I will increase the fusion of the protostar you see in front of us over its limit. It will release a staggering amount of energy. It's important you stand firm, as your hands will form the relics.'

'Mother…' I whispered, hesitant. 'How do I know what to make?'

'You have made the other Gods. You and me together. You know what they are made of; you know what should be retaining their powers. Now, let's proceed. Hold tight!'

As Creation moved further away, her hands opened to the sides, her power started to flow around her body, making it shine. Right in front of her, something else came to life. A pulsating miniature of the same star we were about to turn supernova appeared from nowhere. Small, white dots danced around it, frenetically spinning in every direction. The pure representation of every atomic matter held Creation's core. Right from within, an object of Human nature unfolded. Turning its form, its shape changed. Golden and shining its bindings, a bright white book flipped its pages rapidly, left to right. For every page turning, a flame of power was unleashed.

'As the history of this universe was written by our hands, as we placed the first word in a never-ending sequence of life and power, here we come to write a new chapter. Here we come to strip the destiny from its end and make more history to be told…'

Whatever Creation was going to make for us, she had clearly made one for herself already. The surge of energy spread rapidly across the space, leaping from the pages of her artifact and invading every empty spot, filling them with light and fire. Creation's hands moved in unison, pointing at the unsuspecting star that was soon to be struck by something unexpected.

The flow of power moved fiercely against the giant, feeding it, penetrating its skin, accelerating its gravitational pull. Eventually, once it had reached the breaking point, it let go, releasing the pure power of a new universe around, clashing onto me. I faced the blow with no resistance. My skin turning to plasma, my eyes brightening like the same exploding star, I opened my arms wide, accepting the will of my mother, dissolving into particles of energy. Once every element had found its new form, with gases drifting and matter floating around, a newborn galaxy had come to be. Her book closed again, Creation's eyes closed in a sign of requiem. The first step had been laid, the beginning of our suffered end was written.

After some time, following the long-awaited silence of the aftermath, under the quiet witnessing of my mother, I formed again, slowly coming back to life. My body looking exactly like before, I held a stronger power within my hands.

In front of me, four relics floated in space, gravitating around an invisible centre of energy. A clepsydra rotated upside down, pulsating with green flashes. A long, adorned stick stood upright, its head resembling that of a snake. A shining crown flickered with a crystal light, crying tears of life. And, at last, a pulsating heart in the shape of a diamond sat, resting on a white shell.

Creation waited silent, her eyes fixed on me. The most critical part of her plan was finally achieved. One by one, all the artifacts began to fade, slowly dissolving as if swallowed by the dark universe surrounding us. Finally, when the last relic, the heart and the shell had disappeared, Creation spoke.

'It is within them that my power and your powers shall reside for eternity,' she said, her voice firm.

'These are all Human items…' I said. 'Is it right to be this way?'

'It is to the point my own artefact is also of Human making. You are the key to our future. It feels right for you to shape them as you see fit. Now, let's go. We must act fast. These gifts belong to their rightful owners.'

Chapter Two

Creation's Sacrifice

∞

As it was long agreed, Soul, Time and I met on Talush, Health's protected planet, a world of immeasurable beauty and strength. A land of powerful beings, nature embodied the immortality of her master. While everything around showed the pride and beauty of our mother, the threat of destruction and emptiness lurked in the shadows, already drawing near its adversary. The five of us had gathered deep within a vast forest. The trees were ten times as tall as we Gods, and the bushes and flowers spilled colours of magnificent vitality. At the very heart of the woods, roots and branches formed an incredible storm of beauty and strength. With only the sky as their limit, a gigantic, living structure resembling a tree sat peacefully in the green land.

Everywhere, beings moved back and forth. Following Health's instructions, they were preparing to resist an impending diabolical attack. Some of them reminded me of my beloved Humans. Their strong muscles defining their limbs, their hair long and shiny, they looked powerful and yet graceful at the same time. With deep, dark skin and sweat on their foreheads, they were organizing the counterattack to an ambush that had occurred in the recent days. In the polar regions of the planet, Nothing's army had taken advantage of the perpetual shadow to secretly construct a weapon of destruction.

'I heard the Hoonits talking about something in the far north,' Time said as he joined us at the top of the gigantic tree. His face was shaded by concerns for leaving Runae unprotected, and he seemed visibly unhappy to be there.

'The one we don't speak of has come up with a new trick,' Health replied, moving beside Soul, who was silently observing the beings of Talush. 'People are falling seriously ill everywhere. The disease is spreading rapidly, changing and mutating before we can address and eradicate it.'

'It's more than just a disease,' Soul finally added. 'It's not only affecting their bodies. Somehow, it penetrates their cores, infecting their thoughts and souls from within. It's as if they have lost their own will.'

'It's what they were before you came into existence,' Creation interjected. 'Nothing is causing them to regress, undoing what we have done. This is how they were before you and your sister existed.'

'We need to move faster, Mother,' I said with a sorrowful expression. 'Somehow, these creatures have lost the most vital parts of themselves.'

'Time, Soul, Health,' Creation called, capturing their attention. We fell silent, our eyes and ears focused on her alone.

As we looked on, Creation extended her arms in the air, her hands up, summoning three shining objects from an unknown reality. Suddenly, the entire space around us froze. Every Hoonit in the far-below land stopped their work, captivated by the bright light emanating from the large wooden structure. Rays of warm light filtered through the branches, bouncing off thousands of leaves in an intricate dance of pure magic, leaving them spellbound. At the base of the tall structure, two pointy heads moved away from the same gateway they had guarded for centuries. Their rounded, large eyes gazed upwards. Their skinny, knotty appearance made them look like walking plants.

'These, my children, are yours to keep,' Creation continued, her voice resonating from all around. 'They were forged from fire and energy, strong like your will, made of the same substance as you are. For now, they won't appear to have much power. But in time, they will become the key to our victory in this battle.'

'What are they? What are they meant to do?' Health asked, her eyes reflecting the same bright golden light emitted by the three artefacts.

'If I succeed, these will preserve your lives. It's essential that you never part from them, ever! Allow them to become a part of you, an extension of your power, of who you are.'

'There are only three…' Time interjected, his eyes ever keen for scrutiny. 'Where is the fourth one?'

'I already have mine,' I replied, materializing a reddish stony diamond resting on a white shell. 'I assisted Mother as she infused them with her true power.'

'Your brother gave them shapes that he felt were right for each of you. I think you can guess who gets what,' Creation added with a brief smile as each artefact moved closer to its rightful owner.

As our gathering had been primarily planned by our mother so she could share her intentions, her sudden departure caught me off guard. Her plans felt clear before, yet I couldn't comprehend why she chose to withhold the true nature of those artefacts from my brothers and my sister. As they were now, they were merely decorative objects without any power or magic. Without Creation's spell, they remained empty vessels for a magic that, if in danger, had nowhere to go.

'So, is this it?' Time wondered aloud as our maker suddenly left. She had smiled once more, left the artefacts to their new owners, and then departed, dissolving into nothing.

'I don't understand what they're supposed to do,' Soul added. 'I don't sense any power or essence emanating from them.'

'Love?' Health turned her attention to me, as my brothers had done before her, awaiting an answer.

'I'm not entirely certain of Mother's exact intent. She said they are meant to protect us in times of peril. Somehow, she found a way to bind our energy, our true essence, in these objects. In case we are defeated...in case we die, we should be able to return through them,' I explained, revealing the truth all at once.

'But they're not yet...ready?' Soul inquired again. 'What is lacking?'

'To defy the laws of matter, she must have discovered something quite peculiar,' Time speculated.

'Does it really matter?' Health's enthusiasm remained undiminished. 'We have finally a way through. This is what we needed to defeat him!'

'At what cost, sister?' Time's question quickly dampened her renewed joy. 'What's the catch?'

Health wasn't allowing our brother's pragmatic viewpoint to mar the significance of that news in her mind. She was steadfast in believing that could be the turning point in our long-awaited triumph against evil. A few moments later, the master of time departed from the gathering, hurrying off. He wanted to return to Runae, completing a spell he had set in motion without our knowledge. In his mind, that was the way forward. As us three walked through the breathtaking gardens surrounding Health's kingdom, Soul began to speak.

'I've been contemplating something,' he began. 'What if the worlds we've sworn to protect could do more than merely exist? I've been thinking about what you said, Love, during our last meeting. Perhaps there is good in granting them a power of their own.'

'Do you still fear it might dilute our strength instead of amplifying it?' I replied, handing a flask containing a mysterious greyish fluid back to a Hoonit who looked at me in return, with pride.

'I do, but I also see how it could enable them to fight for what is rightfully theirs,' Soul continued, smiling at the same Hoonit who poured some of the magical liquid onto a small plant, transforming it into a tree within seconds.

'We need to ensure that we, and they, are prepared for what lies ahead. I'm certain Mother's plan will work, but what if it demands a heavy toll?' Health mused, moving her hand near a massive tree, as if inviting us to enter it. 'After all, even with the creation of these nodes, these passages…what exactly are we preventing?'

'You know well, sister,' I replied. 'These weren't created to prevent Nothing from attacking and destroying us, but to make it impossible for his armies to pour from one world to the next. Remember, we can't sever the magic connections between our worlds. They stand at the four corners of the universe, each holding the edge of Mother's making. Our magic and so the evil magic could flow in and out of this very planet if it weren't for this node.'

'That's exactly what I mean,' Health responded energetically. 'We've been thinking too narrowly. If these nodes are the only way through, how did Nothing manage to enter our worlds? He's successfully sending his evil pawns somehow…but how?'

'Time mentioned something about the Cloudy Mountains,' I whispered, almost as if talking to myself. My sister's question—and her worry—had merit. 'And on Earth, we're witnessing increased activity from the Harpies. Soul, what about Varayal?'

'It's exactly the same. Just like here and in the other worlds, diabolic whispers are slipping past my sight. The doors to Varayal are shut, and yet, he is still accessing our lands.'

'I truly hope Mother's new trick will have far-reaching effects. She must have found a way to do more than this.' And with a circular motion of her arms, she created a passage through the thick bark, cutting it as if it were fragile paper. 'Please, promise your next visit will be soon. I have a terrible feeling that something is coming, and it's coming soon, I'm afraid.'

Upon those worrying words, Soul and I departed, each returning to our respective worlds, carrying the weight of an uncertain future on our hearts. Little did we know, it would be the last time we set eyes upon Talush in all its splendour and strength. As we moved through the passage, a thunderous roar erupted from a distance, causing the magical walkway to flicker and then shut down entirely. Caught off guard by shock and surprise, Talush was devoured by rage and magic; a massive wall of fire began to spread across the lands. Health's expression turned horrified as she was thrust to the ground by a powerful surge of energy. From both the west and the east, the sounds of screams and rumbles reverberated loudly. Hoonits everywhere ran for their lives, unable to confront the enemy who had descended with full force, his grasp crushing the core of their planet.

The newfound delight Health had experienced just moments before was obliterated. In mere moments, dreams and hopes were dashed by the diabolical will of Nothing, who had finally revealed his true form. A vast, ominous shadow began to extend across the sky, transforming day into night and bringing a frigid, deathly sensation. Small stones and lifeless leaves scurried about on the ground, gradually lifting, pulled by an eerie, compelling force. As that power intensified, Health's feet lifted from the burning soil, raising her into the air. Animals, plants, Hoonits, and all living creatures floated, powerless to resist. Trees were uprooted from their homes, their foundations shattered.

Dwellings and buildings followed suit, crumbling into dust as their structural integrity dissolved. In the petrified gaze of the God, everything began to disintegrate into a thin, dark substance. Cells and molecules were ruthlessly torn apart, dragged by an unrelenting, malevolent intent. As Creation's masterpiece was rewound to non-existence, our mother appeared by Health's side. Flickering with magic, her hands on my sister's shoulders, she gazed at her with a mix of terror and determination.

'There is no time,' she urged. 'You must leave now!'

'No, Mother!' Health retorted with fury. 'I won't abandon them. They... They all are my children to protect!'

'I haven't completed the spell. You are still mortal,' Creation stated, pushing her will upon her daughter. 'If you stay, you'll be lost forever...'

'The very reason I exist is precisely the reason why I can't leave them behind!'

However, the odds were set against Health's determination. The ground and sky began to warp. Like wax exposed to excessive heat, everything melted away, drawn towards a dark point in the distant atmosphere. They were on the brink of becoming part of the same matter as a black hole that materialized out of nowhere, consuming every particle in its path.

'My child, this is beyond repair. You must go. I need to initiate the rite of power now, releasing the enchantment onto your artefacts. Please, make your way to the node and reach your brother Soul!'

Urged by our mother's plea, Health summoned enough power to wrest herself from Nothing's grasp; her course was clear. She had to reach the node before its magic could be overwhelmed and extinguished, entangling her in Talush until its end.

Creation vanished with a snap, her physical nature left behind, transitioning into her true form of pure energy, ascending above the world and soaring towards her adversary. Her power, immensely potent, pushed her between evil and Talush, her eyes ablaze.

'I warned you before,' she cried out into the void. 'I am the future; these worlds and my creation are things you cannot take away!'

'Your existence defies me, defies all that should be,' a voice replied. Something was forming before the God. 'You shall return to me, and with you, every abomination you've crafted...'

'Your time is over. This is the era of existence!'

A colossal being manifested in front of Creation. Twin hollows stared back at her. His mouth was like a vortex, spinning and drawing life from all around. The God of every making appeared minuscule, like a tiny radiant point into the darkness of the universe. Her determination unwavering, her power paled before the king of obscurity. As the gravitational pull intensified, a spear-like power shot forth against Creation, who struggled for her life. In the attempt to progress with her plan, she willingly drew Nothing closer, who stripped her of her power like flashes of fierce flames. In the fleeting span of a moment, just before the enemy could strike her down, Health interposed herself between them, absorbing the blow into her essence.

'No!' Creation screamed, stunned by her daughter's fate. The God of Health was pierced through, torn into shreds of energy. 'This is not how it shall be!'

With raw power born from grief and desperation, Creation's energy surged tenfold. Her hands outstretched into space, she reached every trace of Health's remaining core, reassembling them before her enemy's eyes. As the weak and barely surviving God materialized once again, Creation whispered:

'Listen to me, run to Soul and heal. Warn him!' Creation turned towards her daughter, sheltering her once more. 'As all fades before coming back, nothing dies but only transforms, as pure life regains its purpose, my plea is set. May my energy find its rightful hosts through their magic. May their creations preserve their essence until they can reunite!'

Health's sceptre appeared in the darkness of the final hour, shining brightly before Nothing's eyes, who'd just witnessed yet another unexpected defiance. Creation released the full power of her being into space, reaching the edge of the universe, flowing into our artefacts, piercing the evil like thousands of poisoned thorns. With a staggering blow, Creation transformed her life into a potent weapon, a spell of hope, an invocation of faith and eternal existence. The mother of everything that existed made the ultimate sacrifice. Everyone's path was laid out once and for all.

As she vanished, a promise was forged. A new chapter of a never-ending war was written in secret; the new era began. She had given away her life to protect her children and everything she had made, inflicting her will right into her enemy's heart. In the empty space left by Creation's disappearance, her own artefact floated dead. Its light gone, its covers shut, Creation's amulet was defenceless, ready to be taken by the enemy. Health had just reached the node when the bright, motherly light pushed on her weak shoulders, causing her to slip through the node. The last thing she felt, passing from one world to the next, was our mother's final breath and wish.

The other side was not more welcoming than the one she had just left behind. If Talush had been torn apart, Varayal was burning alive, consumed by raging fire. Whatever Nothing sent to the worlds, he had done it on both planets simultaneously. The sky was red, the lands raged under an intense battle. Soul stood at the centre of a large valley, close to three tall towers. His home under attack, it was the only place still standing. The people of his world had gathered under his protection, fighting for their lives against the evil's army. Countless bodies lay dead or floated in the nearby river. Some were being resurrected in a different form, returning as spirits standing beside their protector.

With her back to the planet node, the doors closed shut. The tree on the other side turned to dust, erasing the passage through time and space. Unable to return to her own world and with the little energy she had recovered, Health rushed to support our brother when something unusual caught her attention. Someone else similar to her in spirit and power walked those lands. Only a few miles away, someone else had come to the rescue. Time's familiar essence reached her senses through the miles in between them. In her heart she was certain he had come to support Soul in time of need. Despite his resistance and opposition in leaving Runae unprotected, Time had come to stand beside his siblings.

Faced with the choice of continuing her run towards the battle or rushing to meet her brother, she stalled. In that moment something else stirred in Health's ears. My voice called her from afar, troubled and confused. My silent cry penetrated her mind. My presence strong, I existed in too many versions of past and present for her to fully understand and respond to my plea. In between the pages of history, I resounded from both her time and my future. Two versions of myself existed in the same reality, one on Earth, in her present, fighting in protection of my world against Death and the rocky bullet he was riding towards my planet, and the other on Varayal, a future version of me split into two beating hearts, desperate, broken and fragile.

'Love, is that you?' Health asked, her voice barely audible amidst the deadly sounds of war. Her weak essence shifted through realities. 'I can hear you. Where are you?' But there was no answer. All she could feel was the distant echo of my voice.

Trusting Time could support and rescue Soul, she rushed back to the node. If our brother had come to save him, she had to do the same for me. Ready to traverse a myriad of miles, Health opened the door of Varayal and left.

Contrary to my sister's beliefs, Time's presence was not for Soul's sake. His magic spread across the burning lands, manipulating the ticking of every second not to save but to take. He was on a single mission: to take the Tiara of Souls away from our brother, the same artefact that only a few moments before had been transformed into an everlasting beholder of supreme power. Master of everything that was and would be, Time knew he had entered a loop of events that had to unfold.

Next to him, suspicious and gifted with a piece of her master's magic. Revelia caught a glimpse of Time's plan without fully grasping its meaning. At the moment of their appearance, she sensed the presence of my sister, just before she departed. Unbeknownst to any of us, I, my brothers and my sister, existed in the exact same place and at the same time. Different versions of ourselves, different versions of past and future mixed together, close to a vital contact and yet, we missed the great opportunity to be together once more.

The only chance we were going to have for the next thousands of years was lost. In our failure to find each other, we would endure pain, imprisonment, apparent death, and oblivion.

Creation's sacrifice became an unending agony. Instead of rendering us immortal, the spell froze us in an eternal state of defeat. Ages would pass, with us Gods striving continuously to revert our history, only to repeat our actions over and over again.

And yet, the time for a final, definitive confrontation had finally come. Blessed by Daniel's, Noah's and Anita's determination to break the chains of the Gods' entrapment, my siblings were set free, one by one. Through pain and sacrifice, they conjured me back to life, reuniting us Gods in a supreme spell of protection. As the enemy's second coming descended upon us and the remaining worlds, we prepared for the fight of many lifetimes.

When the universe teetered on the brink of extinction, we walked the frail path between life and death, light and darkness. Our faith, love, and desire for survival were all that stood between victory and oblivion, each of us hoping we would be worth granting the miracle that had eluded us for so long.

There we stood firm, we Gods floating in the cosmos, shielding our universe. Our hands and magic stretched to the beyond, resisting Nothing's evil, oppressive power. Down on Earth, the ones we loved and cherished braced for the unthinkable threat ahead. Their hearts and souls crushed by Daniel's departure, they were back home and yet lost. Their hopes shattered, their future vanished with their loved one. Among evil and despair, they prepared to embark on the final journey, a last adventure that would end it all.

Chapter Three

An Unbreakable Bond

∞

Anita, Noah, Trusk, and Revelia stood petrified outside Noah's old cottage as Nothing's violent attack struck from the far skies. Even if opposed and mitigated by the renewed, combined power of my siblings and mine, his eternal magic deformed space and time as if every matter were wax melting under a malignant sun. Defying gravity and every rule of a millennial existence, he pulled and dragged every essence out of their rightful place.

A deafening roar split the air, followed by a high-pitched blast that shattered windows, sending shards of glass flying. Terror-stricken, the four placed their hands over their heads as they kneeled on the road. The ground trembled beneath them as throngs of panicked people ran in fear, their shouts echoing in the chaos. The sky morphed into a haunting purple, and in the far east, a blinding point of light flared, like a sun ten times its size at sunset.

'This can't be good!' Anita shouted, dodging the frantic crowd.

'Revelia!' Noah yelled, his eyes wide with fear as he saw men and women pointing and screaming. 'You're visible!'

Before Trusk could wield his magic, another blast rippled through the land, knocking everyone to the ground. Car alarms blared, and the air filled with the sounds of breaking glass. In the distance, unseen by Human eyes, a war between Gods had erupted.

'What's happening?' Noah gasped, shielding his eyes from the swirling dust.

'It feels like the day in the Ancient Mirrors,' Revelia murmured, her long hair whipping around as if pulled by an unseen force. 'The day of the Great Dawn…'

Cars moved of their own accord, dragged by an invisible hand. Desperate, the people inside tried to drive away to safety, but the vehicles remained unresponsive. Streetlights and poles bent, their bases cracking the earth, while shop signs detached and floated towards the glowing point in the sky. Anita and Noah felt their feet lifting off the ground as the pull grew stronger. They were about to be consumed by the vortex above.

Suddenly, the invisible force released them. It turned into a mere breeze, weakened by the protective power of the Chomp, who stood with arms raised, the Flare burning bright. A shielding veil descended, softening the impact of the new threat. Time seemed to reverse; winds changed direction, the pull became a push, and everything that had been taken was hurled back with fury. Cars and debris crashed down, sparking new waves of panic.

Nothing's malevolent magic had penetrated our defences, extracting the very essence of life from my dear world, and now, it was all being regurgitated in a violent backlash. A massive wave, summoned from the lake, surged through the village, demolishing barriers and smashing into buildings. The ancient bridge was obliterated into rubble by the force of the raging water. Nature itself seemed to expand and push against the people, who fled in terror towards the woods.

'We need to leave, now!' Noah yelled, his voice trembling.

'Can you lift us?' Revelia asked Trusk, who struggled to maintain his power.

'If's foo strong. I can barely hold my Flare…'

'We'll do it the old way.' Noah said, determined. 'We run.'

Fear crawled up their backs as the four ran for their lives. The physical laws of matter were subverted as the ancient enemy had come to exterminate the last living proof of Creation's deceit. Waves of energy pulled and pushed the defenceless Humans in a nauseating loop, dragging them a few feet into the air, suddenly releasing them, and slamming their backs onto the ground. Everywhere, cracks opened up in the streets, scarring the Earth's skin as if it were made of thin fabric. The tranquil waters of the river, the lake, and the nearby sea had turned into yet another violent enemy. With raging power, the waters clashed against walls and penetrated streets. The blue waters turned brown as they flooded Noah's Bridge, dragging away cars and trees, destroying everything in their path. Convulsing under the cosmic pressure of the invisible hovering force, the lands deformed and wobbled frenetically.

Following the terrified crowd up the hill to the far woods, the four companions fell to their knees and backs several times. While the ground moved, they stopped here and there to help those who couldn't stand on their feet. With terror in their eyes and desperation imprinted on their faces, the Humans screamed in horror. As if Mother Nature had surged against her people, she shook the tablecloth of life with no regard for those who found themselves on it, unwanted.

'Can't we use the Flare to shield them?' Noah shouted a few feet away from the others. His hands on an old woman's arm, he had quickly run to help her, holding her upright. Behind them, a few buildings had just collapsed, crumbling into the water. 'You are fine, Mrs. Lynch. Hold on to me, I'll carry you up to the woods…'

'Fhis is beyond my Flare's reach,' Trusk replied, coming out of the invisible dome, in the open.

Another pull suddenly struck from the far sky, lifting Noah and Mrs. Lynch up in the air. Under the shocked gaze of the ones who were shielded by the Chomp's magic, the two fell back on the ground, rolling downhill. With them, dozens of other people followed suit, crashing on the hard soil, only to end up in the hoovering mouth of the wrathful waters.

Trusk's tiny hands met Noah's right as he was about to be swallowed by the ruthless waves. Somewhere beside him, the old woman disappeared. With her, many other lives had been claimed in an instant. Trusk's wings flapped recklessly as he opposed the dark magic surrounding them, finally extorting Noah from its devouring power, bringing him back inside the dome where Anita and Revelia waited impatiently.

'This is…' Anita staggered. 'Where are they? We are not going to survive without the Gods. Nobody will!'

'The Flare won't hold this world in place,' Revelia added, observing the magnitude of the raging destruction. 'We can protect ourselves under it, but it won't do any good if the planet is broken apart.'

'We will be fine. Let's move uphill before the sea gets here. Quick!' Noah pushed forward, but his mind kept revisiting the last few painful minutes. His back and arms hurt, but the true ache pounded in his heart when Mrs. Lynch's face appeared in his thoughts once more.

They had almost caught up with the other fleeing residents at the top of the hill, when a large number of Harpies appeared from within the many trees. As if they had just walked out from the ancient bark, the many evil soldiers gathered in the woods, stretching their hands towards the many people who ran in fear. With their smoky, grey shape bringing the panic of a new terror, they scattered across the hill, grabbing as many victims as they could. Loud screams travelled all around. Sinister clouds formed among the trees, enveloping the fugitives and dragging them into their dark depths. Then, they vanished, and the Humans' shouts abruptly ceased as the victims were snatched away from their world.

Amidst the chaos, a towering Harpy stood motionless. His golden sandals anchored firmly in a patch of withered grass, he remained unmoved, indifferent to the carnage unfolding around him. Far removed from the fray of his army, his dark, contorted face veiled by a dark shadow turned towards his coveted prey. Death, unrivalled in his ability to pierce through enchantments and falsehoods, fixated unwaveringly on the quartet hidden within the Chomp's protective dome. He had returned once more, driven by an unrelenting determination to extinguish their defiance. Though oblivious of the conjuring that had allowed for my return, in Death's unyielding gaze, they remained the same formidable threat. Driven by his master's mandate, he sought to fulfil his duty, indifferent to any divine intervention that could challenge his malevolent resolve.

'You come to me finally, when the hour is right…' he intoned, arms raised to the sky. His hair, like serpents made of dark magic, writhed in warning of imminent danger, revealing a visage that struck terror, a grim invitation to the final confrontation.

'Here he is again,' Noah murmured, halting the group just short of the woods.

'He sees us… Whaf do we do?' Trusk's voice quivered with panic.

'Where are your…Gods?' Death continued, his tone dripping with disdain. 'I would very much like to meet them once more…'

In a silent, suffocating embrace, the Harpies closed in, forming a malevolent circle. Their hollow, lifeless eyes bored into their enemies as they began to weave a haunting melody of enchantment. Death advanced slowly towards his prey. With each step, every blade of grass instantly died at his touch, causing the hearts of the four companions to tighten further in dread. Fuelled by fury, Death's hands clenched. Empty of his trusted weapon, they moved and contorted as if seeking for the artefact that could channel his wicked will, reminding him that his scythe was lost, stolen by the same ones who stood only a grasp away.

'I would like to reclaim my sceptre… It was a gift, a cherished one,' Death mused aloud.

'It was never yours to have! Your gifts belonged elsewhere,' Anita retorted boldly, her fear conquered long ago. Even without Cherish at her side, she stood resolute.

'Silence, insignificant worm!' Algos spat, conjuring a blade of magic with a sweep of his arm through the charged air.

'Look out!' Revelia cried, pushing Anita aside, her foresight once again sparing her friend from harm.

'You are late,' Noah countered, a sweat of pure fear mingling with his soaked look. He knew the moment had come to fulfil the promise he had made to Daniel. 'The Gods have returned—all of them. They might not be here, with us, but you can no longer stop them.'

'And tell me…' Another Harpy materialized beside him in an instant, her warped hand seizing his chin in a vice-like grip. 'Would they not return for you?'

'Mcspherya,' Death called, beckoning his henchwoman back into formation. 'The one called Love has but one weakness. Them. He will return, mark my words…'

As if granted insight by my brother's magic, the four glimpsed their fate unfolding in their minds, their demise imminent as the tall Harpy closed in. They had no means to resist him now. Noah had lost both halves of the artefact and the only other Human capable of unlocking its power. His gaze darted to Trusk, knowing a hasty retreat offered little refuge. The Harpies had already found them. Revelia, unable to foresee the ambush, sensed time and options slipping away.

'But I have to agree with you…' Death continued, his voice chillingly calm, mere inches from his coveted prize. 'We don't need all of them to have him back. One of you will suffice. The rest can rot here, with the rest of this world.'

Before they could utter a word, before they could conceive an escape from the impossible, Death extended his right arm, palm wide open. His fingers stretched, decayed bones and flesh transforming into a swirling black vortex. The magic repeated with his left hand, unleashing his supreme power.

The myriad of shadows under his dominion drew nearer, their eerie chorus growing louder. Whatever incantation they sang, it drowned out all other sounds. Silence engulfed the space, even the roar of the surging waters behind them subdued by their malevolent will.

A devouring force surged from within Death, tearing away at their essence, their very souls and energy. Trusk's Flare extinguished instantly as his light body levitated, skin stretching as if it might tear away towards the adversary. Beside him, Anita stared in horror as her own arms and hands seemed to separate, her spirit emerging from within. For a brief moment, flesh and bone remained behind while her soul ascended.

Two fiery orbs gleamed as Revelia rushed forward, desperately seeking a path through the tapestry of time. Whatever she glimpsed offered no salvation. She grasped Anita's shoulders, their faces almost touching.

'No, stay with me,' she implored as Anita's soul drifted, passing through her. 'Find strength within yourself, please!'

'She's gone, Revelia. Cherish is gone. I can't fight this…' Anita's vacant shell echoed from behind. 'I can't…' Her eyes closed, words hanging in the air.

'It doesn't matter.' Revelia's despair echoed to no one and everyone at once. She glanced around at those being abandoned to their final moments, at the hands of a foe they seemed unable to overcome. 'There is magic within each of you. Fight back!'

'I don't know what you are…' Death began, only a step from her when he laughed. 'I don't know where you came from, but I know where you'll go. You lack a Human soul, yet I am certain we will find a place for you within our realm. Now, come to me, all of you…'

As the dark magic expanded, Revelia's feet left the ground. Her flowing hair responded to the sudden weightlessness. The more she resisted the deadly pull, the higher she ascended, losing control of her own body. Two crimson sparks flickered in her eyes.

Whatever fate awaited the Leonty, she had to witness her end before it unfolded.

A fleeting vision displayed in her mind. Daniel's face appeared, as vivid as memory. His unruly hair, piercing blue eyes, shattered her heart anew. 'You awaited me, wherever the Gods had granted your reprieve. You beckon me forth to tell me there is a better place I'm destined to go?' she mused.

'You told me once there was no other way...' Daniel's voice echoed softly. *'I asked you why she could not find redemption... You insisted that some things cannot be changed.'*

'Are you here to tell me I was wrong?' she whispered. Death's outstretched arms enveloped her fully upon hearing her words.

'I refused to accept it then, and I still refuse it now, my friend.' Daniel's smile graced her vision. *'You saved me. You saved them time and again. You deserve more, we all do. It is time for you to learn the future can be reshaped...'*

'What is this?' Death was taken aback. Beside Revelia, another figure materialized amidst realities. The mortal decree he imposed appeared final, unyielding. If anyone could defy his formidable magic, they had to be divine in nature.

'Who are you?' he demanded, scanning his surroundings in a frenzy.

As the Harpy's attention wandered elsewhere, Noah's lifeless body moved beside Revelia. His eyes now a haunting grey, his soul already surrendered to their executioner, yet he stood motionless, as if awaiting someone's instructions.

'This has always been your journey. You were meant to become the keeper, standing alongside those we cherish, carrying forwards the bonds we forged,' Daniel's voice whispered. *'Remember the promise you made to me and the Seven. Your job is not finished.'*

At those words, Noah's inert body stirred as if moved by another's will. Breaking free from Death's malevolent grasp, he resisted the magnetic pull. With a sudden burst of newfound strength, he propelled Anita and Revelia towards Trusk.

'Trusk!' a voice cried out. 'Now!' Noah's presence seemed to swell tenfold, infused with an unexpected power.

Once again, Death's onslaught faltered. Between the warring factions, an invisible barrier surged into existence, blazing with brilliance. The many Harpies, momentarily blinded, flickered in and out of sight in rapid succession. The ticking of seconds halted. Time was brought back and forth, then gradually resumed its natural flow. As if the spirit of a lost ally briefly walked among them, a face torn between past and present darting across the space, a dome of protection enveloped the trio.

Responding swiftly, Trusk raised his arms overhead; the Chomp's Flare erupted, cloaking his friends in invisibility, whisking them away.

An act of defence had intervened once more, shielding them from the merciless enemy. As Anita's soul reunited with her body, a stark reality dawned upon her. Noah, left outside the protective shroud, stood exposed. The safeguard they had all received had deemed him unworthy. He, who had shattered Death's grip, became the sole victim, trapped in the enemy's clutches. The monstrous Harpy entangled him in a deformed embrace, as if seeking to consume him to the bone, crushing him into oblivion.

'You are now but an empty vessel,' Death crooned, 'as hollow as ever. Ah, yes, I can taste it... So much anguish, so much despair... Yes, loneliness and sorrow. Excellent, truly excellent.' Noah's form dissolved, matter succumbing to Death's potent grip, consumed by the enemy's wrath. With no trace left behind, he vanished from existence.

'Now join the others!' Death thundered, casting a fierce gaze upon his assembled horde. 'Oz, the Harpy of loneliness and misery, walks among us once more.'

A new, evil Awoken One materialized behind Death. His appearance was warped, reminiscent of Noah yet stripped of all remnants of his original form. His physical body dissolved, his soul twisted into darkness, assimilated into Death's ranks as a fresh recruit, primed for the impending, ultimate conquest.

Anita, Revelia, and Trusk huddled together, frozen in shock and horror. Noah was taken away from them when hope seemed utterly lost. There was only one thing they could do, the only thing they had done most of their journey to resurrect the Gods: run.

The blade of Death struck their hearts as swiftly as it pierced mine. Though distant, I felt Noah's soul depart from my cherished realm as if I had witnessed it firsthand. His will still entwined with mine, with Daniel's, propelled him forwards in a determined effort to safeguard me, my siblings, and the entire universe.

'Love!' Time's cry echoed distantly in the cosmos. His form, radiant and pure like plasma in the dark expanse, reached out beyond grasp. Sensing the sudden severance in our magic, he extended his power to find mine, to fill the void I had left. I had relinquished control, my heart drawn away from our battlefield towards my beloved.

'What is happening?' Health's voice whispered to me. The circle of power among the Gods had just revealed its greatest flaw: me. I knew my siblings and so the fate of everything that existed depended on me to contain Nothing's onslaught, yet I couldn't silence the cries of those I cherished most on Earth. *Where does my true allegiance lie? Whom should I stand with?* They needed me desperately.

'Stay with us, brother,' Soul's voice repeated as if floating around my head, mixing with the anguished cries of the three companions. 'It's the only way to halt his advance...'

'We can delay him only so long,' I implored, desperate. 'But what will remain of Mother's creation if we allow his horde to ravage it?'

'We can't be in two places at once,' Health reasoned. 'Remember who you are and why we are here.'

At the sound my sister's words, deep within, I grasped my identity. My loyalty was clear. My heart beat not only for the Humans I swore to protect but for all that Mother had created out of love. I came to existence for everything she had made. I had to protect it all and now everything spread too far and too thin for me to reach it at once. Once again, I needed to be more than I was. I wanted to be everywhere it mattered, I needed to transcend once more, to be present where it truly mattered. *We can be in two places at once... Yes, I can and so I should.* I had done it before, I had failed before because of it. And yet, even my curse was a forerunner of a life partitioned in two.

If Noah's mission was to succeed, I had to grant him and the others the aid they sought and my protected world the brief respite it desperately needed. By pushing beyond my limits and merging my magic with that of the other Gods, my understanding of my existence deepened. My history and my longing to be more than one slowly began to coalesce into clarity.

'Let go and come back to me,' Nothing's immense presence loomed ahead as it spoke in our heads, his voice thundering from within our minds and all around us. His grip on every reality adamant, his invisible tendrils extended beyond Earth, encroaching upon the moon and other planets.

'Love, please…' Soul begged as I struggled to fulfil my duty, my aim at the ones I had left behind.

'It's alright, brother,' Time spoke to me. 'It's all meant to be. Trust me as I trust you. We are at the edge of our destiny, right between existence and demise. You need to know, before it's too late…'

'Why are you showing me all this? Why now?' I asked, while visions, fruit of my brother's unrelenting magic, formed right before my eyes. 'Did you know all of this was going to happen?'

'You are Love, brother. Don't you know every feeling, every emotion of every living being, deep within yourself? And yet,' Time added, before I could reply, 'have you ever stopped hoping there could be more? Do you ever fear there could be less? I know where this is going to lead you, lead all of us… We are so close now.'

'Show me,' I whispered without hesitation.

As his vision of an everlasting tale expanded inside my mind, so our protective magic extended across the solar system and shrouded Earth under a benevolent veil, restoring calm to the land and waters. Humanity now had a chance to seek refuge, and so did Anita and Revelia aided by Trusk's enchantments.

Near the edge of the hill, amid the ancient woods, the Harpies deliberated their next move when the fury of the elements subsided.

'They still have the protection of their Gods,' Strife said as he gazed at the sky. 'It's all gone quiet. It can't be the Humans' doing…'

'Where have they gone?' Algos queried.

'I could see through their powers, but now I see nothing,' Desolos replied, her eyes narrowing in frustration. 'What say you?' she added, turning her gaze to Lëogan.

'My master,' Lëogan began, addressing Death directly and ignoring the Harpy's question. Though his face was a grotesque mask devoid of eyes or readable expressions, his tone conveyed deep veneration and respect. 'To draw him out, we must capture them.'

'We already have one… the perfect one,' Death remarked, eyeing Oz with an unsettling fascination, almost enamoured with his own creation. The others' sudden escape aided by renewed magic seemed inconsequential. 'Now, tell me, what is their plan?'

'My master?' Noah's voice emerged, nearly unrecognizable, his words strained.

'You shared a bond with him, with them. Tell me, what are their intentions?' Death inquired.

'I can't recall...' Oz muttered, gazing at his transformed hands. Though resembling the other Harpies, he retained vestiges of his former Human form. 'They have abandoned me... He abandoned me... I am empty now, an empty vessel...'

'Indeed you are...but fret not. You possess a new purpose, and I won't rob you of it.' Death circled Noah, inspecting him closely. 'Now, tell me, what do they plan?'

'They will flee... They lack the power to confront you, any of us.'

'Not them, you silly, stupid Harpy!' Death bellowed, shocking the others into turning away in terror. 'The Gods. Tell me their intentions!

Chapter Four

Inside the Enemy's Mind

∞

Less than a mile away, in the safe shadow of the other side of the hill, Revelia had stopped running. Her eyes pointed at the near lake, she was screening beyond realities, trying to see their near future. As the Leonty exited the protection of the Flare, Anita pulled Trusk back, holding him to the spot.

'Wait a minute,' Anita said, panting heavily. 'Something is happening to Revelia…'

'Are you OK?' Trusk asked, staring at his friend, his tiny hands reaching hers. 'Whaf do you see?'

'I see nothing, nothing again… Like before we left Runae.' The Leonty's desperation pushed through her words. 'There is a hard line over which I can't see. It's like there is a moment, in the near future when…everything stops. I can't see past that.'

'Do you see why? What causes it?' Anita asked, worried.

'No. It's just the end of the road. I see a possible future, maybe more than one, but they all stop at the same time. It's like I'm…dead and I can't go any further.'

'Don'f say if!' Trusk reacted, holding her hands firmly. He had lost Daniel, Noah, his family and his entire kind. Whatever he had left, the Chomp could not tolerate losing any more. 'We will go home and everfhing will be like Daniel said.'

Trusk's words thundered in Anita's head at once. Just the mention of Daniel's name brought back the harsh reality, right in front of her eyes. Things had happened so quickly, running had become a bad habit and now she had finally the chance to realize what loss she had to come to terms with. Her eyes fixed on the landscape ahead, she could see the past with the power of her true memory. It wasn't Cherish's magic or any of the Gods' making, it was pure desperation.

A lonely car was parked to the side of the road, she was testing the cold water of the lake with her bare feet. And then the rain, the run back to the car, screaming and laughing, with her best friend, Daniel. The journey to that place was the trigger of everything that followed.

Despite their destiny being long written, for Anita that was the moment when everything changed. The door to the magical journey had been there for thousands of years, locked. They had found the key and used it to peek through it, heedlessly. From that little, pivotal moment, their entire story had been rewritten. A new friend had come into their life and she had learned to grow fond of him, only to lose him by the hand of Death.

Broken and devastated, Anita fell on her knees, her hands covering the many tears flowing. Trusk and Revelia moved beside her at once. The first joining her in desperation, the second one holding them together, her face directed towards the surroundings. Something else stirred in the invisible beyond, highting her senses, triggering her magic.

'There is something here… Trusk, hold on to your Flare. Someone is coming…' she said, her eyes as if on fire.

'Is it them again?' Anita asked, sobbing.

A sudden, gentle breeze lifted from the ground, scattering the many dead leaves around. A whisper came right after, a voice of a lost soul spoke of a bond with the ones he loved.

'I know your pain 'cause it's mine too. I know your heart is shattered but, even broken, a heart beats the same…' it said. The three gazed around, afraid and yet hopeful. 'He is gone, thousands of miles away, beyond this world, to fight him. But his mind, his heart is still bound to you. Daniel's soul is keeping him…chained to you all.'

'Who are you?' Revelia shouted, standing up. The firm look on her face spoke of anger and defeat mixed together. 'Where are you? Show yourself. We really have no strength left to play this game any more!'

'You know me. Although briefly, you have seen me before…' And the Awoken One who had been rescued last formed before their eyes. His body transparent, his eyes clear like shining crystals, Eros appeared next to Anita. 'You came to get me out of Runae, out of a lost past where John and I were trapped by the hand of Nothing.

'You are still here?' Revelia asked.

'Where is Daniel?' Anita quickly added. Seeing an Awoken One returning after the conjuring spell quickly ignited the feeble spark of hope.

'We need help,' Trusk interjected. 'Fhe Harpies fook Noah.'

'I know,' Eros replied, taking them by surprise. 'I've been with you since Love has returned. And so is someone else you know…'

To their right, another familiar Awoken materialised. Her face unmistakable, she carried the same duality as the first time they had met her. Her body almost inconsistent, her shape forming and disappearing in a constant loop, she was there and all around them.

Eventually, Iris's shape became more tangible and she spoke.

'We were meant to join him in battle, but Love has never changed. He can't leave what he cares about the most behind. And so I departed him and reached you. My magic and your magic,' she added, looking at Trusk, 'have merged together. Your dome resembles mine now. You are not only out of sight, but also out of time…'

'No!' Anita exclaimed in between gratitude and fear. 'We are glad you are back with us but we can't lose any more years inside your magic…'

'Don't be worried. You lose as much time as you spend inside the Chomp's shield. Nothing more, nothing less.'

'How can you wield Time's magic?' Revelia asked, her sharp mind ready to probe even the most merciful act. 'Why did you let them take Noah? How many others have returned?'

Revelia's questions fired like darts against allies who had disappointed her. Then, as if she wasn't really interested in any explanations, she turned her gaze back where they had come from. The idea of going back and fighting the Harpies, to rescue Noah, had replaced any other thought. As if time and events had merged together, like Iris's and Trusk's magic, the past was representing itself as their new present. Noah, once again, had moved beyond, on his own will, and now they had to take him back from the hands of the enemy. *Una...Nothing...it will never end...* she thought.

'It's just the two of us,' Eros replied, his hands brushing on Anita's arms as he helped her to stand up. 'There is someone else whose soul has departed the world of living... His voice is loud in our heads, in Love's head. But it's just the two of us, I'm afraid.' And as if the Awoken One could just betray his own words in a mere second, he instantly disappeared, followed by Iris, leaving the three bewildered.

'Where did fhey go?' Trusk lifted a few inches in the air, gazing at the landscape. In his eyes, tears appeared once more.

'Wherever they went, it doesn't matter.' The Leonty could not accept the status of things. Whatever future she was prevented from seeing, she could not come to accept their present, their fate. 'We can't leave Noah behind,' Revelia added, her voice low, filled with anger. 'Death can't have him. He is the only one we have left and we need to get him back.'

'Like we did in Runae?' Trusk stopped crying; his eyes flickered as he stared at his friend.

'Exactly like we did in Runae.'

'He is gone, Revelia. He is dead...' Anita replied, defeated. 'Wherever Eros and Iris are, I don't think they will be able to help us.

'If there is something I know for sure'—and the Leonty moved a few steps away—'is that we can fix this. I've seen it happening too many times to give up now. Time, Love, the Gods can undo whatever they want. But we need to get him out of the enemy's hands first.'

'We are no match for them,' Anita said, finally looking back at Revelia. Once again a hint of hope peeked through. 'How do we do that?'

'We have you, and me and this little one. Have you heard what the strange ghost said?' And, at the mention of that peculiar description of Iris, a brief smile appeared on Anita's face. 'They could not see the Chomp's Flare any more because she had put her magic into it. I can tell when past and future are being manipulated. She has gifted us a great help. I say this is enough.' And a smile of pride appeared on her face. 'Although I don't understand how one of them can wield Time's magic… And now that I think about it, she had this power even before we freed the Gods… Anyway, let's go.'

So the group got back on their feet. Ready to start another rescue mission, they headed back to where they had run from. From hunted to hunters, they spun their destiny in a hazardous gambling. Running turned into chasing, their minds desperate to overcome an end that had been forced on them. It was time to act.

When the three reached the Harpies, they found their enemy exactly where they had left them. As if they had been frozen in a still frame, Death and Oz stood face to face. The large Harpy floated slowly on the dead soil, his horrifying gaze fixed on the newborn, silent, as if waited for instructions. Oz had not given him any relevant information beside a few details on things that were already obvious. The Gods had come back, their artefacts in their hands, the fight was brought back to Nothing. And yet, Death penetrated Oz's corrupted mind searching for new answers.

For the new Harpy the torturing connection his master held the grip on flooded freely, unchallenged. There, for a brief moment, Death's own thoughts reverberated in his cracked mind, echoing of fear and disappointment. As Death navigated the obscurity of Oz's core the other suddenly found access into his torturer's thoughts.

The Lord of the Harpies had failed his master shamelessly. He had lost his sceptre and lost control over Health. Oz could sense how Death challenged the simple idea of defeat. After all, he had to fight not one but two Gods. If one was deprived of her artefact and the other one had been split in two, victim of a deadly curse, it didn't matter. They were still Gods and they had been trying to come back to life for centuries, fighting him and his Harpies with great determination. As far back as his wicked memory went, Death had always struggled to fulfil his destiny.

As if the creation of Oz itself could ignite the old memory of his own birth, the large Harpy gazed at the sky. In his mind, his first spark of consciousness replayed slowly.

'What is this, what am I?' Death's first words hung in the empty space of a newly arising evil. He had just formed out of the darkness of Nothing's will, immediately after Creation's fall.

'You are the one that will take everything back where it belongs, me. You are Death, an extension of what I am, the annihilation of every living matter,' a deep voice whispered in the Harpy's head.

'Who are you?' And the Harpy's large, grey entity shaped into a body, shifting back and forth between a tangible form and a ghost. A disturbing face, contorted limbs and golden features appeared in a quick sequence. Next to him, a second, grey creature started to form.

'I AM. And you are part of who I am. I am everything and everywhere. And everything needs to be me, as this is the law of the eternity. Beside you lies the remains of the one who could not be put out. Her nature, her magic is as stubborn as she was. The only way to get back what belongs to me, is to have her gone from existence.' And the second newly formed Harpy contorted in pain. It moved as if melting under too much heat as her soul shrank into a tiny dot, right before Death's eyes.

Death's ancient memories came back to him all at once. The long journey through the thousands of years was fast and unchallenged. He could recall the moment he had come to be as if it had just happened.

'The enemy has scattered across the space,' Nothing continued, his voice a chilling whisper that echoed through the vast emptiness. 'But I am everything and everywhere. Even as we speak, another God falls. There is an...impediment that prevents me from eradicating this disease completely. For now, I will just silence them.' His words reverberated within Death's core, a thunderous command that moved from the depths of his consciousness to the desolate, external world. 'Their maker is gone, but her defiance still walks within my domain, beating through a relic of an insolent nature. Now, I make you the keeper, the withholding essence of their disgusting magic. Hold on to it, make sure it won't see past your corrupted will. Go and join the others I've sent. Make more of them, turn them all!'

The Eternal's instructions had been followed meticulously. With the spoils of a dying Earth, Death had produced forth an empty, dark space he would call home. The same home kept welcoming him for millennia, feeding from him and he feeding from it, in a never-ending loop. As Health's power diminished, Death's grew stronger, allowing him to bring to his side thousands of Human souls. Many were turned into silent inhabitants of his domain, while others were shaped into wicked soldiers.

The oldest fighters he had made were the strongest. Harpies devoted to the mission, they would join the rest of Nothing's brethren, bringing the nightmares of a life without love, without soul or health. They had the power to turn happiness into torment, joy into suffering.

If they all shared the same power and were all under his total control, the one who was born next to him, the same one with whom he shared his origins, was the only one he feared. Almost as strong as their evil maker, the one who was turned from light to darkness lay prisoner in the secret of his dungeons, hidden away from prying eyes. As the memories flashed before his deformed gaze, the large Harpy briefly entertained a worrying thought. If the Gods found a way to come back, challenging his master, they might also discover the perilous secret he guarded.

But hesitation held no ground in the malevolent mind of Death. Desterea was safe, protected by an impossible path. Neither Humans nor Gods knew of her existence, and even more, no one could break the eternal spell that bound them to one another.

After all, I'm eternal, as eternal is my master, he thought as he pushed any fear away. *My duty was to face one God only as I kept this world under my grip. Instead a second one came to his rescue. She, the one who has prevented me from fully being, to have the absolute power of extinction, kept hiding in the shadows, resurrecting their hopes over and over. Even with her sceptre in my hands, reforged by my king into the most formidable weapon, she still lived. She lived to defy my will, to come back and mock my efforts…to take it all away from me. But it doesn't matter,* Death quickly objected to his own thoughts. *I've kept my crown and I will still. I've shaped the history of this world. After the God fell, I had no power challenging me. Even his stupid followers were nothing compared to my army. No matter how many times they have come back, attempting to conjuring him to life, I swept them off this world. I am the sole conqueror!*

'Now tell me,' Death finally spoke again, louder, looking at Oz. 'What's their plan?'

'They will revert everything that has happened and will go beyond…' Oz stared back at his master, unafraid. As if he was looking for answers to secretive questions, he kept wandering in his lord's mind.

'What is it that you are so avid to understand?' Death had captured Oz's intention.

'We all share the same mind, your mind… It's taking a lot of energy to even understand it.' The Harpy's words were slow and measured.

'You have eternity to get to that point. Focus on them now.' And Death moved away, ready to act on his next steps.

'My master…' Oz continued, challenging his king's command. 'If Health is back and she has her artefact with her, how is it that you are still here, that we are still here?'

And to that question, all the Harpies showed the same, terrified look. Whatever Oz had seen in their master's mind, it was something none of them would dare to ask or speak of. The secret of Death's existence, his ability to come back over and over, even after a fatal blow inflicted by the Gods, was not meant to be discussed. Completely convinced his power could not be overcome and that nothing of Noah's mind and soul was left to challenge him, Death dismissed Oz's question, moving further away, his head signalling to the others it was time to move.

Although permanent and strong, the turning of Noah into a Harpy was somehow disturbed. Noah's mind and will were destroyed, as it had happened to all the Harpies that had come before him. In the millennia of Death's making, he had never failed the spell once. If something different was lurking in the shadow of Oz's will, it had to be connected to who he once was, before giving himself up to his new master.

The hidden trio had climbed back to the top of the hill and quietly observed the enemy from far off. Whatever they were supposed to do, it was failing to materialize into a plan.

'I can't look at him,' Anita whispered, her voice muffled by the Chomp's shield. 'There is nothing left of Noah in it.'

'It is still him, Anita,' Revelia replied, determined to rescue him. 'We only have to reverse this magic and bring him back.'

'He is nof dead,' Trusk added, his face showing some hard thinking. 'He is sfill here, fhis is a good sign, no?'

'He is one of them now…how can someone be more dead than that?' Anita challenged. 'But it's true, he looks different from the others.'

'He seems to be holding to a Human shape, doesn't he?' The Leonty gazed through the veil, her eyes attempting the well-known magic. 'It's like he is resisting. I can still see Noah's future if I look at him. At least up until this dark hole I see in everyone's future…'

'You mean he will be back?' Trusk asked, happy.

'I mean his mind. I see his intentions. He is planning something, something dangerous…'

'He is with them, with Death… I see danger all over, even without your powers,' Anita said aloud. 'They are moving. Let's go!'

Chapter Five

Earth Node

∞

Out in the open space, embraced by mine and my siblings' true powers, I found myself hanging on what my host once was, his feelings, his emotions. Daniel being the one who had carried the deed of sacrifice, he had done it by bringing in me a piece of himself. If I had been lying within his heart in the many lifetimes he had lived, the final spell of conjuring had acted more like a switch. Daniel's core was not completely destroyed. Instead, his soul silently took his rightful place within mine. His presence strong, it drove my will to the point of distraction. Feeling the pain and hurt by Noah's departure, I tuned in with his loved ones' struggles.

My ears close to Anita's and Revelia's words, beside Trusk's actions of protection, I rewound my past fast, my memories going beyond the last few decades. That bitter taste of loss, that feeling of being unable to be there and everywhere that mattered, was not strange to me. The excruciating pain of seeing my people, my Awokens, being tormented by Nothing's army was something I had experienced before.

It wasn't long before the journey brought back the memories of the ancient times, right after our dear mother had sacrificed herself, while my brothers and sister succumbed to the evil. A gathering of Awoken Ones sat around a large table, by the tall tower where I resided. Some planned their next moves against the most powerful Harpies who were spoiling the world with their defiance, turning the Humans into prey. Some others kept quiet, waiting for instructions.

White marble ran all across the space, turning into a warm orange shade under the soft kiss of the sun peeking through the large windows. Here and there, some Awokens joined the majestic picture absorbing the same magic, radiating like tiny stars in a room too small to contain their supreme power.

Amongst the many, Iris and Cherish stood next to the wide opening onto the large terrace. As if they kept the balance between two opposite powers, one absorbed the light of the sun, almost feeding from it. Iris, in the other hand, kept looking away, hidden in the shade of one of the tall pillars. Her mind troubled, she looked into the invisible beyond of her worries.

'Hiding has served us well, so far...' she said, interrupting an ongoing argument.

'Doing nothing? Letting it happen, hoping that he won't pursue his final goal?' Cherish asked, annoyed. Next to her Eros moved close.

'This is an evil that doesn't rest,' I replied to Iris. 'We can't take for granted what he will do next, what they will do, spilling over the boundaries of this world.'

'Love,' the one called Asher interrupted. 'What good would come from doing something like that?'

'He is powerful and eternal. He is everywhere he wants to be, but their army is not,' I stated, moving towards the terrace, attempting to look at a faraway, unreachable node.

'Is there also this risk?' Ashrat and her twins said at once, their voices tuned to the same sound, their minds speaking at once.

'You are saying his followers could come to this world from the other three nodes? Can they pass through?' Eolen wasn't convinced.

'They are powerful enough to find a way to use the nodes and increase their numbers here on Earth...' Kathor replied, before I could add anything else. 'We have enough enemies here already. What will they do when they are done with Talush, Varayal?'

'Runae...' I added. 'Time won't resist long either.'

'So, the solution is to destroy the node? What if the Gods need to reach us, reach you?' Cherish moved restlessly, impatiently, in and out of the room, her feet as if floating on the large square tiles.

'This is why I'm not suggesting we destroy the node,' I replied, placing a calming hand on Cherish's shoulder. 'But I need to know where they come from. I need to make sure it's not mother's gate, our node. We should cast a spell on it, making it unreachable by evil.'

'Whatever spell we use, the passage would still be material and therefore reachable,' Eros said. He moved to one of the large windows, his eyes scanning the defenceless world outside. After exchanging a meaningful glance with Cherish, he added, 'It could work if we hide it within our own power.'

'Even then, we all would be at risk,' Iris said, moving towards the inner part of the room where a cold breeze offered relief from the scorching heat. Her face intact, there was no duality within her. The age of a frozen time still had to come. 'I think we can do more than that.'

'What are you suggesting?' Cherish's attention was fully on her.

Before Iris could reply, a bright light flashed across the land, infiltrating through the tower's openings, blinding us all. Moments later, a crack between time and space opened in the near sky, an immense power seeking its target. I stood still, taken in an instant, my Awokens disappearing one by one. The last thing I saw was Eros and Cherish reaching out to each other, their gazes locked in a moment of petrifying fear. In a sudden snap, we were all gone. In the empty room, a shining red diamond appeared, slowly rotating in the air. A large white shell moved beneath it, letting it rest in its opening. Like a gentle, soft touch, the two pieces merged together, the shell closing its folds around the red heart, lying quietly inside.

Like waves in a raging storm, I and all the Awoken Ones reappeared at once, standing in the same spot we stood before the unexpected magic. Our power made stronger, our faces shocked, we stared at the artefact floating before my chest. Somewhere in the cosmos, a supreme sacrifice had been made, reaching me from afar.

With a heavy heart and profound desperation, I realized what my mother had done. The urgency of action collided with the realization of what had occurred, sending us into a frenzy. Creation's act of protection meant only one thing: Nothing was closer than ever, and the chance of a swift, inevitable end loomed over us, catching us unprepared.

'What happened? How did we get here?' Two more Awoken Ones manifested in the centre of the room. Harmonia and Strife had been moved from their distant location.

'You are here,' I said. 'I'm afraid we have no time left. We must act now, faster than we anticipated.' I gazed at the sky. The weight of my mother's decision threatened to shatter my soul into a myriad pieces, too many to even match the number of my Awokens.

'Something has happened in the west,' Strife said, his face unusually dark, his thoughts conflicted. 'The enemy has appeared in the Harbour of the Giants. They bring the black mark of downfall.'

'How did they reach the island of the thousand statues? In the middle of the ocean?' Eros asked, perplexed.

'Does it matter?' Iris asked, her composure unshaken by the dire news. 'They know. They must know the node is on an island. They just don't know which one…'

'The Monsai are powerful, but they are still Humans,' I replied, glancing at Mnemosy. 'They won't survive an evil they can't begin to understand. Their statues speak of veneration, not war. Please, Mnemosy, take Eolen with you.' Without hesitation, the two disappeared swiftly.

'Love,' a voice whispered in our collective minds, interrupting my train of thought. Somewhere far away, Agapei called for help. *'The Tepe Valley is under attack. A new personification of a deadly power has just manifested here…'*

'But you are one of the Seven, accompanied by the others,' Harmonia interrupted, a brief smile adding a hopeful note to the announcement. 'Well, most of the Seven,' she concluded, glancing at Eros. His first act upon returning was to move closer to Cherish, their hands clasped, their essences bound by supreme affection.

'Philiat and Pragma are not with us. We won't last long. This enemy is much more powerful now. Something is giving them strength,' Agapei continued. The fear in his tone crept into us, instantly erasing Harmonia's optimism. *'I can feel their effect spreading like the disease they carry, and their numbers are increasing. Among them, a new evil walks the lands… The incarnation of a merciless end has shown its deadly footprint.'*

'Whom do you speak of?' I asked, my worry joining the others'.

'The enemy whispered a name. They call him Death. That ending power now has a body and will of its own. He seems to be leading the other Harpies against the cities of Gope and Karahan to a point of no return.'

'We won't run!' I thundered, sensing Strife's emotions loudly and clearly in my head. 'Harmonia, control your brother, please!'

Turning my back to the crowd, I moved outside onto the large terrace. In my mind, many thoughts fought for attention. My mother had fallen, my siblings were in danger, and Earth was in check by evil. Mirroring my steps, Cherish followed me into the open.

'Look to your left,' Cherish said, her eyes fixed on the rumbling horizon over a territory that would soon become the Aegean Sea. 'They are turning the world into fire and misery. Their infection will soon reach every known land, and then here, to us, to the node.'

'What are you suggesting?' I couldn't bring myself to look at the far eastern point.

'We can fight them. We will fight. But you are right… They cannot find the passage and use it to reach Runae and the other worlds. You need to take the node away with you.'

'The artefact you have seen… It has much more power than before. Maybe I should push it to its limits and…'

'Turn it into something else,' Cherish added.

'It's still not safe enough,' Iris said, joining us outside, resisting the urge to turn her back to the shining sun. 'I'll find a better solution if you give me enough time.'

'Time is a luxury we don't have,' I replied sharply. 'Even with my brother's power, it wouldn't be enough. We must go now.' Turning back inside, I addressed Eros. 'Call the others. We might need all of you.'

'Love,' Cherish interrupted. 'You sent Philiat and Pragma against the one called Athymos. We can't possibly let her roam free.' At her words, a terrifying feeling overcame me. I was spreading my power too thin to resist the enemy. Soul's statement echoed in my mind. Yet, I had to be everywhere that mattered.

So the Awokens and I soon moved to battle, in face of all odds. Determined to push back the forces of evil at any cost, we joined Agapei, Storgén, Xena, and

Prometheus in the vast expanse of the great desert. As we materialized, our combined power lifted the yellow dust into the scorching air. In the midst of our swirling magic, a dark poison spread across the landscape, heralding the ominous promise of an epic confrontation with our formidable foe.

When we arrived, the two large metropolises of Gope and Karahan were already empty. All the residents of the two once-lush cities had been turned to dust, their souls in the enemy hands, the remnants of their essence ghostly walked the large streets. Vegetation, trees and every life were dying fast, giving up lands to the near desert, merging with it. Every trace of the glorious emerald glass covering every structure, making the city sparkle like a precious stone, was gone. As if the destruction had come directly from the sky, the top of every building, every home, every symbol of beauty and strength had been stripped away, revealing the bare metal and stone underneath.

At the horrifying havoc, the Awoken Ones had gone into shock. Silent and saddened by the evil making, I stopped right after the city gates of Gope. The large, golden frames crumbled together with the silent stones they stood on. The Harpy's wicked power had gone beyond the kingdom of living. Like Agapei had warned us, their influence had grown so much that they could turn every matter into non-existence.

'So much pain is now mingling with silence…' Agapei appeared, responding to my presence. As I stood by his side, I could see in his look the clear, heavy sorrow.

'They are not silencing life,' Storgén added, manifesting next to me. 'This is the annihilation of every matter.'

'I can still feel them,' I replied, touching the few bare standing walls of what once was a large entry point. 'They were here not long ago. Their emotions still float in the air…'

'And so was the enemy,' Cherish said as she brushed her fingers on the crumbling walls. 'Look at their evil hands, leaving traces of dark magic all around this place. They are still vivid and tangible. Some are still smoking out of their diabolic spell. They are not far.'

Almost like a premonition, Cherish's words proved to be right. A few moments later, at the turn of the very centre of the destroyed city, a loud scream shrilled in the air. A large gathering of diabolic entities roamed the area, dutifully carrying out their tasks. Some Humans spared from the unmerciful raid squeezed together in horror. With their faces covered by their arms, they cried as they awaited the same end reserved for their relatives, their people. Among the visions of an upcoming end, they ignored a far more terrifying outcome. They were about to face something worse than death. They were the chosen ones, the ones that could bring more power to their new master, the ones that would help him to complete his mission.

'We are going to bury this whole place and the memory of it after we have dealt with you,' the one called Algos said. 'There is going to be nothing and no one that will remember you.'

'But don't worry,' Desolos added; a wicked grin flashed on her smoky face. 'You'll come with us…'

Old and young alike, the group was about to be turned into newborn Harpies when I stormed in, followed by the Awoken Ones. In the blink of the prisoners' eyes, a raging battle unfolded, ethereal beings fighting each other, light and dark mixing in a raging storm. Flashes of magic moving in every direction, my Awokens pushed against the enemy , cleansing the space with every inch of power they held. As our powers clashed against one another, a few Harpies disappeared unnoticed. In between the smoke and dust filling the air, they abandoned the battle to then reappear beside the Humans.

'Your lord is waiting for you,' Desolos said, as she teleported at their back with the swing of a foggy arm. 'Now, listen to his call.'

'No! You won't have them!' Ashtra moved in between the hunters and their prey. Her hands stretched in the open.

'One of you against five of us?' Algos laughed, ready to attack.

'One? So you Harpies can't really see the truth with your own wicked eyes?' Ashtar materialised next to her sister, followed by her other twin, Ashrat.

The three sisters shielded the Humans left alive with an unexpected resistance. With the power of a trio, they merged into one, inflicting a bright, painful light into the Harpies' core, making them bleed a dark vapor from their cuts.

At the centre of the destroyed city, I moved swiftly against the many enemies. The more I erased, the more would appear in a quick sequence. Assisted by Cherish and Eros, we pushed forwards in all directions. As we moved further away from one another, a swirl made of grey fog and dust rose in the air. Its shape took form from within the twisting whirlpool of dark energy acquiring limbs of its own. At last, a face appeared. With eyes stretched to the sides and no mouth or nose to be seen, the Harpy of Madness and Agony manifested.

'Your mind is mine!' she shouted as her left hand surfed the air in a malevolent gesture. A trail of strings twirled towards Cherish whose attention on the enemy ahead had made her blind to the attack coming from behind. In between her and Lytas, Eros moved fast as he fell under the Harpy's magic, trapped and enveloped by her evil power.

'I see...' Lytas said, her voice filled with the satisfaction of discovery. 'Oh, the memory of her...her presence conquers your every thought… Well, let me show you how it will end.' And the Harpy pulled her hand back, snatching Eros with it. As if the invisible strings of evil could drag his core out of his intangible matter, he screamed, releasing a wave of fear all around.

I could see his thoughts being crumbled, I could sense his feelings being crushed, distorted by the nightmares the enemy played in his head. A vision of Cherish being tortured unfolded before his eyes as if it were real. Forced to watch his loved one die of a painful end, Eros's desperation thundered all across the city.

'Take your hands off him!' Cherish said as she preceded me in the attack. Her presence glowed bright amidst the dusty wind twisting around the Harpy and Eros. As she got close, a blast of energy released all around, dispersing the evil spell, making Lytas dissolve in the air. As the yellow sand fell back on the dry ground and the wind subsided, the two reappeared before us. Cherish held Eros in her arms as he looked at her, terror still lingering in his eyes.

'Don't worry… I'm the Awoken of Memory after all. I'll reinstate your true memories. Close your eyes, my love.' And she softly moved her hand on his face as if caressing him with the gentle touch of a restoring power.

'Your witchcraft won't stop us!' Desolos's shouts reached us from afar. Her mouth enlarging in a disturbing sound, she had released the full desperation of a sad whistle. Her mouth, wide open, turned into a horrifying hole. Like a song enchanting a suggestible snake, the shrilling melody hit the three twins, capturing them in a dull, frozen spell.

'It won't work this time,' Harmonia declared, her voice a beacon of hope. Her face shone like a tiny star, her light radiating courage and resolve. She stood alongside her brother, their united presence pushing back the melancholic sound of desperation, returning it to its grim owner. A wide, transparent veil of shimmering light ran across the battlefield, enveloping the Harpy and enclosing her in a cage of pure, bright will.

Despite her entrapment, the Harpy wore a suspicious smile. Her gaze fixed on Strife, whose expression had turned unexpectedly sorrowful, as if he had exchanged roles with his enemy. He felt Desolos's insidious power reverberating in his ears, slipping through the cracks of his weakening mind.

Close to him, the Harpy's smile widened, a sinister reflection of her delight in the success of her evil actions. She seemed almost jubilant, a personification of contemptuous satisfaction, her happiness a stark contrast to the turmoil she had sown. The veil of light shimmered, its brilliance both a barrier and a testament to the fragile hope that still lingered in the air, even as Strife struggled with the encroaching darkness within.

'Something is happening to me…' Strife twitched and fell on his knees. His hands on his ears, he shouted, 'Make her stop!'

Captured by the long desire of something different, something of a dark nature, Strife's eyes turned grey. His light diminished as he gazed at the twins. Able to move unchallenged, in between the trust of his siblings, he swung his arms straight ahead, his energy forming a sharp, pointed blade. Like a flash darting through the air he struck Ashtar in her core, splitting her apart, her power dissolving into the dusty air. Right in front of the shocked face of the twins, almost instinctively, Harmonia screamed my name, begging for help.

In the brief instant of never-ending pain and sorrow, I moved by Ashtar and her sisters. My eyes, as if on fire, looked at Strife, who struggled to maintain his true nature, his body convulsing between good and evil. As I gazed at the true enemy, Desolos looked back at me with delight. She had struck us from within, using one of us in a treacherous, cowardly act. Her smile reached her deadly eyes as she bent her body in a mocking bow, a clear message that evil could reach us whenever and however it wanted.

'Now, show me your dark side,' Desolos said, raising her arms in the air, waiting. 'Because it's obvious you have one,' she added, glancing at Strife, who was slowly turning into a grey shadow.

'Harmonia,' I called out, ignoring the Harpy's remark. 'Take your brother away from battle. You and only you can contain the pain he is going through. Take him home, now!'

Without hesitation, Harmonia moved beside her brother, folded her arms around him, and disappeared. Behind me, Ashtar's sisters staggered, their hands on their chests. The same piercing blade that had erased my Awoken replayed its horror on them. With their unbreakable link dragging them towards the same fate, their chests started to bleed rays of light, stains of power marking their bodies as it slowly left them. They had lost a piece of themselves, a piece of me. Under the Harpy's attack, they found themselves betrayed by our own kind. The weight of the event claimed a price against our true nature. They had been challenged by an enemy too powerful to fight, and so they slowly let go, succumbing to an end tainted with the harsh colours of betrayal.

Losing the twins was painful to both my eyes and my heart. I could feel their energy dissipating—partially returning to my core, yet leaving behind a trail of their now orphaned magic in the vastness of nothing.

Turning back to the Harpy, I thundered, 'You are not welcome here! You have never been. Whatever the source of your power is, I will eradicate it from Earth, for it is true that I am the protector of this world!'

My body enlarged, my essence turned into a pure glow. The Seven suddenly joined me in the fight, their arms raised, their hands to their chests. My artefact emerged, spinning on its own. As the shell opened, the heart released an overwhelming flare of energy, scattering around the area, engulfing Desolos, Algos, and the other nearby Harpies. A moment later, when my power reached the edges of Gope, clearing the path to the gates of every evil, a new resistance, the new enemy we had heard of, revealed itself.

Chapter Six

An Indomitable Enemy

∞

Standing untouched, large and dark, a piercing hole floated in the wake of my bright light, bringing the cold and emptiness of a night without stars. Death, the leader and master of the Harpies, had finally made himself known to me and my Awokens. His name finally had a face, yet his figure remained obscure and impenetrable. His evil actions had hands yet unseen, contorting into a mystical dance. His long hair moved with its own will, like thousands of snakes, slithering around his deformed face. His arms long, his legs enlarging at every step, he wore shining, golden metal wrapped around his features. An *X* standing on its side covered his large chest. His head appeared grotesquely distorted, with no nose or mouth—only a spinning vortex where his lips should have been.

'All of this for nothing,' he started; his voice was low, his steps measured. With no fears in his moves, he dragged his long, dark cloak as if he wanted to slowly savour the taste of his upcoming victory. For every inch he moved closer, he expanded in size. 'They will all come back. In fact, they are already coming back...'

'If they are, they will soon find their own end again, by my hand. And so will you,' I replied, ready to fight.

'Tell me...do you know who I am?' he asked as he got closer.

'You are the one they call Death. Another diablery sent by the one who does not find the strength to face me. Tell me, how did you enter this world? How did you enter this city?'

'Thanks to the King of Emptiness we walk freely anywhere he needs us to be. Even within your protected abode, we have access to lands, matter, hearts. Here and everywhere. Here and in the other worlds...' And Death stopped, a few steps away from me. 'We will walk those lands too, soon. We know about the sacred waters...'

Death laid his menace right in the open. The most worrying threat up until that moment was sent right to me as a torment. The enemy knew the passage's location and it would use it soon.

'You cannot pass through the Gods' gates. None of your thugs can.' Desperate to prove him wrong, in the deepest secrecy of our shared minds, I told Iris and Cherish to depart and reach the node. *If he is telling the truth, you must stop anyone who tries to break through. Go now, please, hurry!*

'We can and we will,' Death replied. 'But even if we couldn't, little it matters. We are already there... He is already there...we only need your door to unify our forces, to finally merge these worlds into our destructive power.'

'Where?' I thundered.

'Everywhere,' he murmured as he smiled. 'We are part of him and we are one. We are the anticipation of his unchallenged victory. Two worlds are already gone, two more will soon follow. You'll see...'

Tired of being tested, I had no words left to spare. All I wanted to do was to act, attacking the enemy at once. I stretched my arms and let the power of my own core clash against the large Harpy. Wobbling and shifting back and forth, Death absorbed the blow, breaking apart into thornlike fragments, his matter decomposing and yet rebuilding back again. As he was turned to dust, so his dark particles and evil will came back together. Something held his core to a status of perpetual existence, a blueprint of magic able to remake itself over and over. His smile appearing on his re-formed face came to mock my desperation.

'It's not possible!' Kathor thundered in my head. *'We used our full strength… He should be shredded to pieces.'*

'Our power was effective but his matter is holding to something out of existence, Xena added. *It's like an echo of something else moving within space and reality.'*

'Let me tell you what's going to happen. Let me tell you what we are going to do to your world,' Death continued. 'This world must go back where it belongs. But we won't rush our hands as we had done with Talush…Varayal. No, you and your power need to be challenged in a different way… You see, he could infect and kill to move against Talush; tear and extract every life to move against Varayal; but you? Here? No… This world is sustained by emotions, by memory, by belonging…'

'He is buying time… We should leave and join Iris and Cherish,' Eros let out.

'So this is what we are going to do,' Death continued. 'We are going to erase every life, one by one. We will bring hate and sorrow where you planted love and happiness. Imagine this: your people and their stupid lives buried under feet of soil, suffocating in desperation. Then, when you beg for us to stop, and you give yourself to me, then we will mercifully end you and your world, forever.'

'You won't cross the node!' Iris's voice resounded in my head.

'There are too many!' Cherish shouted.

The struggles of the other two fighting against the Harpies by the node spoke clearly in my head. I could not entertain Death in conversations nor fight at the expense of my Awoken Ones so I kneeled and placed my hands on the ground. My gaze fixed on the enemy, my mind moved beyond, over the hills of the far north, by the island where the passage stood unprotected, under an imminent threat. Without any further ado, we vanished from sight, raising a sandy fog all around the ground, hiding the instant disappearance of the Humans we brought with us.

At the other side, we landed on soft, green grass. My Awokens left my core and moved across the fields, some rushing their feet to the large lake nearby, some taking care of the survivors who had been moved from their city in ruins to the opposite side of our world.

'Good, you are here,' Cherish said, worried. 'We managed to push back a few Harpies, but one slipped through the node.' And a malevolent twirl darted in the air, against her.

'It's too late, ha ha ha,' a Harpy mocked as he floated closer, his hands stirring in intricate movements.

Another attack flashed across the space from him to us, bouncing off the shield Xena had just raised in the air. A few more Harpies emerged in quick succession, moving like invisible ghosts. At every appearance another spell released against us.

'Only one?' I replied, moving towards the shoreline of a quiet lake. The surface looking calm, it was like danger had not infected its purity, like the evil had not just stormed in.

'Yes. But I don't know where the Harpy is heading.' she added. 'He could be in Talush, Varayal or Runae. Iris followed him. I couldn't stop her. She just...went.'

'If what Death said it's true, there is no Talush nor Varayal any more. Why don't you just die!' I shouted as Algos manifested in between me and the portal ahead. A flicker circled around the invisible passage. Whoever had entered it, they had just landed on the other side.

As I pushed back the Harpy once more, making her disappear, the fear of an imminent danger ensnared my heart. An electrifying power shook my body, paralyzing my limbs, making me crash onto the soft grass of the lonely island.

'Something is coming...' I whispered as a multitude of Awokens spun off my being. 'Something is burning in the skies...'

'Where?' Storgén added, as he moved beside me, his hands on my shoulders, his gaze fixed on the immense blue. Above the peaks of a wonderful city made of glass, silver, and gold a trace of cosmic power flickered in the sky, small yet bright.

In the far distance, the words of an unexpected wonder spread among a gathering of people. With their heads raised and chatter growing loud, the Humans discussed a meteor visibly glittering against the bright morning sky.

'Nothing is willing to annihilate his own army just to destroy this world. What he couldn't achieve directly, he made the universe carry out his malevolent act. No soul, nothing will escape the impact,' another Awoken chimed in.

'I still bear the duty to protect this world,' I asserted. 'I can't simply let it happen. Even in this eleventh hour, I still possess the power to shield this planet from being reduced to dust!'

'Love, the impact will be too immense to evade.'

'I understand, Kathor. I respect your insight into the sheer potency this will unleash upon us. You are, after all, the Awoken of Power. We need to turn that energy against it, not shy away from it.'

'Even if we were to fight, it would necessitate all our powers, your entire strength,' another voice spoke.

'What does the Awoken of Hope have to say about this?' I asked.

'It is the only way, yes, master. We have to return it to you if you want to have a chance.' And the one called Asher looked at the others, reminding them that was the only option they had.

'So, we shall!' Kathor replied. 'We will give it back, no hesitation. There is no good ending in the final pages of our existence. We might fight better as one.'

'We will, but on one condition,' I said. 'Whatever happens to me, I won't let this world end. People will survive, Humans will rebuild. But I can't let them live without love. They must have it. It belongs to them! The Seven will stay, not part of the whole, this time.'

The group was taken by surprise. Many raised their voices, objecting to my decision. If they were going to make it, if Nothing was going to be stopped, it would require every inch of strength they had in their hands, especially the strongest ones.

'Love, are you sure this is the right thing to do?' Cherish asked, her voice low, her worries passing through.

'I am. I would ask you to stay too, to give them the power to remember, but you are the strongest beside the Seven. I'll need you by my side.'

'Master, how long before the impact?' another Awoken asked, staring at the blue sky. A shining dot blinked in the pure blue above, leaving an almost invisible trail behind.

'Eight days, and it will be colossal…' Kathor replied before I could speak. 'It will crash in the northwest, by the great glaciers, north of the green valley. It will spread fast, melting the ice in a few seconds. The world could be washed away, if not completely destroyed.' And her hands pointed to the far land, over to the stunning golden city that stood quietly on the horizon.

'We will contain it. We might not be able to stop it entirely, but we can contain it,' I said.

'What about the other Gods? Any chance any of them are still out there?' Cherish asked, moving close to the edge of the crystal lake.

'If they are, they are facing him too. I can't hear my sister's voice any more and neither can I hear my brother Soul. We are on our own, I'm afraid.'

'Love,' Cherish continued as she gazed back at the node. A golden circle formed all around the passage. Someone's power held its magic in between realities. To our surprise, it flashed three times and briefly glowed wide. A gentle breeze passed through and, suddenly, the portal shut down.

'Iris?' Cherish called. 'I thought it was her?' she added as we waited for her reappearance.

The one who insisted in hiding the passage had succumbed to the pressure of an unstoppable bravery and slipped through the node, hunting for the one enemy who had preceded her. And yet she hadn't returned.

The Harpy had just reached the node on the other side, his appearance already bearing a deceptive disguise. White hair and a white beard appeared on what now resembled a Human's face. Shortly after, he was confronted by someone clearly unprepared for a foreign invasion. Unaware of the danger his presence represented, an Aqualymph materialised at the edge of a tiny island, at the centre of their ancient sea. The expression on the stranger's visage spoke of a friendly request for help. Gifted with the power of a thousand lies, the wicked Harpy had already put his magic to work. Among the many residents of the blue waters, a few walked right in front of him, their bodies slowly taking shape as they dragged the very soil from the ground into their matter, becoming one with the surrounding nature.

'I'm Aura,' one Aqualymph said. 'The God of this world has put me as a gatekeeper. We were not expecting anyone. This gateway is open only to the Gods. Who are you?'

'My name is Lëogan,' the man said, attempting a smile. 'I'm here because my world is in danger. I come to ask for help…'

'What world are you speaking of?' The Aqualymph looked at her guest with suspicion. Something wasn't right.

'Earth. We are under attack! We need your help, your power, your magic to face the enemy!'

'If what he says is true, we need to bring him to the council!' another Aqualymph suggested.

'Yes, please. I need to talk to them!'

Those words were the first lie spoken by the one who would soon be known as the Snake, whispering into the innocent and suggestible minds of my brother's world.

Soon after, he would corrupt the hearts of many—Aqualymphs, Humans, and Leonty alike. Unaware of the enchantment cast upon them, they were instigated against one another. Humans were convinced to wage war against the Leonty, while Aqualymphs were pushed to abandon their land, joining the new rising power in the north, and eventually allying with the evil forces led by the Crimson Queen. In the secrecy of his malevolent mind, the Snake sowed the initial seed of Nothing's conquest through the hand of his chosen ones.

Not long after they had left the node, Iris found herself in the vastness of nothing. The calm waters were silent. Strangely, no one greeted her arrival. Unable to reach the other side of the shoreline and surrounded by a dense, thick fog, she shouted for Time.

'So you are of Love's making,' Time suddenly appeared behind Iris, startling her.

'You are here,' she replied sharply, unchallenged by the presence of another God. 'Love's memory is also my memory. I can see you in my mind. I know you…'

'I was expecting this moment. I've been expecting it for quite some…well, time.' The God stared at the Awoken One, inspecting her closely.

'Love is fighting Nothing's army. His power is reaching heights of worrying proportions. They know about the gates. One just walked through the node a few seconds ago.'

'I know. I've seen it,' Time responded. His tone was calm, as if flattened by a boring discovery.

'And you let him through? Why?'

'Because I've seen him cross the node too many times for you to even begin to understand. It must happen this way.'

'I have no idea what you are saying, but I'm sure you've made a mistake,' Iris pushed back. Time's indifference to the gravity of her news surprised her. 'I'm not sure you know the evil of Earth, but one is surely capable of bringing chaos and destruction,' she added, looking worried.

'He is not here, is he?' Time's calm response transformed as his words travelled from him to the Awoken One. In Iris's ears, he was being dismissive. 'Don't occupy your already troubled mind with what is now our business. The Aqualymphs will take care of the future in store for them, for all of us.'

'So where are they? Those...lymphs?' Iris asked, pushing back against Time's sense of security.

'Leave this matter to me. My sight goes beyond yours. He was, after all...expected. And so were you.' And the God gazed at the far, purple sky above, lurking in the invisible folds of the years ahead. After a long silence, he resumed, 'You will be a way through in a plan that will take millennia to see fulfilment. You need to go back now and join your master in battle.'

'Before I go,' Iris said, moving closer, 'Love is determined to cast a spell on the node to prevent any evil from passing through. But I have the feeling this won't be enough. We need to make the node impossible to find. Help me. Help us!'

'Can't your kind stay and watch?' Time replied without looking at her, almost annoyed by the request.

'As if that would be enough…judging by the fact nobody was here when I walked in?' Once again, Iris was pushing her own will on the God.

'I see where this is going now. It does give me hope knowing that some possibilities have been…overlooked, even by me.'

'What does it mean?'

'The gates could indeed be hidden, but not solely within Love's magic. It needs more. A folding of time, in a lost past. That's when it needs to happen,' Time replied, raising his arm. The gates opened again, as if mercilessly inviting the Awoken One to leave.

'Help us!' Iris pleaded, moving closer to the flickering magic.

'There is something you can do. Something you must do alone. Something you must do in the future ahead. But beware, your actions will cost you dearly! You will have to let the days run their course, no matter the pain it might cause. Then, and only then, you will be able to do what you wisely proposed.'

'Tell me!' There was no hesitation in Iris's heart and voice. She was ready.

'I've seen pieces of countless possible futures. Too many to count. But they all share the same ending for me. However, your presence here, now, confirms something I had heard in the mad whispers of a witch. There is a way to create a timeline where I could return from my prison. Love needs to do it himself, and to do so, he must face his greatest defeat. When, and only when, his core and artefact have been broken, take whatever piece you have left of it, of him, and use this spell to hide it from the enemy.'

A green glow manifested from within Time's presence. A spinning vortex enlarged right between his hands. Emerging from the twirling magic, a small wheel began to form. Its delicate structure shimmered as it moved from one bearer to the next, acquiring an ethereal string with each transition. Finally, it glided gracefully around Iris's neck. As it touched her, it sank into her form, fusing seamlessly with her essence. Green strings branched out from the point of contact, spreading like veins of magic across the left side of her face. Her left eye glowed brightly for a moment before turning grey, as if it had suddenly died.

'Now, Awoken One, you must remember. Don't interfere with the flow of time. Do not share our understanding with anyone, not even my brother. Do what you are now called to do, when and only when you have the heart with you!'

'The heart…' Iris whispered.

'The heart.' And, in an instant, the Awoken One was transported inside the gate, back to Earth. Her heart pounded, her eyes revealing a new magic, while her face struggled to contain the duality of past and present.

'Iris!' Cherish hurried towards her. I followed suit. 'Where is he? Where is the Harpy?'

'He was already gone, lost in a strange land. I met Time. He said we can leave the matter to him. He said everything was…expected.'

'Is my brother in danger?' I asked, worried. 'Is Runae facing enemy attacks too?'

'What happened to your face?' Cherish added.

'I'm fine,' she replied. Her cold tone, although aimed at dismissing my suspicion, was familiarly hers. 'I don't know. Time seemed…well…serene. He was strangely unconcerned. I asked him to help us, but he sent me back.'

'Sounds like my brother, alright. OK, we need to close the access to the node before we move against whatever is coming,' I pushed.

'We can still hide it from sight,' Iris said. 'I can use my magic to conceal this place.'

'We have no such power. And if we did,' I quickly replied, without questioning where Iris's idea had come from, 'it would mean leaving you behind, watching over this spot. We can't have that.'

'Let's transfer its property to your own artefact,' Cherish interjected. 'Move it within your essence. If you need to walk through it, you will be able to do so with just the power of your mind.' And with Cherish's suggestion, Iris's understanding of Time's words came to her at once. Whatever he had asked her to do, it would not only protect my relic but also the node.

So the time came when another spell was cast on the vessel of my power. A new magic fused with that of our mother, adding the ability to be undetected, hidden in the very core of my being. Blind to what the future would bring, condemned to a life split in halves, I put my trust in the very item I was soon going to lose.

Chapter Seven

11200 B.C.

∞

The potent magic of the cosmic passage had returned to resting within my artefact when I gazed back to the sky. Hurried ahead by the new devilry sent by Nothing, I dismissed the worrying notion that a Harpy had just slipped through the node. With the portal made impassable by the new spell, I had prevented him from coming back and, with it, made impossible for Time to reach me.

With no hesitation, I sprinted up through the atmosphere, over the innocent lands and the powerless clouds. Followed by the Awokens, I left Earth and passed its lunar companion in the split of a second. As we pierced through the solar system, a hostile, gleaming rock welcomed us, its intentions dark and malevolent.

As it sped fast towards us, its trajectory spoke of a clear threat against the world we had left behind, aiming at the people we had vowed to defend. The closer we approached it, the vaster it became. The colossal stone dispatched to overcome Creation's design carried the signature of our enemy. Although Nothing's attack was executed by proxy, his lethal weapon preceding him, I could clearly perceive the enemy's obscure power surrounding it.

'Something is pushing its will on it. The speed is too high, the heat is too strong for this kind of asteroid!' Kathor shouted, as her body shifted in and out of our magic.

'There is darkness all around it,' Cherish added. 'I can almost see its hands pressing. Over there, where the space is piercing through, the evil is there!'

'Nothing is not just sending a mere emissary of death. He is accompanying it with its own power.'

'We won't be able to face it alone. Call all the Seven!' another Awoken shouted.

'No. We will face it now, the many of us,' I replied.

'Over there, where space is torn asunder, evil's presence looms!'

'There is a terrible evil walking right on its surface. We can't face this alone. Summon the Seven,' another Awoken cried out.

'No. We'll confront it now, with our combined strength,' I countered.

As we reached the scorching surface of the speeding projectile, we encountered our most formidable foe. Bodiless yet mighty, its will was the essence of everything that existed—dark, vast, and intensely diabolical. Its rage against us was palpable in every aspect we perceived. Amidst the trembling soil of the celestial body, another presence approached us—steady and untouched. His familiar golden feet hung in space, his large hands extended a deadly invitation, his face distorted by an unsettling grin. There was no body, only a dark, dusty mist accompanying it, taking the place of limbs and will. The hurtling rock had a rider; the master who we had recently left behind in Gope awaited our arrival. As he advanced, his form grew more ethereal, vanishing from sight, returning to nothingness.

'And so, another one comes to his end. The first abomination, the first...God created by something no longer wandering this void.' A voice resonated, thundering like a blend of metal and fire. 'Your creator is gone. Why don't you follow her footsteps?'

'We care not for your words,' I responded. 'Skip the pleasantries and return to the abyss from where you came. This world is beyond your grasp, and that of your master!'

'Ha ha ha ha. We are already here...we are already there. This is the sole existence permitted.' His laughter echoed, a dark disdain for all we stood for.

'Awoken Ones!'

The clash was cataclysmic, beyond prediction. We collided with a wall of pure emptiness, our powers rebounding to their respective sources. The adversary moved with elusive speed, untouchable, unstoppable. Every strike we launched proved fruitless as we crashed into the rocky soil, shattering upon impact. Suddenly, Death's large figure manifested once more. A long set of dark filaments extended from his fingertips to the asteroid we rode. As if he drove the carriage of extinction himself, he laughed repeatedly. A few Harpies emerged from his obscure body and launched themselves against us.

Like against a wall of pure, white magic, their assault left untouched. We stood still, one next to the other, our energy rising like a second sun. Next to me, Cherish gazed at the enemy resolute as her stems of light whipped in the raging wind. To her right side, Eros held the spot between her and many other Awokens. To my left, Agapei held the hand of Storgén and Storgén the one of Iris.

Caught in a standstill against time, we found ourselves unable to overcome the enemy, vulnerable to our own defeat. Time was of the essence, no room for hide-and-seek. In a matter of hours, we would reach

Earth, returning to where we had come from, mounted on the steed of death and devastation.

'It's leaving a trail behind. His Harpies feed from him,' Cherish's voice whispered within our minds. *'We only need to face one, only him. We are many.'*

'Alright. Let's do it!' I replied.

Multiple beings left the ranks, scattering all around our enemy, taking Death by surprise, catching him unprepared. The dance of war turned on our side. We trapped him in a circle of pure power, limiting his moves, as we prepared to strike the final blow. And so we reached him, like tens of bullets tearing his essence apart, pushing him through the cracks of the asteroid. Our power drilling down to the core, using the evil as the tip of a piercing machine, ended him completely.

Unknown to our ingenious minds, the sinister evil had driven us right where he needed us. As we dived into the interiors of the stone, cracks ran quickly all around, reaching the fragile surface. With a deep, thundering sound, Nothing's weapon broke apart into two fragments. Its trajectory unchanged, the solitary menace split into two colossal projectiles, both aimed at our most cherished realm.

'You never learn,' a disturbing, deep voice resounded from within the cosmos. Watching our every move, Nothing was nearer than ever. As the emptiness of his growing presence grew large, a cold, sinister omen played in my mind.

'There are two of them now!' Asher exclaimed, fear-stricken.

'This is beyond repair. We can't stop them both,' another Awoken added.

'Where there is Love, there is power,' I replied. 'I would do anything for them. Anything to shield them from this merciless malevolence.'

My light blazed brighter and my power expanded as I reached all the Awokens, connecting their souls and magic back with mine. Our essence stretched from fragment to fragment as if we could embrace the infinity. Our invisible hands seized both segments of the lethal rock, each one of us expanding beyond our collective power.

Cherish closed her eyes as her hands looked for mine, her magic made thin by the urgency of our sacrifice. I could barely feel her soul connecting with mine when she slipped away. With her, Eros was pulled away by the rocky bullet. As we sped past the moon, Nothing's evil will pressed against ours, pulling the two fragments apart.

There I searched for her, for her touch desperately. A companion of a lifetime, the keeper of memory and herald of protection was taken away from me in an instant. And so I surpassed the limit of every existing matter and I stretched beyond magic. I could see Eros holding Cherish in his arms as they plunged down, entering Earth's orbit.

'And this…is…it!'

Nothing, the supreme architect of every evil, the prophet of our mistakes, awaited that precise moment. Anticipating the leap of faith he knew I would take, his power surged against us, penetrating a core made too slim to resist. As I gazed at my loved ones slipping away, I was caught unprepared. Nothing's dark blade lacerated our matter as if it were a fragile veil. As if he claimed us for his own, he turned us asunder, generating a cataclysmic burst of energy.

In the surging explosion of our matter, I felt the soft embrace of a familiar voice. What felt like a new magic emerged from space to confront the evil we could not conquer any longer. Health's spirit permeated the space, reaching every piece of my shattered soul, attempting to reverse the enemy's attack.

'By the grace of the beloved mother of us all, it comes to you the balm to dying wounds. May you find the path to your heart and heal. My brother…'

'Sister…' I whispered, as I collapsed into a burst of glittering dust.

Health's supreme power merged with mine as I scattered across the atmosphere, the powerful blast of our combined energy dissipating into the void. Fragments of our magic rebounded through the dark expanse, permeating Nothing's essence, distorting it, corrupting it. Like dying Gods, we offered the ultimate sacrifice. We vanished into our collapsing will, plummeting towards our demise, the image of the Humans we cherished dissolving in our lifeless gaze. In our final, fading breath, Health grasped my soul, her whisper weaving a tender farewell.

The crush of our divided magic pounded like two bullets shaking the very centre of the Earth twice, destroying it. Like the dead meteors turning into dust, so were we, our souls gone, our beings ripped apart and left behind, sinking into the depths of ice and the Earth's crust.

With our collapse, two large cavities formed, the blast eradicating the life of our dear world, putting an end to nations and kingdoms, Humans and civilizations. The rising of the raging waters came right after, pushed by the blow, flowing out of their ancient banks, newly formed oceans claiming the long-waited lands back in their folds.

Health's pulverized sceptre glittered all across the small, familiar island of Noah's Bridge. Descending like a supreme conqueror, Death landed right in the same spot, on his face a grin of pure satisfaction.

Harpies appeared beside him in great number, rejoicing in a long-awaited victory. Their words like a lament of a dark prayer, they intoned a disturbing melody.

'Go now,' Death said to the gathering. 'Go and reach every corner of this world. As they die by the hand of an eternal winter, bury their cities, erase every trace of their God. Make sure every temple, every building erected in his name, disappears under feet of soil. Let the waters take the rest…'

A few moments later, Death stood alone. His henchmen sent on his mission, he roamed silently as he gazed the destruction unfolding on the planet.

'This world and everything within is an abomination.' A deep, slow moan reverberated in his dark mind. 'I have come to reclaim it all, to bring it back to where it belongs. Yet, something resists me now, a disease spreads inside me, against my will. I opened a way through in this world and yet, I cannot fully annihilate it, cannot undo the creation of these…these beings who call themselves Gods.'

'You have achieved your desire, you the Supreme Emptiness.'

'I have not,' Nothing continued. 'The end of my enemy has been temporarily averted. I will now delve into the depths of my own existence, to eradicate the spell cast upon me.'

'My Supreme Emptiness,' Death said, perplexed. 'You have already destroyed the creator of the Gods. You merged her power with yours when I came into being. I hold her secret within my power. What else can they possibly do against your terrifying will?'

'I did so. She shall remain dead for eternity. However, her children wield a stubborn magic that cannot be extinguished.'

'You have bestowed upon me great power, my Great Emptiness. But this world is vast, very vast.' Death looked up into the sky, hoping to catch a glimpse of his benefactor.

'At your feet lie the remains of one of the two who dared to violate my true essence. She is dead but these Gods will attempt to return, seeking to impose their will on what is right and true. Through their magic, they will seek amulets containing their powers. You must prevent their return. Open your arms, now!'

Without hesitation, the Harpy obeyed. His eyes transformed into large, rotating cavities as he received a second, precious gift. His hands contorted, his feet and legs expanded, and he transformed into a giant, dark being. From the ground, hundreds of golden pieces, the remains of what once was Health's artefact, merged, reshaping the surrounding nature into an obscure vortex. A long branch broke from the dead tree by his side, joining the unfolding dark magic. After a few moments, a long sceptre materialized before its rightful owner. A shining, metallic blade curved at its top. Death's supreme weapon was finally complete, ready to execute the merciless act.

Chapter Eight

Those Who Never Left

∞

Protected by Trusk's magic, Revelia and Anita had walked for miles. Following the Harpies, they had crossed the village once more and were headed to a very familiar place. In the silence of the cold evening, the enemy chanted a melancholic song. Their words cryptic, their voices deep, the sound carried the oppressive weight of an obscure spell able to turn life into death and death into a new form of life. As they moved slowly through streets and alleys, the Humans that had fallen under the impact of Nothing's attack rose again. Their flesh and bones left behind to rot under the ticking of time, their souls were ripped and dragged into the fold. The Harpies' song to guide them, they were enslaved and led to their new home.

As their final act unfolded together with the assault carried by their master in the faraway skies, they spread in the village like a dark fog, bringing the bitter taste of death, penetrating homes and buildings with no resistance.

The three stopped at the large square, next to the tall church, their forms still hidden by the Flare. In a dwelling to their right, several people gathered together in panic. Some walked among the scattered debris and shattered glass, swiping it away as best as they could. Some others entertained fully panicked conversations, their voices loud.

'We must warn them,' Anita said as she gazed at a few Harpies entering a home not too far from where they stood. 'They'll hear them...'

'I don't think it's going to make any difference,' Revelia replied as three more Harpies emerged back into the street, their hands displaying intricate movements. As if they could lead the dead and living alike just by raising their fingers, they looked as if they led an orchestra of evil assembly.

To Trusk's surprise, right in front of the building Anita had just pointed out, a stirring glow moved across the crumbling façade.

'Fhere... One of fhe Awokens!' he let out.

'Must be Eros or Iris, let's go,' Anita said, taking Revelia's hand. In the Leonty's mind, they were only wasting time.

As they approached the entrance now reduced to a mere hole in the wall, the flimsy, white shadow dissolved. To their shock, several men, women and children lay at the other side of the wall, terribly injured. Some, under the excruciating pain, had fainted. A few held still in between life and death, their laments reduced to a low murmur.

The place large, the remains of chairs and tables clearly recalled what once was a restaurant. At its centre, half of the bar counter was gone. Above the portion that had remained intact, a TV hung precariously from the ceiling. As it slowly swung left and right, it displayed vivid images of remote disasters. The voice of a news reporter came and muted in sync with the flickering, intermittent images.

'Dublin, it's gone! Completely under… The ocean has risen at least twenty feet and moved all the…to Kildare.'

'This is a nuclear attack,' one man said as he looked at the television. 'I'm tellin' ya!'

'Oh shut up, Eoin,' a woman grumped. 'They would know it by now, don't you think? Give me a hand with this table here, we need more space.'

'Please, water…' a voice whispered, struggling to talk.

Anita, Trusk, and Revelia walked silently inside the place, in shock. The horrifying scene carried the weight of a reality they had too easily dismissed. They were all focused on their own quest, their own lives. Now, as they slowly moved across the large room, guilt twisted their stomachs.

'Where you here when t…happened?'

'I was alright! It's shock…solutely shocking! Came in and went in fi…nutes. Me ma called me from…the time I…it was all gone.'

'It's confirmed that all major co…cities have been inundated by water. The Thames and…Seine have swallo…London and Paris in…same way…'

'It's happening all over the world,' Anita said as she gazed at some of the people lying on the dusty floor. 'We have to take them out of here, at least the ones that can walk, before the Harpies get any closer.'

'I'm afraid they can follow them anywhere,' Revelia replied. 'But it's worth a try?'

Without any concern over exposing their magic, Anita moved out of Trusk's veil and quickly manifested in front of the group. For a brief moment, the eyes of a little girl found her. Her tiny hands pulling onto a woman lying unconscious next to her, she called for attention. To Anita's surprise, her sudden appearance had been dismissed by everyone else, as if she hadn't presented herself out of nowhere.

'You can't be seen…' Eros's voice whispered from behind her. 'Iris is extending her power over you, please get back inside the shield.'

'We can't leave them here, in their hands.' Anita's forms were as fleeting as a passing ghost. Next to her, the Awoken One gazed at her with sorrow. 'And tell her to stop taking us off our timeline. I'm done wasting my days like this.'

'I know what you feel because it's what I feel too. Yet, your actions would be pointless. There is something far more important for you to do. Please, Anita…go back inside. They are coming.'

'Let them.' Revelia joined the other two, out in the open. 'If we can't outrun them, we can only fight them.' And she and Anita exchanged a look of growing determination.

Anita and Revelia moved at once. With no concern for the fear the presence of the Leonty could trigger in an already scared group, the two suddenly appeared in the middle of the room. Screams and shouts erupted almost instantly. With the unexpected magic and Revelia's strange look, panic ran from every corner.

'Please, stay calm. Keep quiet, we are here to help,' Anita begged, her face showing fear and guilt mixed together. The more their voices rose, the quicker the Harpy would come and find them.

'Who are you? What is that thing?' one man called out, his finger pointed at Revelia.

'It's hard to explain but, please, it's important you keep your voices low. Someone is after you, after all of us.'

'Not a nuclear attack, it's the aliens then!' Eoin shouted.

'It's not going to work, Anita. Please, I beg you…' Eros whispered from behind. His presence was undetectable but his words resounded loud in her mind. *'They are coming. They will all die…'*

'And so we will die with them!' she let out, resolute. To the unaware audience, she looked as if she talked to the walls. Gazes of shock ran across the room, the few who had questioned their presence went mute.

'Agapei? Is that you?' Iris materialised in a snap, triggering a loud gasp to the silent observers. Whatever nightmare they had witnessed up until that moment, it was all forgotten. Compared to the manifestation of a supreme being, their struggles were erased and supplanted by new worries.

Next to Anita, a bright glow appeared, flimsily floating in the dusty space. Its move slow, its light flickering, the Awoken One moved close to a few people who lay unconscious on the floor. Two arms and hands formed out of the ethereal light when a voice said, 'They need help. Some have left the land of living but there are others here who could still make it…'

'Were you with us all this time too?' Revelia asked. 'Within Anita?'

'Not really. Someone is summoning us. Someone who's able to force Love's will. He is releasing us out of his essence without opposition.'

'Can you help us?' Anita moved closer to Agapei, her hands gently brushing on an old woman's scars. Red, dried blood covered most of her face, and yet, she was still alive, her eyes glittering at the sight of the Awoken's magic. 'Can you help them?'

'I believe Time has revealed something of a great importance to Love. He needs us to let things follow their path. And your path leads you to Noah. He must come back…'

'Love wants us to leave them behind and go rescue Noah? Can't we do it all?' Revelia asked. She gazed over the opening in the wall. Her eyes became like a raging fire as she explored the near future.

Several visions mixed together with little logic. Although versed in foreseen future events, Revelia struggled to focus on one mind at time. Too many played a part in their upcoming moves, too many events formed and dissolved before the Leonty could grasp them. Like she had said before, intentions were all that mattered for her magic to work. Without a will to inspect, someone's desire to examine, she felt powerless.

And yet, the darkness she had explored before manifested once more. Within it, a bright sparkle blinked repeatedly, growing and shifting until it transformed into a large, white book. As the stiff covers creaked open, the pages flapped rapidly, like the fluttering wings of a thousand birds. A moment later, the book halted. On the open page, a name appeared, glowing with a ghostly light. The revelation of an inexplicable future marked the new vision, casting its significance into her mind like a brand.

The name pulsed with an intense luminescence, brightening the surrounding darkness. Revelia felt a profound connection to the name, as if it held the key to the future she had to shape, the battles she had to fight, and the sacrifices she had to make. It was a sign, a guidepost in the vast, unknown landscape of what was to come.

The future playing in her mind quickly changed as the Harpies moved unopposed, unchallenged. She could see them spreading in the space like an unstoppable disease. Then the darkness of an endless night enveloped them. Tiny blue lights flickered in a large room filled with a myriad of books. Noah's voice resounded in Revelia's head, desperately calling for help. And yet, the vision shattered in the blink of her red eyes, supplanted by Daniel's face. He smiled at her briefly as their gazes met. He looked exactly like she knew him but the perception of her own self had changed. The ages of an eternal being had passed, trailing its signs on her face.

'Inside the Flare, now!' Eros shouted as he pulled Trusk off his spot and moved him next to Anita and Revelia.

A few seconds after they had disappeared inside the Chomp's magic, a multitude of Harpies entered the derelict restaurant. Their twisted hands moved at the rhythm of their enchanting murmur, sliding over the people who were long gone. Under the terrified stare of the few alive, their souls lifted from their bodies like fragments of an obscure power.

With tears flowing and anger mounting in her head, Anita turned her gaze away. Standing still, powerless, was something she could not accept. As the idea of facing the Harpies head-on surfaced in her mind, a flicker, a glimpse of pure imagination displayed before her.

Daniel looked back at her as if he wanted to tell her too many things at once, an eternal collection of thoughts that struggled to come in the open. His mind and so his heart were there beside her and yet his body hadn't followed. He had no means to speak, no way to tell her. So he nodded, trying to convince her to restrain her instinct to go and fight an enemy she could not overcome.

'Daniel?' she cried. 'Daniel, you still here?' but he could not reply. All he could do was look at her, begging her to stay within the dome with just his gaze. They had been friends for so many years, Cherish and I had been together for an eternity, and both we and they shared a connection beyond words, the ability to read each other's thoughts was at work once more.

'We need fo move. Even inside fhe Flare, I don'f feel safe here,' Trusk said.

'I see it. I see our next move!' Revelia exclaimed, resolute. 'Let's go!'

As they all left to run outside, Daniel's ghost briefly gazed at Desolos whose deformed, enlarged mouth opened. An oppressive sound travelled the short distance between her and her victim. Even without a heart of his own, he felt the desperation raising. His soul mine to have, his emotions mine to feel, I felt it too as the man's will was ensnared from him, turning him dead, a wicked expression on his face left as testament of the atrocity.

Daniel hesitated to move further, back in my hands, but his stay was short lived. As the Harpies left the dwelling behind, he dissolved like a distant memory.

In the space of an hour, the enemy had already ransacked the village and moved towards the edge of the large lake. They left the shoreline and walked right through the waters, cutting the surface in halves, floating in between the sky and the abyss. The small island their destination, they had finally put some distance between them and their invisible stalkers.

'What do we do?' Anita asked, looking at the Harpies disappearing in the dark. 'Can we trust the Flare will keep us safe if we follow them?

'I'd say we try. I believe this is what he wants,' Revelia quickly replied.

'He?' Anita asked.

'Noah…and somehow I believe someone else wants it too.'

'We should and we will,' Trusk was determined to not lose sight of Noah's steps.

With their arms around the small Chomp's hips, Revelia and Anita moved up a little, lifted by their friend's wings. Barely flying above the surface, they soon caught up again with the Harpies as the latter left the waters to reach land. Their numbers had doubled with the ghosts of all the Humans they had captured, and Death led them to the centre of the island, in search for their way back home. At the presence of a grey, large tree, he finally stopped. His deformed hands moved on the ancient bark and it suddenly cracked open; a hole enlarged rapidly. One by one, all the Harpies slipped through the black veil of the evil gates, bringing their prey with them.

'Whaf do we do now?' Trusk whispered.

'We got this far…' Revelia said. 'We can't give up now.'

'How do we know your magic will hold?' Anita looked at the Chomp but Trusk had no assurance to give.

'We have to believe it will,' the Leonty insisted, pushing to move ahead.

'This is such a bad idea…' Anita muttered, vividly picturing them being teleported straight to hell.

As most of the Harpies disappeared through the passage, a last one silently waited for all their collected souls to walk in. With his sight blind to the renewed Chomp's magic, he eventually followed suit, closing the wicked gates at his back, unaware of the presence of unwanted guests.

An absolute darkness welcomed them to the other side. Impossible to distinguish left from right, top from bottom, the three froze in their spot. Swallowed by a dark night, all the Harpies vanished, leaving the intruders lost halfway through life and death.

'Well…'After a long silence, Anita finally spoke, her voice low. 'I was expecting fire and flames. Not this…nothing.'

'Where do we go? I can't see anything,' Revelia added.

'My Flare is sfill working,' Trusk added, his power reflecting on his friends' faces, brightening them up. 'Buf inside fhe magic only.'

'If you are suggesting we should lower the veil and use the Flare to see the space around…it's another bad idea.' Anita quickly replied.

'Can't you see their traces?' Revelia asked, her hands moving into the emptiness, trying to connect with the very space around them.

'It was Cherish who could see their power… Not me.' Once more, since the Awoken One's departure, Anita felt powerless.

'Are you sure she's really gone? After all, the others came back. Speaking of which, where are they?' The Leonty's face looked puzzled. Something else was invisibly pulling the strings around them, and a glimpse of power had caught her attention.

'Eros? Iris?' Anita called. After a few minutes waiting for an answer, she continued, 'If we get out of the dome and they see us, how are we going to escape from this place? How do we open the door back to our world?'

'One worry at a time,' Revelia replied, her eyes flashing red. 'Noah is about to step into his own death…'

'What are you talking about? He is already dead,' Anita let out, her face showing the pain still fresh in her heart.

'No, he is not. I can still see his future playing ahead. It's like he is still holding on to his true nature, somehow. He is about to do something very, very dangerous. Something that will trigger Death's anger. That's when he truly dies.'

'OK, lef's go.' And at that unbearable threat, Trusk lifted his magic at once, leaving them in the open space, visible.

The Flare suddenly shed a light into the surroundings, breaking against the rocky walls and the narrow tunnel ahead. Like a giant snake, the way through curved left and right, ending in a long set of stairs. At its bottom end, a wide, circular opening waited quietly, its perimeter enclosed by several archways. They all looked the same. As if the enemy had built too many ways in and out of their abode, more than a dozen passages brought the group to a sense of loss. One archway, larger than the others, contained a wobbling dark matter. Like ethereal doors, a black surface moved slowly from the centre to its sides.

'Wherever we go, please not there...' Anita whispered.

'Noah could be anywhere,' Trusk said.

'There are marks on top of each door. Do they look like numbers to you?' Anita asked, her eyes narrowed as she tried to focus on the distant enigma. 'Three thousands, four thousands...'

The three stalled. The Harpies were gone and everywhere around doors led to unpredictable outcomes. Whatever road they were going to take, they had to choose wisely. Anita gazed at Revelia silently, waiting for instructions, but the Leonty had none to give. They held their spot in between pondering and acting. Fear and determination were equal opponents in a race against time.

Suddenly, a loud chatter spread out of the first opening to their left. Several Harpies were about to walk out into the large dark room. Going back under the influence of the Flare would have turned the three blind once more. Yet, they could not stay in the open, visible and unable to face the enemy right in their home.

Chapter Nine

The Books of the Dead Ones

∞

'In this one, to the right, quick! A few of them are about to walk right in. Let's go under the Sháten Déil's magic,' Revelia urged.

They slipped into a larger chamber as Trusk's magic enveloped them once more. The floor was paved with cold, black stones, and the ceilings soared high above. Suddenly, the three intruders could see through the darkness. In the corners of the freezing room, flames with a strange blue tint flickered on tall, golden holders. Softly dancing on their spot, their light roared and swelled as if fuelled by an unseen hand. Waves of light cascaded from the flames, traveling across the room as if with a will of their own, only to vanish against a multitude of shadowed walls. The eerie illumination painted a scene both haunting and mesmerizing, a testament to the room's ancient power. 'I've seen this place before…' the Leonty said while they halted next to the entrance.

Thousands of stony bookshelves ran from one side to another, creating a complex labyrinth of intricate shape. Every single inch packed with strange, large books, the place immediately gripped Anita's heart, drawing her towards the unexpected revelation. After she pulled the other two closer to the fascinating discovery, she brushed her hand on the cold, white bindings.

'I can't believe my eyes,' she gasped, her mouth wide open, in shock. 'I've never seen so many books together in my whole life…'

'Why do they have books? Why would Death need books?' Revelia gazed at the vast number of bookshelves.

'3960… 3990… 4420… Whaf are fhese numbers here?' Trusk asked, turning off his magic, their spot blessed with the Flare's light once more. Indistinguishable from one another, in the compressed amassment of knowledge, the many stony bookshelves seemed fused together. And yet, the Chomp's eyes fixed on the sequence of numbers. After directing the light of the Sháten Déil at the top of the bookshelves, he added, 'Fhey look like fhey're in order…'

'But they all look the same…same binding, same age…' Revelia added.

'They are split by numbers in sequences of thirty?' Anita's mind was piqued, hunting for answers.

'Fhirfy whaf?'

'Thirty years, I'm afraid… More or less thirty yacs,' Anita replied as Revelia slowly moved back to the large doors. Her ears tuned in with the enemy's moves, her eyes flashed red, a cunning anticipation of their hostile whereabouts. 'It can't be a coincidence. Thirty years like the time Love needed to come back. This…all of this might contain the knowledge of our entire history.'

Without thinking twice, Anita pulled one of the books out of its millennial place.

'Whaf are you doing?' Trusk blurted out, worried. 'Puf if back!'

'I need to know…' Anita replied, almost as if trapped in a spell of attraction and desire.

Initially resisting the unwanted dislodgment, the tome eventually snapped out of its place, sending a small cloud of dust right in front of their faces. On the front cover an *X* bent on its side held the number 29. Its binding glued together by an ancient, dark magic stood against Anita's curiosity, holding itself shut.

'It won't open…'

'Possibly because we are not meant to?' Revelia asked, sarcastic. In the depths of her mind, every action they took, every move they made, led to an end she failed to foresee. 'We should leave…'

'If fhese are like fhe ancienf mirrors fhey mighf have magic? Maybe fhere is a spell, words you have fo speak fo open if?' Trusk asked as his gaze trailed to a blue flame floating a few steps away.

'There is nothing written on it, just a number.' Anita's determination was stronger than any magic and certainly moved unchallenged by the Leonty's words of worries.

Eventually the book gave in and opened, releasing the same blue light running across the room. At the discovery of a diabolic revelation, Anita's eyes enlarged, a terrified look descended upon her face. A long list of names ran in a spectral sequence, wobbling on the mystical pages as if made of smoke. Next to each name, a tiny crystal shone brightly.

Before she could put words to the horrifying idea that had just formed in her head, two Harpies walked in. As if they had been alerted by the unfolding magic released by the actions of the unexpected thieves, they walked right towards their enemy. *If these books contain Death's power, he must know I opened one,* Anita thought.

As the Harpies moved from row to row, getting closer, Trusk wrapped the other two under his veil, making them disappear. To his surprise, Anita was still holding the stolen book in her arms.

'You need fo puf if back,' he pressed. 'Fhey can'f see us buf fhey can see fhe book is missing…'

'You don't understand,' Anita replied. 'I'm afraid I know what these are for… These books contain the many souls Death has taken away since…well, who knows since when.'

'In these books? He is actually trapping the dead in these?' Revelia could not believe the evil magic they were witnessing. 'Nevertheless, he is right. You must put it back.'

Resistant to the idea, Anita finally gave up and placed the heavy tome back in its rightful place, right before the Harpies turned the corner.

Proceeding as if they could still be seen or felt, the invisible group slowly moved away, putting some distance between them and the Harpies. At the edge of the room, under their stunned eyes, one of the flames had suddenly brightened again, puffing from its top in a brief sequence. A few flashes followed, releasing a grey cloud into the nearby space. Its colour turning white and gaining consistency, it suddenly changed form, taking the one of a newly shaped book. On its fresh, untouched face, a shining number was printed. Lifted by the dark magic and led by its own destiny, it flew across the room, finding a welcoming spot in a large, almost empty bookshelf.

Anita's words replayed in their minds. They all knew what they had just witnessed. The newest addition to Death's collection had just formed before them. It contained the names of all the people who had been dragged down into the cold hell they now stood in, held prisoners by the Harpies and their undying spell.

'Do you think it can be undone?' Revelia asked, looking left and right as they crossed another section of the room. The entry archway was close by.

'You mean by us?' Anita gazed again at the many shelves surrounding them. 'I'm not sure. I wouldn't say we could just burn them to set them free. Something is holding them in here.'

'This is what Noah is looking for,' Revelia suddenly stopped walking. 'He is about to ask Death... Who's Desterea?' she asked, pausing for a brief moment. 'I'm not sure I'm seeing this right. He says this name before he gets killed...again. Noah has found something in their shared minds; something that is holding this entire place together.'

'He is here with a mission then?' Anita's hope rose a little. There was still Noah's stubbornness and determination behind Oz's actions.

'One that won't last long,' the Leonty replied. 'We need to get to the other side of this hall. It's happening somewhere in there, soon.'

'What a waste of time! Lëogan, let's go,' one of the two Harpies shouted, a few steps away, making Anita gulp.

The very first Harpy she had met was nearby. That name resounded in her head like a cannon. Last time she heard that name, she had witnessed Time erasing him from existence. And yet, he was back from death like the rest of them.

'Hold on, Némein,' Lëogan replied. His voice had not changed. Slow and deep, it penetrated the matter of everything around him. 'Something, someone was moving in this room… I recognise this…smell. But how can it be?'

'What smell? What are you talking about?' Némein inquired, almost as if mocking him.

'You wouldn't understand. There are things I've seen and felt somewhere else, away from Earth. This…feeling of power, a magic I learnt to recognise and fight against. The one who overpowered my magic…she had this scent on her green skin, following her.' And Lëogan moved closer to the entry, his head shifting as if multiplying of faces projected his own self in different directions.

Even under the effect of their protective shield, the three held their breath, terrified. Almost as if the Harpy could see through their magic, he scanned the place carefully, moving around like a hungry hunter.

'He is the one, Revelia,' Anita whispered. 'He is the one that walked through the node from Earth to Runae and convinced the Aqualymphs and the Humans to attack your people... He is the one Una killed by making him jump out of a window...'

'Is he still alive?' Revelia's expression filled with anger. 'The only good act my sister ever did. And he erased it by coming back?'

'That wouldn't be the only time. Not long ago Time himself destroyed his core right in front of me...and yet he is back.' As Anita continued, another familiar Harpy entered the room. The one called Algos walked in to call the others at the presence of their master.

'You two. Death wants us all together. He is ready to make his final move. All the Harpies from down below are already there. Let's go.'

'Hold it, Algos. There is something in here. I can feel it.'

'Idiot,' Algos blurted out. 'There is nothing in here. It's that...Oz that is causing it. Death knows something didn't work right with that one. Now, let's go.'

'Did you hear?' Anita rejoiced. Once the Harpies had left the room, the petrifying grip on their hearts finally released. 'Noah is still alive!'

'And they know. We need to hurry.' Revelia pushed the other two out of the room, following the very enemy they desperately hid from.

As they crossed the dark hall, the Leonty stopped briefly. Her eyes pointed at the only thing darker than the rest. A large, black matter wobbled in the main archway; something called her from the near future. Ignoring the hint and worried for their friend's fate, she resumed her run to the next room.

Slightly brighter than the dark hall, the large room expanded to an invisible infinite. The Harpies' forms were barely visible against the empty background they moved in. Their numbers high, the vast majority stood up, their horrifying faces pointed at a long table. A few sat by it, gifted by the immense honour of being part of a privileged elite. At the far end, Death occupied the place of a sovereign, his chair made of the same black stone that ran across the pavement; his hands were clenched. Although his figure was almost impossible to distinguish from the nothingness enveloping him, the golden metals covering his body shone brightly.

As the audience waited for him to speak, two dying flames silently waving at both ends of the room flashed at once. Blue rays of light moved towards the large Harpy, penetrating his ethereal skin, lightening the two large cavities in his face, turning them into cold fires. As if the dead that had been collected fed his hungry power, at every released wave, Death's form enlarged, turning him more tangible and eviller.

'The new one may come into the open,' he started. With no resistance nor fear, Oz walked into the middle of the room. Between him and the other Harpies, a sense of upcoming judgment widened the empty space, keeping him apart from the others. 'As you said, the one called Health has come back. She is wielding the weapon that used to be mine. Tell me, how do I take it back?'

'She is in the far space, with the other Gods,' Oz replied, after a moment of hesitation. 'How can you take it back if you can't leave these lands?'

'Matter of fact I can... We can,' Death replied, untouched by the Harpy's implication. 'I was born out of cosmic power. I conquered the space and rode planets and moons as I came here. Even my Harpies can leave, if they wanted to. You did leave this place. Isn't it true, Lëogan?' And a grin filled with evil satisfaction appeared on the Harpy's face. 'You see, right before the great destruction by the hand of Nothing, we managed to find the node and crossed it. Lëogan slipped through the gates and reached one of the other worlds. Its name... Runae...'

'You were righf,' Trusk whispered to Anita.

'We went and followed our mission there as much as here,' Death continued. 'There was very little resistance. It was so easy to turn the hearts of the many who had never been challenged by darkness. One by one they were turned against each other. We set the field for our master's return. Once he was done with Love, he was going to rip that planet apart. Exactly as he had done with Talush and Varayal. But, somehow, Time resisted, his world resisted, graced by something unexpected.'

'I know the history of Runae,' Oz interrupted. 'The Human that existed before me was there. He knew what happened. He knew about the queen Nothing put in dominion of those lands…'

'My best work!' Lëogan stated with pride, capturing Revelia's attention. Suddenly, in the most distant place in the universe, her sister's story and the fate of her own kind came back to haunt her.

'Yours?' Oz asked.

'Oh yes… Even if Nothing had already found access to that world, it took me a long time. You see, they possessed magic beyond comprehension—especially those who prayed day and night. Their prayers were filled with enchantments, and their magic kept Nothing's power confined to the Cloudy Mountains. To succeed, we had to ensure they would all die. Oh, it took a long time indeed. Many years passed before their hatred for each other could turn into action. But it worked. It was I who enchanted the queen of those water creatures. It was I who had the Humans move against the green ones. If it wasn't for me there wouldn't have been a supreme queen…a queen of the absolutely nothing! Ha, ha, ha!' And a loud laughter spread across the room. 'I brought her exactly where she stood, when she took the crown for herself.'

'Enough!' Death shouted. 'We are not here to recall useless memories. We are here for a different reason… Tell me, Oz… What is it that you are truly looking for?'

'We need to leave,' Revelia said, in tears.

'I'm sorry,' Anita replied. 'We didn't know either…'

'It's not about my sister. Noah is about to confess his plan and get destroyed because of it.'

'No!' Trusk bellowed, his voice bouncing back from within the security of his veil.

'I know his confession. I've just seen it. We can do it ourselves. We can carry his plan and move the attention from him to us. But we need to do it now!'

'Let's go.'

Anita didn't hesitated. She knew Revelia too well to doubt her ability to prevent a horrible future from happening. She was right. Noah was still there somehow and had gone into hell with a mission. Whatever that was, it was going to cost him his life. It had to be for a good reason. It had to be good enough to change their fate and the destiny of the entire world.

Back to the main hall, fallen into the darkness of the empty place, the three stopped in front of the large, black magic. Waiting for Revelia's lead, Anita and Trusk stood a few inches away from the wobbling doors. After stalling for a moment, the Leonty took their hands and pulled them through. The resistance of the evil spell was sticking to their skin, like gum holding to their flesh, it was opposing their will, slowing their moves. Their push intensified, their bodies stretching to their limits, when they finally made it through the other side.

To their surprise, the Chomp's Flare turned off instantly, their invisibility removed at once. In the silence of the dark, a sobbing sound welcomed them in. A few steps into the unknown and the path had been lightened by several floating, speeding lights. Like dots roaming without a direction or will, small sparks of blue light moved left and right, projecting shadows on a circular corridor. As they travelled into the unknown, some changed form, taking the shapes of Humans. Like ghosts, they followed their own desperation, back and forth, searching for a way out. To the far right, at the end of the path, an opening left the space to a small, circular room.

'Help me,' one ghost lamented.

'I don't want to become one of them,' another one cried as it appeared and disappeared in a snap.

'This is where they keep the ones they didn't put in the books,' Anita said in shock. 'These are going to become the next Harpies.

Taking them by surprise, a louder moan travelled from the far right to them. It cried desperately; words of liberation begged above all the other voices. Resolute and hastened by Noah's intentions, the group moved towards it. Led by the cry echoing in the space, they walked straight inside the tiny room. There, to their surprise, a Harpy sat chained to a stony throne. Hands and wrists resembled the ones of a Human being but the rest of the body contorted in smoky spasms.

'I thought they were all with Death...' Anita whispered as she made a sign to the others to go back. 'This must be where they turn them?'

'Whatever that thing is, it's the reason why Noah will die,' Revelia replied. And she slid slowly by the side of the cold walls. Somehow, the enemy ignored their presence.

'Die for a Harpy?' Trusk asked, following her.

'There is something different with this one,' Revelia added. A moment later the strange Harpy abruptly stopped crying.

'Are you here to free me?' a voice resounded inside the room. For a moment they believed the Harpy had spoken but the sound of her words came from every direction.

'Who are you?' Revelia asked.

'I'm Desterea...the first one...' And the Harpy's form ceased the contorting shaking. Her face formed out of the grey smoke, her shape resembling the one of a woman.

'That name...' Revelia gasped. 'I heard that name in my visions.'

'The first one?' Anita asked, moving beside the Leonty. They stood close to the enemy and yet something felt to them amiss. This one felt different.

'The first one he took. The first victim, the first prisoner,' she replied, raising her hands, showing them her wrists, chained together. In between the binding spell, a key hung.

'Why are you here? Why are you not with the others?' Anita continued, stepping closer. Prudence was long forgotten.

'Because I'm the first one. My true soul, my true nature was hidden from me. I can't tell you much more. He controls my mind, my words… I am the origin…'

'The origin of what?' Revelia quickly gazed around. Behind the enslaved Harpy, a stand occupied a corner at the other side of the room. On its top, another book lay muted, trapped in similar chains.

'His origin. The origin of Death. I'm the first one he enslaved, the first one that gives order to his kingdom.'

'Why does he keep you here, chained?' Anita was fighting the idea she could be just a victim. *After all, she is a Harpy. How much can we trust her words?*

'Because the spell binds my soul in there, in that book. The first book. That book keeps the order of everything he has done, the order of every soul he has taken; the order of who he is. In the wickedness of his sick mind, Death has shaped it like a dark, evil copy of what once used to be mine and now lies in his hands.'

'Death has an artefact too!' Anita let out, her face showing the sudden realization. 'His spell is similar to the Gods' one. The secret to his immortality might be nestled in there!'

'This is what Noah is after,' Revelia added. 'His plan is to penetrate the enemy defence line and strike him from within…'

'Madness,' Anita pushed back. 'But yeah, he knew what he was doing. I suspect this is the reason why he didn't disappear like Daniel did. He must have stayed behind to come here.'

'If we open the book,' the Leonty said hurriedly as she looked at the other side of the room, afraid Death could end Noah's life at any time, 'can we free you?'

'There is a stone inside…beside…my name.' Desterea's voice trembled as if she struggled to reveal her own secrets. 'Remove it and crack the stone open and release my spirit into the sky. Bring the book into a world he can't reach.'

'Let's do it,' the Leonty said, her fingers already sliding onto the newly discovered relic.

'No!' Anita's hands moved on Revelia's. 'We can't do it just yet.'

'Why nof?' Trusk asked. 'We have nof much fime!'

'If what she said it's true, we could make a mistake. If we take this stone out of the first book, I'm sure he'll know. What are we going to do then? How are we going to get Noah out of here?'

'If we take it would we not break the spell? Set them free?'

'Revelia, think about it. Noah's name is in there...' And Anita moved away and started walking around the room. 'I wish I had Cherish with me still, she would know what to do...' And she paused for a moment. 'Let me think...'

'We need to hurry,' the other one pressed as her eyes ignited again. A vision of a short future erupted from within her thoughts. The dark, blind spot in her magical abilities, the darkness surrounding their days ahead spread like an encroaching night.'

'Noah's soul was taken only recently,' Anita resumed. 'He must be in a new book. Perhaps the one we saw forming when were hiding in that room...'

'If we get it.' Revelia turned to the Harpy. 'If we get his crystal, can we do the same thing we are supposed to do with yours?'

'I don't have a body to come back to. My spirit, my soul can exist beyond real...' Desterea suddenly stopped as she moaned as if in a great pain. 'He needs his body...to come back.'

'Alright. Back on our steps we go.' Revelia looked towards Anita and Trusk. 'Once there, pull the Flare's magic onto us. We need to be fast. And you.' She turned around to the Harpy. 'We will be back. I promise. We will get you out of here.'

'Please,' she begged. 'Don't leave me here!'

No matter how desperate her plea sounded to them, there was no mercy that could sway them away from freeing Noah. If they had the chance to release Death's first victim and bring down his dominion, it could not be at the expense of Noah's life. Convinced they could bring him back from the very hell they all had entered, the three walked back into the main hall and, as they traced back their steps, Trusk's dome reappeared, bringing them under the protection of invisibility.

To their right, the thundering of Death's voice resounded like whips of a hateful punishment. In there, Oz and his wrathful new master entertained the others with the display of a merciless spectacle.

Chapter Ten

The Origin of Evil

∞

'Once more, tell me what you came to do here!' Scream of an agonizing pain followed. Oz was being tortured under the pleased eyes of the many Harpies.

'We have very little!' Revelia hurried.

'They know,' Oz replied with a broken voice. 'You have come back even after the battle...They know Health's return has not erased you from existence, but they don't know what I know...'

'So you are here to take her artefact! How did you manage to survive? How's your Human mind still playing its tricks on me when your soul is in my hands?' Death questioned, holding his fist high, inflicting an excruciating pain on his victim. The Harpies around had gone silent. The two talked of something of which they had no previous understanding. 'I've destroyed your Human body, crushed your soul, but you still exist! How did you survive?'

The three finally reached the large room filled with the history of the dead ones. The vastity of the space was fighting against their rush, confusing them. There was too much to go through, too many books and shelves to examine. If Anita was right, Noah's soul must have gone into the most recent book, together with the ones that had died since Nothing's recent attack. Yet, as they had fled the Harpies in haste, they had no recollection of where the dark magic had unfolded.

'We need to find the highest number in this room?' Revelia asked.

'No. Let me think… Each bookshelf contains thirty years. Each year is a different book. Thirty at max, then a new book goes in the next bookshelf… We are two years past Daniel's and Noah's thirty…'

'Hurry up, Anifa!' Trusk shouted, looking back at the entrance. Oz's screams could be heard from afar.

'We need to find this last thirty years' bookshelf! Or even better, we need to find an almost empty one, because we have just turned into a new thirty-year sequence,' Anita said, running across the aisles, her eyes zipping towards the top of each shelf.

'We splif and go fasfer!' Trusk urged, turning off the Flare.

'But stay close! We are in the open now.' And Revelia moved to the next row. Afraid they could lose each other in that labyrinth of death, she walked backwards, her gaze fixed on the other two.

'Here!' Trusk shouted a few moments later, from the far left. 'Fhere are only fwo books here.'

'2010!' Anita said, looking at the top shelf. 'This goes from 2010 to 2040.'

'There shelves are mostly empty…' Revelia whispered as if talking to herself. 'The future hasn't formed yet…the future…'

'Let's make sure it never will.' And Anita pulled the second book from the top shelf. A shining number two was carved at the centre of its cover, a few inches over the *X*.

The bindings new, the pages not even cut, the book had been barely used. Confident Noah's name would be listed in there, Anita forced it open, releasing its blue hues in the near space. Several pages had been already used, filled with hundreds of names, and more, new ones were being written right in front of their stunned eyes. Like the ticking of an unmerciful clock, the dead ones of the world were collected there, one by one as they left the bodies behind. For each name that slowly appeared, a blue flame approached, sinking into the page, its eery, diabolic ink pressing against the surface.

For every page, two columns held a sequence of thirty different names. As the pages were getting filled, a golden frame enclosed them around, sealing the making of its master before moving to a next, new page.

'This magic…it's so fast. How many people are dying by the second?' Anita asked, in shock.

'This is beyond everything I ever imagined possible,' Revelia added as their bodies got surrounded by a blue haze. Thousands of flames hovered around them, their journey delayed by Anita's careful inspection.

'Here, Noah's name,' Trusk said as he floated inches from the cold floor, behind the other two.

'Hold on, this reads Noah Fletcher…and here, another one,' Anita replied, flipping a page back.

'How many Noahs are there in your world?'

'It's not a common name but not rare either. What was his last name?' Anita looked up, as if she tried to dig into her memories, back when she had researched Noah's history.

'You will not take her!' Death's thundering rage crossed the walls and the ethereal boundaries of that place, shaking the group at once.

Dust fell from the stony shelves and from the high, rocky ceilings. As if the entire space was a mere extension of its owner, the ground shook at Death's every word. The pavement quivered and cracks opened up, revealing a sequence of a countless number of floors diving down into the depths of Earth.

'Anifa, hurry!' Trusk urged as he lifted them into the air before they fell into the open mouth of the evil's home.

'I need to remember his family name,' Anita replied, desperate.

'I don't know what that means,' Revelia exclaimed. 'Just take them all!'

'McCarthy! It's McCarthy!' she suddenly said. 'Here, I found it!'

'Let's take the stone and go.' The Leonty gazed at Trusk, whose Flare glowed again, reinstating the protective veil around them.

'Let's hope it's the only one…'

Anita placed her fingers on the tiny crystal beside the sought name and, with a slight pull, lifted it off the page, releasing a wave of light down to the fabric of the magic book, making it glow. At the other side of the hall, Death's eyes suddenly brightened. Connected to his own spell, he felt the subtle change in his own power, decreasing ever so slightly. As if someone had unexpectedly robbed him of his own spoil of conquest, his anger waking to a new, wrathful fear, he swung his arm and lifted Oz into the air.

'Who else did you bring with you, you miserable Human? Who's taking my souls away from their rightful place?' An astonishing power rose from his core and seared in the space, staggering the other Harpies.

'Fhey know!' Trusk gulped at the thundering of Death's roars.

'They are coming. To the first Harpy, fast,' Revelia urged Trusk who pulled the others by their arms, making Anita drop the evil book into the abyss.

Hidden by the Chomp's magic, they hovered beside the entrance as they moved aside, letting dozens of Harpies walk through. The largest one led the hunt, moving fast across the aisles. In evident contrast with the invisible thieves, Death knew exactly where to go. In the deepest of his corrupted, diabolic core, he could feel every single particle of power ticking silently in its own resting places. Finally reaching the spot where the stone had been taken, he turned around, his figure growing bigger, his gaze at the far-down place below where the book had fallen into. His shadow penetrated the many layers of his domain; Death was furious.

'I want his soul back!' the Harpy yelled. There was no need for the dead's warder to reach and inspect the tome. He had no need to unfold the pages of the many prisoners; Death knew exactly whose soul had been stolen.

'He knows it's Noah's,' Revelia whispered. 'We need to go and get him.'

Preceding the Harpies, the three swiftly turned the corner and ran across the dark hall. On the other side, inside the room where the enemy had convened, Oz lay on the ground, in between quickly forming fractures.

'Noah, if's us,' Trusk said, lowering his shield, bringing the other two into the open.

'Noah is dead…' the Harpy lamented. He didn't move or show any surprise at their sudden appearance.

'No he is not,' Revelia added. 'We have his soul. We need to get to the first Harpy and run. But you have to come with us.'

'Something is happening to me…' Oz murmured, finally turning towards the others. His eyes stormed with an unexpected golden light. 'My mind is fighting against many others, deep inside…'

To their surprise, a glowing figure rose at the Harpy's back. Like they had witnessed not long before, an Awoken One emerged from the depths of his host's heart.

'You had one with you all this time?' Anita asked as she kneeled next to Oz. At the comforting sight of that familiar magic, the spectre of fear had released the grip on her heart.

'Fhis is Daniel's magic,' Trusk added, as Philiat appeared in front of them, his presence growing tangible.

'You need to bring us out of here,' he said, his voice almost like a whisper. 'I can't protect his heart much longer. Take him now and leave this place of misery at once…'

'You never left, didn't you? You never joined the others. This is why Noah was left behind, after the Gods conjured Love. How?' Anita asked, helping Oz stand on his feet.

''Cause the ones we love are never truly gone. Daniel himself asked us to stay behind, with the ones he would not see suffering, right before he resurrected our God.'

Like the other Awokens had done before, Philiat suddenly disappeared, leaving the three with a suffering Harpy on their hands and an incoming threat ahead. Energised by knowing they had not been left alone to fight the enemy, they moved back into the hall, bringing Oz with them.

Sweat on their foreheads, haste on their feet, the four crossed the hall just before the many Harpies filled the space with their evil presence. Although they had moved freely, invisible to Death's eyes, they could not fool the master of magic, not in his own house. A brief disturbance in the dark, black doors told him where the enemy headed. Their plan all along, Oz had managed to keep a piece of his original host in his heart, bringing with him the ones who had stubbornly pushed their insolence against the king of hell. On the other side, Revelia led the pack to the first Harpy. Chained still to her spot, Desterea resumed her lament and started to cry.

'Please, let me out. He is coming…'

'Anita, get the book, quickly,' the Leonty said, her hands moving frantically around the Harpy as she tried to release her from her confinement.

'He knows we are here,' Oz mumbled, falling on his knees. 'His anger…his hate is so powerful…'

Like she had done with the other book in Death's evil collection, Anita forced the relic open. A staggering, grey energy erupted from within, releasing a dark magic all around. Light and smoke mixed together as a figure emerged from within. A moan hovered in the air, followed by a deep voice.

'I am the master of every Human soul. I own every beginning and every end. For a spell that can't be broken, as nothing can be destroyed, only reshaped, I release only what I'm given instead…'

A vortex of energy spread across the room, lifting the Chomp into the air. Next to him, Oz's form dissolved, replaced by Philiat whose magic shone like a tiny star in the endless nothing in which they stood. Revelia's body rose from the cold stones as she floated in the air, her grip on the same chains keeping Desterea securely confined to her spot.

As if untouched by the very same magic released from the relic, Anita held the book firmly in her hands. The white pages danced as if turned by an unseen hand until eventually it stopped. There, a name formed.

Engraved in golden letters, the most disturbing secret unfolded before her eyes.

'This is impossible…' she whispered.

'Anitaaaa!' Revelia screamed while she stretched one hand towards Trusk, pulling him close to her chest.

'By the power of the silent nothingness I've been gifted with, I turn the spell of creation against its master,' the voice resumed, thundering in the space. 'No Human soul can replace the one held in the first stone on which I build my kingdom. A soul for a soul, this spell shall not be broken…'

'We can't release her!' Anita shouted as she slowly moved against the storm unfolding. 'She is Creation… The Gods' mother!

'How? We did all fhis for nofhing?' Trusk replied, in shock.

'The spell can't be broken,' Anita continued as she reached Desterea and the other two. As if the eye of a powerful hurricane moved with her and the relic she held, the mystical storm ceased and the two friends slowly descended onto the cold ground.

'She is Love's mother. She must have been cast here when she moved against Nothing,' she added. 'Death and Creation are linked by this book…'

'There must be a way to break this magic. Like we did for Time, Soul and Health,' Revelia replied, gazing at the book where the name Creation glittered in a bright light.

'The voice said the only way is to have another soul taking her place. Not just any soul. A non-Human soul…'

Revelia's and Trusk's eyes met. Whoever had cast the spell upon Creation, they knew no inhuman soul walked the Earth. With Love, Daniel, and Noah gone, there was nobody else that could make that trade but them.

'We are not Human…' Revelia whispered as if talking to herself. 'We could…'

'No!' Anita bellowed, pulling the book away from the Leonty's hands. 'We are not going to lose anybody else!'

'I'll do if,' Trusk replied, resolute. 'Mofher and Fafher are gone. Runae is gone…' And tears surfaced in his round dark eyes. 'I'll do if.'

'You can't.' Revelia's hand moved onto the Chomp's puffy cheeks. 'They need your Flare and your strength. They need you and your good heart…'

'I said no!' Anita pushed once more. 'Beside, no Human soul might easily mean the one of a God. It's obvious Death cast this spell. He knew there wasn't going to be a God to challenge his magic. You are not Gods. None of us are.'

'You are wrong, my friend.' Revelia smiled as the long-sought understanding finally reached her. 'Time has given me a piece of himself, remember? When we entered Varayal, he gave me a portion of his power…' And the Leonty paused for a moment. 'There is a reason why I can't see past a point in our future. Darkness is all I can see… The same darkness surrounding us, here, surrounding her.'

Chapter Eleven

What Begins Will Surely End

∞

As if the God of Time had stepped right into that dark space, in between the intruders, the merciless ticking of every second came to a halt. Their ears dull, their faces locked in the same expression of shock and horror, Revelia, Trusk and Anita froze. Desterea's eyes fixed on the paved floor, she begged them to complete the ritual. The first book still in Anita's hands, her original name shone beside a bright flame. Blue and golden waves mixed within the white page.

'Please hurry!' Desterea shouted, desperate.

In a trembling thunder, the space around turned to dust. The evil walls, the very shape of that old prison disappeared, replaced by an ocean of pure dark and emptiness. All around them, the full number of Death's army stared at their prey, their hands down, their heads all pointed at the enemy. Among the gathering, the largest one held his right hand in a fist. In it, the dark power of eternal slavery twisted with a wicked magic.

'So you even dare to violate my own kingdom?' he thundered, his deep voice getting lost in the black horizon. 'You really thought you could defeat me? The master of all Harpies? The one who came to channel Nothing's power, way before your fate was decided, long before you even existed? You really thought you could take away the gift my master and only rightful king gave to me when your own God had fallen?'

'Give us Noah back!' Trusk said, firm, as he poised in between the Harpies and his friends.

'You mean him?' Death mocked. At the swing of his arm, a grey cloud formed before them. Oz reappeared within the dark magic of his obscure abode.

'We need the Harpy if we want to bring him back,' Philiat whispered while his presence flickered ever so slightly behind Revelia and Anita. 'We must bring him out of here...'

'We know your secret,' Anita said as she walked a few steps towards Oz. The terror squeezing her stomach did not stop her. Even without Cherish by her side, once again she faced the same enemy she fought in

Castlecross. 'We know who this is.' And she pointed at Desterea. 'We'll free her like we freed all her children!'

'You escaped me once, but I won't make the same mistake again. You are in my own home now and there are no Gods to protect you, this time… Begone, creature of defiance!'

Death's arms stretched wide, signalling his army to move towards Anita and the others. In the blink of an eye, they were surrounded. One among the many surged forth, his creeping smile a shadow of a past made of lies and horrors.

'We meet again.' And Lëogan laughed. 'I told you… you were better forgetting, did I not? And what do we have here…someone resembling the queen who could not hold to her promise…'

'Stop playing with our feast,' Desolos cried. 'Leave them to me…' And a grotesque expression appeared on the Harpy's face. Her jaw dislodged, deforming, turning her mouth to a large cavity. A shrill moan reached their ears when suddenly Anita and Revelia disappeared. Inside Trusk's dome, his two friends found themselves in the company of three Harpies.

'We can'f fighf fhem all, buf we can fighf fhese ones!'

Philiat, Eros, and Iris shone brightly inside the Chomp's shield, blinding the enemy. 'Hold on right there,' Iris said to Lëogan as a green glow manifested from a small pendant. The tiny wheel released a flash of magic, trapping the three Harpies in a frozen moment.

There, Eros and Philiat penetrated their matter, their rays of pure light dissolving the darkness they were made of.

'We have to get the Harpy and go,' Philiat repeated.

'There are too many, how are we going to do it?' Anita replied.

'We are out of sight and out of time,' Iris interjected. 'We can't get him if we stay out of sync with time. The Chomp needs to get us out. We act swiftly and we go under the Flare again.'

As if the group had quickly agreed on the Awoken's proposal, Trusk switched off the Flare and they instantly reappeared among the Harpies. Welcoming them back, their irate master loomed enormous and terrifying.

'I have enough of your tricks!' And his figure grew larger, almost as if enveloping them all like a dark veil. 'The witch goes first!'

His contorted hand reached Anita and he pulled her into the air. She screamed for help while the rest of the Harpies moved against the group.

'Go and join the others in my collection!'

Death's eyes brightened with a blue gaze as his spirit reached Anita's face. As if he was about to kiss the life out of her body, his face transformed into a hovering hole, engulfing her body.

'Stay with me…' Eros moved next to her, embracing her with his warm power as the two slid through the nothingness, inside the enemy's core.

As Anita's head, arms and legs disappeared within Death's presence, a piercing whistle cracked the horrifying scene. Right next to Desterea, Revelia held the first book in her left hand. A resolute expression on her face, her eyes gazed as red as a raging fire. In her right hand lay the stone that eternity had kept confined in the depths of Death's domain. An entire existence made of countless days, centuries, millennia rolled inside the Leonty's mind as she finally was granted access to the future she was prevented from seeing.

Anita reappeared untouched; her large enemy froze in disbelief. Not only had his greatest secret been discovered, they had found a way to break his spell. There, determined and firm in her resolve, Revelia said, 'You know what torments my gift has given me all these yacs? The sorrow of being allowed to watch the future unfold and not be able to oppose it. My friends have given me what I needed the most. They showed me I…can…change it!'

And Revelia swung her arm in the air, throwing the shining stone towards Trusk. The moment the crystal touched the Chomp's hand, the relic shook, its bindings contorting as if convulsing under an agonizing pain. A bright light surged from its pages and spread across the space like a flash.

A few moments later, the intense spectacle dissolved. There, where Desterea sat, something else stirred, wobbling within itself. Slowly, a new Harpy formed. Her form slim, her hair long and rigid, a dark copy of the Leonty materialised. Her wrists chained, her head tilted down, the terrible trade of a life for another had been made.

The shock of Revelia's actions had petrified both factions. In the midst of their clash, the unexpected exchange of souls had triggered a silent halt. Anita's gazed at the Leonty's double. In her mind, every trace of Death's attack against her had been muted, supplanted by the growing desperation. It didn't matter what she had done that for; it didn't matter if that was the reason why Noah had descended to hell. It had cost her a great loss.

There, in the depths of Death's devouring power, they had been dragged to their end. In both flesh and spirit, he was reaping them all, one by one. As she briefly looked at Trusk, she cried tears filled with desperation. It lasted a mere second, just enough time for the Chomp to exchange the same look of sorrow. Then, a vast, bright light broke through the foundation of the emptiness they stood in.

The ground quivered as a new God surged among the ones who had come to rescue her. The soft embrace of Creation's magic swept across the space, pulling Anita, Trusk, Oz and the Awoken Ones towards her. A moment later, they were all propelled towards an infinite top, breaking through the green grass of Crossing Island.

The fresh air of the early morning caressed their faces, carrying the clear sign they had been rescued right when every hope was lost. And yet, Anita knelt on the ground, crying. Next to her, Trusk held her arms, sobbing. As she moved to look around them, Eros manifested once more, his presence large and bright, covering anything behind him.

'I'm losing them all,' Anita sobbed. 'One by one, I'm losing everything…'

'Don't look!' Eros said as he stretched his presence around the two companions. 'None of you, please. Our mother's power is too strong for mortal eyes. Keep your gaze on me…' he added. 'Keep your eyes on me… Keep your eyes on me…' he repeated with a soft voice. The more he talked, the stronger Anita's emotions resounded within his divine soul. She had reached the limit of breaking, almost as if her heart could shatter in thousands of pieces at any moment.

Yet his voice repeated in her ears, keeping every fragment held together. Like a fabric made of magic and emotions, his words tied the many open scars she had, holding her in between healing and surrender. And his voice carried her beyond the pain and desperation.

'Keep your eyes on me… Keep your eyes on me…'

Chapter Twelve

The Last Stand

∞

The weak light of the rising sun glittered on the surface of the large lake. Against the oppressive swirling of black and blue hues spinning at the zenith, the new morning struggled to come to life. In the far skies the raging battle of resistance between us Gods and Nothing could be seen clearly from Crossing Island. Here and there, flashes of electrifying power ran across the atmosphere, followed by large circles of darkness. As if the celestial canvas was pierced in multiple parts, holes of emptiness spread randomly all over Creation's masterpiece.

The green island rapidly grew smaller under the growing power of a liberated supreme God. A few steps away from Anita and Trusk, Creation woke up to a new existence. After millennia of segregation, the freedom of walking right on the very earth she had crafted, loved and cared for, magnetised her form, boosted her core to her limits. A soft moan, almost as if she intoned the cry of a long-craved liberation, spread in the surroundings, lifting the spirit of every matter, every soul.

'The beauty of my children…' her voice echoed. 'The joy of life, the strength of pure existence ignites my soul.' And Anita and Trusk were pulled up, lifted by the surging energy of Creation. 'I come back thanks to my own making. The love and protection I gave them has been granted back to me. Thank you Anita. Thank you Trusk.'

The two gazed at each other in disbelief. The greatest power in the cosmos had just called them by their names, like long-lasting friends. Whatever power Creation held over the very fabric of every matter, it worked instantly. The pain and sorrow so comfortably nested in their hearts was removed at once. Their bodies had virtually become young again, the scars and aches of a long battle were swept away like dust against a fierce wind.

As if bound to a vow of protection, Eros kept close to Anita, his gaze fixed on her, his presence covering her sight to the powerful magic unfolding beyond. His eyes glittered with a renewed power while his hands held

Anita's shoulders. They both floated a few inches from the green grass, next to Iris whose energy kept Trusk in the safety of her timeless spell.

'I must go and join my children now. Time has come for me to end this reckless expansion of the enemy. And yet, I find myself in need for help once more. To you all,' Creation continued after a brief silence. 'I ask for another leap of faith, another task of incredible magnitude.'

'What is it, Mother?' Eros asked, his eyes still locked on to Anita.

'My soul and my power are back once again, and yet my artefact in which I stored my immortality lies in the hands of the enemy still.'

'How did that happen?' Iris asked, unafraid of interrupting. Her face, featuring the horrifying duality of past and present, showed a firm expression, briefly making Trusk feel uncomfortable.

'There was no time…' Creation replied. 'I had no time to cast the spell on my children's artefact in the safety of our cosmos. Health was dangerously wounded and Nothing was already tearing Talush apart. So I acted swiftly, releasing my magic right when I was vulnerable, when I was a mere step away from him. As my matter spread in the universe, as the spark of life entered the Gods' artefacts, I stood in between life and death. There, before I could come back, forming once more, he took it. He took the relic, he took my soul and my power. In that moment, the enemy you just freed me from was made. In that moment, Death came to be, created with one purpose only, to enslave me and this world under a never-ending incarceration.'

'So Death had not only one but two artefacts…' Anita whispered.

'He had indeed. My daughter's and mine. And both were defied by the enemy's dark power. Both were turned into diabolic weapons against their rightful owners!'

'His scythe was Health's sceptre…' Anita added.

'And my book, the book containing my soul, everything that created and exists, the book of living…'

'He turned it into the book of the dead ones,' Anita concluded. As if they were completing each other's sentences, Anita entirely dismissed the fact that she was in the presence of the greatest power in the universe. Instead, she fed her thinking process from it, doing what she did best: fitting the right pieces into the right places. 'But he still owns that book,' she said to Eros. 'He still has his spell on it. And Revelia is trapped in there now.'

'And you, creature of great intelligence, you are right,' Creation replied. 'This is what I must ask of you. As I ascend the sky and join the others, I need you to break the evil curse and get the artefact back to safety. Only then I'll be able to do what I wanted to do for a very long time…'

'How do we gef if?' Trusk asked, his face clearly displaying the rising concern of having to go back into the abyss of Death's kingdom. 'And how do we give if fo you if we gef if? I can fly buf nof fhaf far in fhe sky…' And to that last remark, Anita could not help herself and she smiled.

'I don't need my artefact to go into battle against Nothing. I need it in safe hands as we enter the never-ending loop of making and un-making, creating and destroying. We will never be able to defeat him. I know this much. Yet, we can surely make impossible for him to go any further!'

'You are going to fight him for…ever?' Anita replied, in between surprise and realization. 'You can't destroy your true opposite. Without him, there is not you… I can't believe how everything we know, everything I knew was right in front of my nose.'

'Right in front of all of us…' Creation concluded. 'Now, I must go. Please,' she added, briefly gazing at Eros and Iris. 'Protect them at every cost. I have the feeling my son will not allow any more pain. I can feel his sorrow, his thundering heart from down here.'

Like an explosion of atomic proportion, the air and lands shone bright as Creation lifted from the ground and rose into the sky. A whirlwind of power and magic blasted all around, shaking the foundation of that small island. Yet, like a merciful and caring maker, her darting like a bullet towards the universe caused no harm to people and nature alike.

'I don'f undersfand…' Trusk let out once the tranquillity of the lonely island was restored.

'Creation didn't create only four artefacts for the four Gods. She had one for herself. She knew she would never defeat Nothing. They exist because of one another. She was born out of his matter. Nothing and Creation are what we call matter and antimatter. Light and darkness as you would call it,' she added, noticing Trusk struggled to understand. 'She will die and reborn as much as Nothing will win and lose. But we need to take the first book out of Death's hands if we want to defeat the Harpies and help the Gods.'

'Why could she nof fake if herself?' But before Anita could answer his question, Trusk's eyes widened at the vision of a gigantic, dark shadow running all over the sky. At its centre, Creation's trail of pure light could be seen piercing the nightly advance she had gone to challenge.

'The dome, quick!' Iris suddenly shouted. 'They are coming!'

'Not this time,' Anita replied, resolute. 'The time of running and hiding is over. Seven,' she stated as if talking to an invisible entity in front of her, 'I know Daniel told you to stay behind. It's time to fight!'

But Anita's words had become lost in the cold air. A moment later, the Harpies appeared as if crawling from the same hole they had surged from, carried to safety by Creation. They all moved at once, led by the one who commanded them. His arms stretched, Death's presence had increased tenfold.

'Give us the book!' Anita demanded.

'Give us back Revelia,' Trusk added.

'Creation and the other Gods are back, you…' But Anita's words trailed off as she was suddenly lifted into the air and thrown away. A single swing of his arm and Death had pushed her violently to the other side of the island. There, Eros had instantly teleported, his soft embrace and golden smile finding her before she could crash onto the ground.

'You didn't think he would give to you, did you?' And he disappeared, together with the one he had sworn to protect.

'I have an idea…' she replied as if she was untouched by Death's attack. In a snap, they reappeared next to the Harpies, who roamed frantically around a tiny spot.

'They are here!' Strife said, as he moved in circles, hunting for the ones who had gone under the Chomp's veil.

'Trusk, you were right…' Anita said right after manifesting inside the dome, taking the Chomp by surprise. 'But not the way you think. You must go back and take the book. Just the book, you understand?'

'Whaf abouf Revelia? And you? If I go fhe Flare will nof profecf you!'

'Don't worry about me. Go back and get the book. Trusk,' she repeated. 'I know it's going to be hard, but you can't free Revelia unless we get the book first.'

'How are we going to break the spell?' Iris questioned. At her back, just a few inches away, the Harpies slid like an evil smoke over the invisible barrier.

'I don't know…' She sighed. 'I'm surrounded by ancient magic, powerful beings and I'm the one who has to know everything…' she let out. 'Where is Cherish? Daniel, we need Cherish as well!'

To the Awokens and Trusk, Anita had given in to madness. She talked to people who were not there or were no longer. Yet, in her eyes, the true power of revelation, truth, spoke clearly. She was determined to be listened to.

'Anifa, Daniel is gone…' Trusk said as he pulled her arm, trying to get her attention. 'If's only you and me now…'

'Oh no, believe me. He is here. Daniel, you owe me one! Remember when you decided to make us reappear in Castlecross, by your house, in the garden? My arm still hurts if I think about it.' And, under the confused gaze of the others, she kept talking to the nothing inside the dome. 'If you are dead, you don't mind sending me your gift from Connemara? Not that you are going to need it anytime soon…'

'Anita, please,' Eros interjected.

'Once we move out of Trusk's dome, it will be just the three of us. If we can't get the help of the other Awoken Ones, we might need some kind of protection… Nevertheless, let's go. Trusk,' Anita continued, holding on to the Chomp, 'whatever happens, know that I'm happy we met and I will always be grateful for meeting you. Now, go!'

Determination imprinted in Trusk's face. As he had proved many times before, he was ready to act. Without hesitation, he sprinted into the air, bringing the protection of the Flare with him. Suddenly, Anita, Eros and Iris appeared among the enemy. To their renewed diabolic joy, Strife, Desolos and Algos turned their attention to the ones they were after.

'Finally…' Death moaned. 'Erase them from this world…'

Gifted with a portion of Time's magic, Iris moved in front of the other two. The tiny wheel flickered with a green light as she briefly moved them out of sync with their present. Their forms blinked a few times. Like passing ghosts through dimensions, they were and weren't in a short sequence. Irate and tired of being deceived, Algos pointed his skinny, bare-bone fingers at his face and towards his foes.

Dark splinters darted through the short distance between them, repeatedly missing the target. Eventually, as his attack increased in size, a few pierced through Iris's ethereal body, shredding her intangible body as if fragile paper. Her magic halted and Eros and Anita froze on the spot. Hurt and weak, the Awoken staggered back and fell on the ground. At the surge of the Harpies, Eros turned around and hugged Anita as his core expanded through the land, blinding the enemy.

'They won't touch you. I promise. You are mine to protect!' And an excruciating scream of pain followed as he was repeatedly stabbed on his back. His eyes turned to pure fire, he glowed bright, engulfing Anita in his magic. Yet, the Harpies were too many for him to stand still and, slowly, his energy started to dissipate.

Alone and without anyone else to protect her, Anita stood surrounded by the obscure gathering. As if they had been silently asked to step aside, they moved away, making space for their master to walk among them. His walk slow, his golden sandals erasing the life of the grass he walked on, Death smiled.

'I have to admit it's a pleasure to end this with you. You have escaped my judgment for too long. You, a pathetic mass of matter, moving against me, the unmatched, the end of every beginning...'

'Give me the book!' Anita shouted as if she hadn't paid attention to his words.

'The book...' Death repeated. 'As if you could do anything with it. My spell is bound to me. And I'm Death. I'm eternal and you are the last one standing...'

And he laughed as he moved close to Anita, making her feel the oppressive power of annihilation, the anticipation of his final attack.

'Join the others now…' he whispered almost as if he was granting her the mercy of a quick resolve, the end of all her troubles and pain.

Chapter Thirteen

The Eternal

∞

The dark fluid wobbled a few inches from his flat nose when Trusk stopped. Passing through the evil gates would instantly turn off the Sháten Déil's power. *How many other Harpies are left watching over the precious relic?* he thought. *Is it safe to assume they are all out in the open, fighting against Anita? Anita…*

Her face popped up in his mind, the last standing friend he had left. Bravery had become her. She, the one who, not long before, desperately wanted to leave Runae and go back home was alone, fighting the most terrifying enemy. He could not wait any longer. After holding his breath for a moment, he walked through the mystical doors.

On the other side, the silence of the vast emptiness brought him relief. The space was as void of life as it was the first time they had entered the depths of Death's home. Like a mockery of their past action, the scene repeated itself exactly the same. This time, Desterea carried the deformed look of someone he knew well and loved.

As he entered the smaller room to the right, the Leonty's remains had completely transformed into a creature of evil, and sorrow gripped his tiny heart. She didn't move nor acknowledge his presence when he approached her. Defying Anita's command, he stepped next to her and placed his hands on her floating form. A weary lament resounded within the Harpy. Broken words and a sobbing weeping followed.

'Revelia…' he cried. 'If's me, Frusk…' But the Leonty's true spirit had left the reins to a newborn, wicked monster. Her head twitched and, after contorting in pain, she gazed at the shocked Chomp. Her ruby eyes a long-forgotten memory, two black cavities stared at Trusk.

'Get that pity look away from me!' she shouted, making him fall back. 'You are the reason why I'm here. You, like your father before you and his father before him… You had the gift and failed to use it to rescue me, to rescue all the others that needed the most!' she screamed.

'Revelia...' Trusk's broken voice carried the petrifying truth. His best and closest friend was gone. Her words twisted the reality they had shared and she now used it against him.

Next to her, on a pedestal, the white book stood untouched. The chains holding the Harpy prisoner had not yet formed back on its cover. The dark spell spreading fast, a ghostly shadow crept from her to the artefact, sliding through the cold stones, climbing up the stand. The ticking of time immediately brought Trusk back to his mission. He swiftly moved past his friend and grabbed the large tome in his hands. As he turned around and approached the exit, he gazed one last time at the Harpy.

'I'll save you... I'll gef you ouf of here.' After briefly looking at the book, the Chomp rushed through the dark gates and up the large hole through which Creation had set them all free.

There, where Trusk's dome stood, before leaving Anita and the Awokens exposed, a new sphere of dark energy whirled with fury. As if a black mould had risen from the bottom of the lake, infused with the evil spark of life, it rotated around the same spot, over and over. Here and there, flickers of a golden magic could be seen through the crack of the enemy attack, as the Harpies surrounded their enemy, their hands and bodies fused together like one mass only.

Invisible to the Chomp's eyes, Anita stood still, her hands covering her face, afraid of facing the inevitable end. And yet, she remained untouched, a bright cloak flapping around her, keeping her apart. The ghost of a lost friend floated right in front of her, his words softly whispering a comforting melody.

'He knows...he wants to come and save you but Nothing is so powerful... They stand in between us and the emptiness he brings within him. But I'm here...'

'Daniel, please, the cloak won't last long,' she begged as she felt Death's claws penetrating the divine fabric of the relic.

'Hold on, just one more second...'

A blinding explosion followed Daniel's last words. From within the dark dome, flashes of light darted into the outside, breaking the collective power of the Harpies. One by one they were stripped away, their evil essence shredded and dispersed across the island. Seven bright columns manifested all around Anita. Legs, arms and faces appeared in a short sequence. The seven closest to Love shone like diamonds kissed by the rising sun.

Under Death's irate gaze, a myriad of other Awokens floated in the space, glittering like the surrounding lake. The three twins, Harmonia, Eolen, Mnemosy, Asher, they stood resolute against their opponent. Lastly, right next to Anita, Cherish manifested in a snap. Her look sharp, her determination cutting the air, she spoke.

'You did good. Way better than I could.' And she smiled. 'You survived all this and rescued our mother's artefact,' she added with a renewed joy as Trusk reached the two, the white tome bringing the sign of a long-craved victory.

'You think you can defeat me? My army?' Death roared. His form had grown so wide it covered the entire landscape. As his figure rose towards the infinite, the edges of his power engulfed the other Harpies, taking them within his evil core. At every soldier he absorbed, he grew faster and larger. 'I'm everything. His power is my power. As he stands undefeated, so will I!'

Death's attack expanded across the land, clashing against the many Awokens who, in turn, glowed with a pure light, shielding Anita and Trusk from harm.

'He is calling them all...' Daniel whispered as he gazed back at Anita and Cherish. 'He is taking all the Harpies from the world and summoning them here!'

'Good!' Xena interjected. 'It's time we put an end to this charade.'

Yet, the Awoken's resolve felt out of place. Even with us Gods battling Nothing in the far cosmos and all the Awoken Ones standing against Death, the Harpies had a power beyond resistance. Everywhere hands made of smoke and sorrow surfaced out of their master's core, dragging the Awokens from their spot. If they managed to emerge back into reality, they would soon be captured again. Electrifying bursts of opposite powers sent the thundering blast of each one's battle into the surroundings. In the invisible embrace of darkness, the Awokens fought to freedom.

As Cherish moved to join the others, a new presence made itself seen. Walking slow and carrying a face devoid of any emotion, Athymos emerged from the collective vileness. The one who had spent the eternity away from both sides, had finally shown the expected alliance. Behind her, a Human body followed suit, dragged like a marionette to a destiny she could not control.

Under the astonished gaze of Daniel and Anita, Victoria walked close. Before she could speak, Harmonia reappeared, an unusual terror displayed on her face.

'Take them away,' she shouted to Daniel. 'She is...' But the Awoken was dragged back inside the devouring power of the enemy. As she dissolved, her brother's grin flashed next to her, his hands carrying her into the fold.

'Victoria?' Anita blurted out as she stood only a few inches away.

'I remember you...' Athymos spoke for her. Her face grey, her mouth locked open, there was no expression in her visage. 'You resisted me… You escaped me once, but not any more…'

The same events that had unfolded in the old alley back in Rome, replayed right in front of Anita's eyes. The Harpy's right arm lifted in the air and her petrifying power darted through the short distance between them. This time Anita had no protection but a shredded cloak hanging lifeless at her back, its power exhausted. As the spell reached her, it bounced back, spreading on the ground, cracking the soil in dozens of rifts.

'No this time, Mother…' Daniel replied. His soul a pure flicker of the imagination and yet his presence carried the magnitude of the very God he hosted all his life.

'Mother…' Athymos mocked. 'As if she ever wanted to be one…'

'As if she ever stood a chance!' he replied. 'As if she ever had a moment free of your wicked power. You fail to see the greatest truth of all…'

'And what is that, I might ask?' And Athymos's obscure face pushed against Daniel's. The two ethereal beings were not held by a material substance and yet their matter felt large and heavy. As he turned his gaze away from the Harpy, Daniel's eyes met the empty ones of Victoria.

'All the Harpies gathered here, they all live their own corrupted existence. Why are you still hanging on the

Human body you enslaved for so many years? Why are you not leaving her behind?' Daniel countered.

'I don't care about her as much as I don't care any of you, as much I don't care about your questions…' Athymos's hands grabbed Daniel's soul as if she could touch and squeeze its very core. 'But she's the one who won't let go… Even now, when there is no hope for any of you, she still tries to tame me. As if she ever could!' And Athymos lifted Daniel into the air, a black vortex spinning inside his bright interior. 'Now that he draws near, I can finally exist out of a Human body…'

'Let him go!' Victoria suddenly spoke, taking the Harpy by surprise, halting her final, deadly move. 'He is my son!'

'Mum?' Daniel's voice echoed like a dying whisper. Under the petrified gaze of Anita and Trusk, Victoria moved on her own, her hand stretched to reach the ghost of a lost child. Whatever past they had shared, whatever void had reigned in between them, Athymos had finally departed their symbiotic enslavement, her power made strong by Death to sustain her dark will. Victoria was free. Free to be a Human with her own feelings, free from the oppression of the malevolence that had conquered her heart.

A blinding light descended from the skies, as I plunged back into my dear world. The voices of the ones I loved, the ones Daniel loved dearly, spoke of an enchantment that no duty, no enemy could silence any longer.

I moved with the swift touch of an indomitable resolve when I spread my arms in the air and I penetrated the matter of the evil, consuming Athymos from within. Her core, devoid of emotions, felt like a quick walk into an empty, dark field. Her presence, her power didn't matter to me. Her core was as unimportant as a life spent without feelings. I moved through her dismissing even the annihilation I had brought to her, my aim at the one who I wanted to erase for good.

From here, there and everywhere, I moved. The thin essence of the Harpies was burnt away under my raging power as I got close to Death. He had neither face nor body any longer. The gigantic form enveloping the space was pierced in a multitude of holes. There my Awokens emerged, one by one coming back to me.

'You can't defeat me. My spell is eternal,' Death moaned as he struggled to maintain his power.

'Now!' I shouted, my eyes staring at the sky.

Another flash inundated the space and Time materialised next to Anita and Trusk. A few moments later, Health and Soul appeared alongside.

'We need to act fast,' Time prompted, looking at the two companions.

'Mother is holding the line against Nothing but she needs us more than ever,' Health added.

'The corruption in Mother's artefact is linked with Death through the souls of this world. There is only one way to break the spell...' Soul continued.

'We need to do exactly what we did with Love. Do you understand?' Time asked.

'Freeze time and space in a single moment...' Anita replied while Trusk silently agreed to something he hadn't really understood.

'We move at once. When I tell you to go, you cross the node and bring the artefact away from Earth to Runae. Half of the work is already done. Revelia's soul is holding the other side of the conjuring. She knows what to do, so be ready,' Time urged.

'Hold on!' Trusk said before the Gods moved away. 'Daniel and Noah?'

'Trust us, little Chomp...' And Time darted next to me, together with Health and Soul.

'Remember what I showed you, brother,' he said as Time's eyes brightened against the darkness of the enemy.

'I do,' I replied. 'So you are finally ready to admit Daniel was right?' I added, smiling.

The pure power of our magic expanded all the way to the far horizon. Turning matter into pure plasma, we shaped the very fabric of nature with the touch of our being. As my hands entered Death's essence, a shadow surfaced to freedom. With the swing of my arm I pulled Oz towards the ones who desperately wanted him back.

As he reached the others, the heart and the shell appeared at the centre of the island, glowing brightly. In the short sequence of a flashing light, the node opened up, the tiny image of what lay at the other side glittered before their eyes.

'Now!' I thundered.

Without hesitation, Anita sped through the field, the precious book in her hands as Trusk followed her, running towards the portal. Guided by Soul's magic, Oz sprinted right behind them, followed by Daniel's and Noah's souls.

As if anticipating our plan, Death's deformed body bent on the ground, his dark matter sliding on the grass. The few remaining Harpies emerged, their hands trying to catch the fugitives.

'Fasfer!' Trusk shouted, as he lifted Anita into the air.

'I swear, if we make it, I won't touch a book again for the rest of my life!'

The moment they moved from Earth to Runae, the portal vanished instantly. With a subtle flicker of his eye, Time had discreetly crafted a safe haven in his crumbling world. Aligned with my brother's power, I grasped my artefact, sealing the passage between the two planets.

As the final spark of teleporting magic faded, the colossal presence of Death convulsed, trembling as it began to dissolve.

'You…' he started, his voice deep and resonant, echoing across the space like a creature's dying breath. 'You've taken it…when?' One by one, the Harpies, hovering like the grey mist of early morning, began to dissipate, retreating back to their master. His figure shrank, gradually becoming a miniature version of the immense threat he had been until we severed the link between him and his defiant spell. 'You think you can defeat me by just taking it away?' he added, his voice tinged with pain.

'It's over, master of the Harpies,' I retorted. He had finally shrunk to our size when my eyes met the dark voids on his deformed face. The once-radiant armour he wore had dulled, reflecting his imminent defeat. 'You've reigned over my world for too long. You stole our mother's artefact, used it to enslave her, and built an empire of despair. But that ends now. Your power is no longer!'

'No longer…' Death repeated, gazing at the sky. 'You think you can erase me, destroy me? I'm an extension of my master, and he is eternal. I'll live as long as he lives. We are bound together.' His words sent a chill through us. Health and Soul turned to me, their expressions troubled. Even in his defeat, Death wielded his malevolent power over us.

'Brother,' Health said, 'I'm afraid he's telling the truth. Even without Mother's relic, he still draws power from Nothing. My magic can't surpass his, as it isn't his own. He was made out of Mother's demise, not mine.'

'Nothing will soon follow; don't worry about it, sister,' Soul replied. Though the rising sun struggled against the dark celestial events, its light pierced my brother, making him shine like a pure diamond. His confidence was evident in his words and demeanour.

'No,' Time interjected before I could speak. His gaze carried the weight of knowledge and understanding. 'Our path lies before us, shaped by what can and cannot be. Even I, close to mastering the manipulation of opportunities, must accept that we can only go so far.'

'What do you mean?' Soul asked, his optimism challenged by Time's cryptic words.

'Nothing can't be defeated…' I said, my words hanging heavy in the air. A wicked smile spread across Death's face, his grim visage of void and dark magic striking deep into my core.

'Ha ha ha! You finally realize you can't fight our existence. We will always be.' Death laughed again as he faded away, followed by his army.

Embraced by our shining light, their dark presence receded into the abyss they had come from. My siblings and I pushed against their weakened power until every trace of their malevolence had gone back into the depth of their abode. There, we extended our arms and sealed the passage with the magic of our combined power. As if a mystical lake formed over the large hole, a bright expanse flashed twice, sealing the enemy's way out.

'We did it all for nothing? We sacrificed so much, only to see it happen anyway?' Health asked as we moved back to the node. 'Our worlds, the many lives lost, all for this?'

'No, sister. It was vital for Death to believe it, to hear us saying Nothing is unbeatable. We have one opportunity only, and it tethers on to a very slim hope Time and I have. Mother created Runae, Talush, Varayal, and Earth as corners of a domain filled with life, shielded by Nothing's power. We enjoyed the peace of being apart from him for too long. That won't be possible any longer. All we can do now is save what we can, protect what still stands, and hold him right where he is until the time is right,' I said, moving towards the edge of the island.

'So we join our mother against him in a never-ending fight in the hope that what you both saw will come to pass?' Soul sighed as he moved next to me. His crystal eyes held unspoken words, regrets, and a sense of defeat we all shared. The moment when Time had come to take the Tiara from him repeated vividly in his mind. Our brother had condemned him to an eternity in slavery, imprisoned inside a cave filled with the cries of the many lost souls. Even if Soul knew he had no chance against the King of Emptiness, ifs and maybes echoed strong. Before he could speak his thoughts out loud, Time didn't hesitate to bring it all to light.

'There was no other way. Among a universe of possibilities, in one and only one lies the way to victory. And we could still fail. We must close the loop we created when we came to exist. We were never meant to conquer him and the entire cosmos. We and Nothing will exist for eternity. We must exist within his vast obscurity. Our destiny is to protect what is left. We have to lock this timeline in a never-ending circle of opposition. This way, not everything will be lost. But, to do so, we have to eradicate his presence from this side of the cosmos.'

Soul's expression was a blend of resignation and determination. 'So we are to be the guardians of this cycle, forever bound to fight without the hope of triumph?'

'Yes,' I replied, my voice steady. 'We fight not for victory but for preservation. Our battle ensures that life continues, that hope remains. It's a burden we must bear, a duty we must fulfil.'

Time stepped forward, his presence a beacon of certainty amidst our doubts. 'Remember, we were never meant to conquer. Our existence is a testament to resilience, to the unending struggle against the void. In our opposition, we find our purpose. In our defiance, we preserve the light.'

As we stood on the precipice of our shared fate, the weight of our roles settled over us. We were the guardians of time and space, the protectors of creation. And though our fight would be eternal, our resolve would never waver. We would stand against Nothing, not to win, but to ensure that life, in all its forms, would endure.

'So we shall!' Health replied firmly.

'Hold on, sister,' Time stopped her before she could shift to an intangible, divine being and rise into the atmosphere. 'Not yet.'

'There is something we need to do,' I added.

'Tell us,' Health and Soul said in unison.

'She is coming back,' Time replied, gazing ahead at an invisible spot on the horizon.

Chapter Fourteen

A New Praetorian

∞

'Mum? Tell me the story again…'

'You should be asleep by now. I know you are still excited about your seventh birthday party but it's a school day tomorrow. Come on, be a good boy.'

'Please, Mum? I want to hear about the Gods again…'

'OK…' Anita exhaled, stuck in between annoyance and acceptance. *How many times will I have to do this?* she thought. 'I'll tell you just a little bit, but try to fall asleep. Here, baby, get under the duvet. Now,' she resumed as she lay comfortable in the large bed, next to her son. 'Where did we stop last time? Oh, yes! The great war far away in the skies…'

'And how the Chomp went back home too, Mama. I like that part…'

'I know you do, Daniel. I can tell you about Trusk and Revelia tomorrow night. For now, let's go back to when the Gods rose up against Nothing.'

'And how the girl with no name met her angel boyfriend…' Daniel added as he was already close to falling asleep. At their back, the ticking of a wintery rain on the large bedroom window enhanced the atmosphere of an upcoming evocative story.

'OK, where did we leave off?' Anita started after she smiled at her son's remark. That question sounded funny to her. In the innocence of that request, she found the amusement of a truth it was yet too early to share.

'The four Gods left the small island in Noah's Bridge and flew up in the sky, way, way over the moon. Past the sun and all the planets, they joined Creation. She stood there, hands and arms stretched over the beyond. Her magic was so powerful that a second sun appeared on Earth. When the four stood next to her, their power increased tenfold.'

'And Creation said they were going to stop Nothing from getting here…' Daniel interrupted, yawning.

'The Gods stood resolute,' Anita continued. 'If it was true that Nothing could not truly be defeated and they could only establish an eternal balance between light and darkness, day and night, good and evil, they had to show him how their resolve would not falter.'

***

'Within me you found your own existence.' Nothing's deep voice crossed the cosmos. 'How can you resist me when you belong to me?'

'I don't belong to you, we don't belong to you,' Creation retorted. 'We were born out of a spark of life. We parted ways from what you could not be any longer. Go back to your dark, remote corners and let us be!'

'You will never cease to multiply and spread, tormenting my everlasting night with the vision of tumults, hate… I've seen what your creation has done to itself. They can only destroy themselves. And you know why? Because in the secret of their being, they crave to come back to me. To erase themselves into the nothing they truly belong to.'

'They do that because of the very evil you've sent,' Time responded. His core slowly grew in magnitude. His long cloak formed around his shoulders as his power rose in the dark universe. 'We have seen your servants too. We defeated them every time. Even Death lies powerless by our hands!'

'Go back and we will not seek revenge,' Health added as she replicated Time's magic, followed by Soul, whose energy shone brighter than ever before.

'Revenge…' Nothing mocked. 'As if you could ever challenge me. Come back into me, you insolent…'

The pure matter of the universe disintegrated all around his presence. Every particle and every atom collapsed into itself as Nothing's power grew larger, expanding his devouring mouth against the Gods. There, quick with her resolve and filled with the desperation of what millennia of imprisonment had meant to her making, Creation reached her daughter Health and her sons Time and Soul.

A brief gaze to Love carried the look of an unspoken pact. Everything they had managed to accomplish, everything Time had meticulously planned and orchestrated reached that final moment when they would finally confront the enemy. Three artefacts manifested in the open. Gravitating and spinning on their own, they left their owners to reach Love. The clepsydra, Health's sceptre, and the shining tiara moved in the same hands that had created them. As if their beginning and end had the same origin, they all departed from their owners and moved next to Love. As they touched his ethereal skin, they dissolved, their power fusing with the one who was going to stand apart.

'What is the meaning of all this?' Nothing said as his shocked gaze was so large that it could have embraced the entire universe. 'I know your spell…there is nowhere you can send your amulets to safety…'

'We don't need them for what we are about to do!' Creation replied, sharp.

'Tell them I'm sorry…' Time whispered as he turned around and briefly looked at Love. 'I've always cared for them. Everything I've done, I did it so they could know…one day.'

'The promise I made, brother, I will keep. He'll be back…' Soul added.

'Keep them safe, keep them within the embrace of your power. If immortality can't hold them, Love will. Let the memory of the ones they love, give them what I can't,' Health whispered.

'Brother,' Time concluded. 'You know what to do…'

As if a ritual prayer had been said for a last time, the four Gods turned their back to Love and fused together. Their energy like thousands of supernovae, they shone with a power never seen before. In the clash against the one who owned it all, the two powers twirled together, their extremes contorting in a convulsive spectacle of light and darkness. Then, after what looked like a brief moment, an enormous partition flashed all over the universe.

The Gods' powers creating an impenetrable barrier, they sacrificed their existence to become something else, something more. They rose themselves in protection of the souls they loved, to give them a future, to give them life.

The incredible display of magic left Love staggered. Mystical tears flowed on his silky, transparent skin as if pain and suffering had manifested like a new God. Everything his brother had told him had just come true. Every action they had taken, every loss they had endured, had brought him right there, to witness the fall of his mother and siblings. All for the protection of what lay behind.

Two worlds was all they could save. Two worlds who would soon rewind their memories to the point of oblivion. Two worlds where the only power, the only supreme protection would always and for eternity be Love.

***

'Now,' Anita whispered as she gently kissed Daniel on his pink cheek. 'I wish you knew the meaning of everything I'm telling you, my boy. I know one day you will. But for now, you are just mine to love, mine to protect…' And she slowly got up and left the room. A final glance to her son triggered a peaceful smile. In her mind, that was exactly what a Praetorian was meant to be. And yet, she was also much more. She was a mother, and also the true representation of the Awoken of Memory and Protection.

'Is he asleep?' Eros asked as she closed the door behind her.

'Yes, he is, my love.' And his form wobbled, his Human body dissolved to then reappear in his true, spiritual form.

Walking across the corridor into the kitchen, he raised his hands to her shoulders and kissed her on her neck, cheek, mouth. Even as a heavenly ghost, he shifted across dimensions, reaching her tangible body as they had done before, many times before.

'After all these years, it still gives me a pleasant shiver…' Anita said, smiling. 'When Soul and Health granted us to be together, I thought it was going to end… you know, afterwards…'

'I was never going to end, Anita,' Eros said as he hugged her. 'Love knew you were mine to protect. In you I found more than what I was, more than Cherish and I were. In you I found my purpose…' And he kissed her, softly.

There, in the Awoken's mystical embrace, Anita closed her eyes and gasped. His touch was as powerful as it had been since the first time he had appeared in Noah's Bridge, among feelings of sorrow, desperation and loss. Able to sweep her fears away, Eros enchanted her soul, turned her body into a raging fire. Her skin electrified by the touch of his ghostly fingers, Anita felt the desire of a present lust mixing with the memories of a troubled past.

As the two lay on the large white couch in the sitting room, her clothes being removed with the swing of

Eros's magic, the memories of the aftermath of Death's defeat replayed in her mind, when Anita and Eros were granted the gift of a lifetime. She had just walked through the node, back on Earth. As she reappeared in Crossing Island, the three Gods and I welcomed her back.

'It's done,' she said. Her face firm, the emotional scars of everything she had endured spoke for her. Yet, a brief smile followed before she added, 'We took Revelia's stone off the book, here…' And she stretched her hands towards us, revealing the white tome sitting in her palms. 'I left the crystal in Runae with Trusk. I don't think the two pieces should ever come to be together on Earth ever again. I don't think Death's spell will ever, truly be over…'

'Thank you, Anita,' I said, smiling as I moved closer and gently pushed the book back towards her chest. 'There is something I must ask of you…'

'Whatever it is,' she quickly replied, her determination clearly manifesting in her tone, 'I won't do it… Unless you bring back the ones I lost. Daniel sacrificed everything for you to come back, all of you. And so did Noah and Revelia…'

'This is exactly what we need to do, it has always been,' Time interjected as he took her hands. '*Make sure she remembers*…did I not say that when you left Runae?'

'You weren't referring to Cherish?' Anita asked, her mind already travelling ahead, making conjectures of her own.

'No. I wasn't.' And Time briefly paused and gazed at the sky. Flashes of an astonishing power spread all around, urging the God to hurry. 'We must act fast. We are at the end of our road and at the beginning of yours. We must do one final thing before we join Mother for eternity…'

So my brother moved his arms in a circle, his magic opening the portal once more. Soul moved next to him, his eyes closed, his hands joined as if praying. The surface of his shimmering body glowed twice in a quick succession and the spectre of a lost friend surfaced from the depths of the island. Her wrists and ancles chained still by the evil spell, the one who had taken Desterea's place joined the gathering of supreme beings.

The two eyes of the snake spiralling around Health's sceptre shone as if connected with Soul's magic. She moved next to the Harpy and placed the tip of her artefact on the enemy's head. A melancholic moan of suffering and agony spread in the air as the ghost of a lost Leonty was pulled away from her prison. Two identical copies, one made of light and one of darkness, convulsed as if determined to opposed my sister's healing power. Eventually, with a resounding snap, Revelia's true body was freed, floated around for a brief moment and departed through the node.

'She'll find her soul,' Health let out.

'Let's go. We move quickly.' Time asserted as he followed Revelia into Runae.

We emerged on the other side in an instant. As if the same island had shrunk in a second, the landscape looked almost the same. The blue sky was replaced by violet and green hues and in the far corner of the horizon, Nothing's attack against Creation could still be seen. Vast and indisputable, the two's presences and powers embraced the visible universe.

Right after the node had shut down, the little crystal in Trusk's hands lifted on its own, spinning fast. Resounding with the body she had left behind, Revelia's soul cracked through the hard matter of Death's diamond and burst into the warm air. Her green skin and the dark marks of Una's domain slowly reformed as a spectacle to the group. The hard, long hair shaped as if drawn by a mystical pencil and at last, her ruby eyes glowed with a renewed liberation.

Before she could even realise her coming back to life, Anita and Trusk were all over her, hugging her, happiness quickly turning into flowing tears.

'I see the future again…' she said, visibly happy. 'I see us… I see my sisters? How?' And she gazed at Time who in exchange responded by raising his hands, his power already at work.

'I must say,' he replied. 'It's almost like an insult of cosmic proportion for me to be the one who says there is no time. But still, someone will carry my will when I won't be able to. As I join Mother in our eternal tribulation, you, Trusk and Noah will continue what I'm about to begin.'

As if we had just been teleported inside the Chomps' old building, by the Ancient Mirrors, the landscape twirled and dissolved, formed and reshaped in a lightspeed succession. Oz's forms vanished and the true owner of his soul reappeared next to his friends. Freckles on his face, the stormy blue and green eyes tearing as he came back to life, Noah found himself surrounded by the hands of the ones he loved.

'We made it…' he whispered, his voice broken by an overwhelming joy.

'Noah,' I said as I moved next to him. 'Your determination, your will, your stubbornness towards what we all believe has kept me alive, has granted us a future that was about to shatter under Nothing's malevolence. There is no thank-you that will ever be enough. Yet, we ask of you something greater than you have faced so far.' And the green clepsydra spun from Time's chest and moved next to Noah, its green light tuned with the colour of his eyes.

'I go now,' Time continued. 'I trust you'll know what to do with the power I'm granting you. For the many things ahead you are unsure of, trust Revelia and the future she'll seek. For the many things you can't believe possible, Trusk will guide you with the wings of courage and protection. Brothers…' Time added, gazing at us Gods. 'Time is of the essence…'

And my brother turned into a stream of light as he sprinted into the sky and disappeared. His magic still at work, the world around us kept the rewinding of Runae's history, the artefact in Noah's hands channelling the power of unmaking.

'Anita,' I resumed. 'To the one who witnessed so much, carrying the weight of a never-ending past within Cherish's memories… To the one who will carry them still into our future, you are granted the promise you have made to Daniel.' I swiftly moved next to her while two of my strongest Awokens appeared beside me. 'In the greater scheme of incomprehensible powers, Daniel managed to see through. His soul, his heart didn't only keep mine safe, he went beyond. He embraced the true representation of what I am, what my mother is. He gave himself to me so I could see, so my brothers could see. Because there is no greater power than love, greater than creation itself. It holds the reason of existence, the reason why we all managed to survive the second coming of the enemy. His soul, his bond with the ones he loved enchanted me and the Gods to a supreme truth: there is nothing worth saving if the ones we love are not preserved. So he'll come back to you, when the time is right…' And I glanced at Eros and Cherish. 'They'll be by your side as I keep the stronghold of this world protected by Death, until the right moment when we'll all be ready to wipe his essence out of this world.'

'So it's true,' she interrupted. 'He can't be defeated…'

'Exactly as his master. So as my brothers join Mother, I won't follow them. Mine will be the only power to hold the two worlds together, mine the responsibility to fight here what they will fight there. We can't destroy Death yet but Love will be the ultimate weapon against his erasing power. We'll wield love as the only way to survive. Until…'

'Until?' Anita asked as I briefly stopped, thinking to how the future would shape ahead.

'Until he is ready…' I replied, smiling.

Soul walked next to us and gently touched Anita's face. Health followed as she kissed her forehead, her magic secretly at play. 'When the time is right, he'll come back to you,' she repeated. 'My job here is done and so is Soul's…'

And my siblings dissolved like Time had just done, their trail of pure light departing as fast as the beating of my heart.

'What did they do?' Anita asked, looking at her hands. Somehow she could perceive a new magic running in her flesh and bones.

'Nothing yet.' And I smiled again.

And so the moment came, when the souls of those who fought hard could find the time to rest, reassess, rebuild, love again. If Noah, Revelia and Trusk had left Anita behind, making her feel the full potency of their absence, she didn't feel lost, alone. Next to her, Eros followed her like a protective shadow. Determined to feel Cherish in his heart once again, he stood resolute against my will, my command to go and seek every passage, every open gate through which Death and his Harpies could resurface on Earth.

'Wherever she goes, I'll go!' he had stated, right after my siblings had departed.

'Cherish won't be with her forever. How do you think she's going to feel the day we'll all go?' I had objected.

But there was no words I could master that could persuade Eros from being anything different than he was. It was fascinating, worrying and yet, satisfying in seeing a piece of me becoming more than simply an Awoken. He wasn't an extension of who I was. He had become more. Somehow, whatever secret magic he withheld, it felt very similar to Daniel's. I could not control the rightfulness of their actions. *Is this Mother's true magic?,* I thought as I departed, living Anita and Eros behind. *Is this what I am? A power that transcends every control? A power that can live out of its own embodiment? Yes, this must be the answer. This is the reason why Time's plan is so…accurate.*

'What do we do now?' Anita asked Eros. All around silence had come to conquer her heart with a pure sense of emptiness. 'Everybody is gone…' And she turned around and walked to the edge of the tiny island.

Right where she stopped, a precarious, small boat resurfaced from her memories as if real in her mind. The same boat that had brought her and Daniel back to Noah's Bridge. After seeing the kiss between Daniel and Noah, after the disappointment, the shock, they had gone back to the inn. She shook her head and gazed at Eros whose form flickered under the sun's strong light.

'We go home?' the Awoken replied. His almost invisible hand moved into hers.

'What home?' It's all gone, isn't it?'

'Home is not a place, a building, Anita. Home is where you feel safe, loved. And I'll make sure anywhere would feel this way, to you, to me.'

'So you are really staying with me…why?'

'Because my place is with you, if you want me…' And a soft smile appeared on Eros's face.

'Was there something between you and Cherish?' she asked, her eyes fixed on his.

'Can you tell?' he replied after a moment of silence. Describing with words the feeling he had for both the Awoken and her host was difficult.

'Cherish's memories always came to me when I needed them the most. Sometimes when *she* needed it the most. I know now what she felt for you…'

'Is it wrong? To be wanting you so I can also have her again? So I can make sure you are safe?' Eros's voice trembled as he asked that question.

'I had less noble reasons to be with someone else, not long ago… And to be honest, who am I to judge an Awoken of Love on this subject?' Anita added, smiling. 'With the hundreds and hundreds of books I read, there is no research I can do that can make me understand what it means. If there is something I know now, it's that some things can't be learned. They can only…be felt.' After a brief pause, she added, 'Will my house still be there?'

'I think time is being rewound as we speak. Sure, we'll find out soon.'

Eros extended his arms, silently asking her to come closer. As Anita's body touched his, her face placed on his ethereal chest, he embraced her and the two dissolved into a flash of light. A moment later, the sting of a humid, strong scent of the sea reached her senses as she opened her eyes and gazed at the vast ocean.

They stood silent for several minutes while Anita stared at the infinity of the blue horizon. The large beach had shrunk to a thin line, the grey sand sunk under the heavy flowing of the tide. Like the recent past now gone, so were the imprints of three friends who had walked freely in a summer afternoon. Both Daniel and Noah were gone. Their innocence, their naivety about what was going to come were also much-loved friends who had gone forever.

'How does someone rebuild a life, after all this?' Anita whispered, almost if talking to herself.

'Even if you can't see it now,' Eros replied, softly holding her. 'It's all here still. The waters will recede, the beauty of living will appear again. You only need to trust it will. I promise…'

And as a lost past was reforged into a new present, so the months eventually rushed ahead. A stronger bond between Eros and Anita had surpassed its supernatural connection with Cherish, spilling into their tangible reality, reaching Anita's heart. The stronger Eros's feelings for Anita became, the more time he spent in Human form, by her side.

Day after day, her desire and need to have him closer grew stronger. Whatever emotions Cherish loudly spoke in her mind, Anita had made space for her own feelings, her own attraction to flourish. And then desire became passion, and passion turned into an overwhelming lust as Anita moved on Eros's body, conquering him, owning his whole essence with the power of her movements. If the Awoken inhabiting her soul once again wanted it or Anita's own desire spoke to drive her actions it wasn't important to her. They all wanted to be together, physically, emotionally.

It was impossible for her to understand how she had found in an Awoken, in a time of danger and sorrow, the soulmate of a lifetime. And even more, Anita's surprise in finding out she would carry a child, fruit of a passionate love with an ethereal being like Eros, had come with shock and confusion.

And there she was, merging her true essence with his once again, in between the memories of the life they had built together, she knew their son was the making of the Gods. Her promise to Daniel spoke loud in her mind. She could see the silent forest in Runae growing large as the two ran away from the others, right after Eros had been liberated. There, amidst pain and an indomitable will, she had said the words now ever present in her mind: 'If you come back, I'll be your Praetorian.'

Chapter Fifteen

A Mother's Choice

∞

It was a sunny day, warmer than anticipated for a mid June in Ireland. Daniel sat at his desk reading the essay over and over. Although his mother had raised him surrounded by books of every kind, teaching him all the things she thought would be important as he grew up, his mind refused to cooperate.

He gazed around the room packed with anxious teenagers. Some were writing already, others carried a visible worried look on their faces. *What am I going to do when I'm out of here?* he thought. He had grown up free from rigid expectations yet closely guided by his parents. School was almost over. A few hours and he would be free. *Free from what?* he asked himself as he looked back at the white sheet of paper.

'Heads down, the clock is ticking…' Mrs. Doyle said as she walked in between the desks lined up for the final exam. Two rows ahead, to the right, someone Daniel had been wanting to know for months lifted his head and turned around, briefly meeting his gaze.

His sandy hair moved to the side as he looked back at Daniel, smiling. A thrilling shiver ran down his spine, electrifying him. Colours and sparkles of light darted across Daniel's eyes as the sun peeked through the window next to that beautiful boy. As if the bright rays would lift his presence to a greater beauty, a nervous smile crept across Daniel's lips.

A strange yet familiar feeling emerged from within his thoughts. As if his already laborious imagination unleashed freely, pictures and images of them together popped up in his mind. Details and features of an impossible present formed right before him as he envisioned glimpses of a life lived with him by his side. Large paintings decorated walls of a large home they lived in. Two dogs and a cat lay asleep on the floor. They were suddenly made older, surrounded by many friends as they sat around a dinner table.

Daniel smiled again and turned his gaze away, perplexed. That wasn't the first time he had very vivid visions. Anita had told him his creativity and imagination were things he had to cherish deeply. Yet, the attraction and the feelings he had for a boy he had never found the courage to talk to triggered something beyond what he was familiar with. He wasn't only seeing himself next to him. He felt as if a lifetime spent together whispered of memories he couldn't possibly have. He had done it so many times. He had pictured himself next to that boy, introducing himself, getting close to him. Then they had become fast friends and, perhaps, even more. But, in reality, every time the opportunity presented itself, something held him back. Introverted and driven by fear, he shied away from him.

'Ten minutes…' the teacher announced at some point.

In between dreams and a cacophony of thoughts, Daniel had managed to write a good length. *Mum would be proud of this work,* he thought. *What did she say? We are going to get something for our holiday in Italy after school…can't wait!*

So the most dreaded test was finally over and the collective joy of the relieved students broke freely through the exit doors as they left the room. Amidst the pressing and pushing of the many, a white sheet flew across the corridor, landing right at Daniel's feet. As he moved to pick it up, another hand touched his.

'Sorry…that's mine,' the other boy said, smiling. At the sight of the one he had spent the last hour dreaming of, Daniel blushed. The charged jolt resumed instantly.

'This is incredible…' Daniel let out as he gazed at the elaborate drawings on the white sheet. 'Did you make it?'

'Yeah,' the other one said, a northern Irish accent sneaking through. 'That's what I'm going to do, one day. For work, I mean…'

'An artist?' Daniel asked as the two followed the crowd out of the building. In the far distance, Anita had just parked the car and hurried towards her son.

'Yeah… I'm John. We never managed to introduce one another.'

'Daniel…' And the electrostatics in the air were almost making his messy hair stand upright. If something was at play, it wasn't certainly just pure attraction.

'Daniel? Let's go, we are late!' Anita said, a disturbed look briefly appearing on her face. 'Sorry, we really need to go,' she added, pulling Daniel by his shoulder. Her eyes glanced at John once more, a mix of sorrow and delight mingling in her heart.

'Ma, was there a need for that? I was talking to him…' Daniel lamented as he entered the car. 'I swear sometimes you really embarrass me…'

'Every parent does that,' Anita replied. 'I'm just sticking to my part in this story.' And she smiled as she turned to look back at John. Seeing him again, so young yet still vividly resembling the man she knew, struck a blade into her heart.

'I feel like I'm back ten years old. I swear this is the last time you pick me up from school.'

'I don't see how it could be any different. School is over. I certainly won't drive you to college in Dublin…'

'I'm not sure I want to go to Dublin, to be honest,' Daniel said all at once. As if that sentence had no impact on his mother's expectations, he let it out without thinking. All he could think of was John.

'Excuse me?' Anita said pulling up to the side of the road. 'What happened? Did you finish the essay?'

'Of course I did, Ma… All good,' he added after seeing Anita's expression dangerously changing. 'I'm just not sure I know what I want to do yet… I was thinking art might be a better fit for me.'

'Art…' Anita blurted out.

'Yeah, art.'

'Yes.' And after seeing Daniel's swift relief she quickly added, 'Yes, not yeah. How many times I have to tell you? Why art? I thought you wanted to pursue social studies…' But in the secret of her mind, Anita knew the answer already. She had showed up just in time before Daniel and John could get past the simple exchange of names. His presence, their past, were suddenly interfering with their present.

'I don't know. I'm just not sure,' Daniel replied as he gazed to the other side, his eyes staring at the world outside but his mind travelling beyond. *I want to talk to him again,* he thought.

'Is it because of a boy?' But Anita's question was left unanswered. 'Is it because of a girl?'

'Maaa,' Daniel protested.

The whole conversation around college was left aside as the two went shopping for swimwear and a few more items to bring on their holidays. A few hours later they were all ready at the house and dinner was almost ready.

A couple of suitcases stood upright in the hall, next to the front door. Three tickets hung in balance on top of one of them and the destination could clearly be seen.

'It's ridiculous I have to fly inside a machine when I could just be there in an instant,' Eros said as he set the table. 'Daniel,' he shouted. 'It's almost ready!'

'I know, love, but surely we can't tell our son you are not coming with us and then just show up in Sicily…' Anita replied, smiling. 'By the way, is there a chance you could speak to Revelia before we go?'

'Something happened?' Eros left his duty unfinished and moved by the cooker, next to Anita. After pulling her chin with a soft touch, he added, 'What is it?'

'Nothing. I'm just…well, Daniel met John today,' she confessed. 'In school. I didn't even know they went to the same school. I thought he was brought back to his true past. Why is he here, in Castlecross?'

'Despite what Love told us, you are the one who insisted he should have a life as close as the one he had.

This is exactly how you do that. It's going to happen, eventually. Maybe this is a sign we are doing everything right.'

'But it's too soon. Noah's work isn't finished. Beside, there is so much I have to tell him first… I know what Love said, yet I don't want it to happen. He deserves better. He deserves to get back what he had.'

'I know,' Eros replied as he pulled three plates out of a cabinet. 'But you also know you can't have it both ways. Either we let his future unfold as it should, with him walking back all the steps until…' And he stopped, briefly. 'Or we keep our ground and keep him away from it. But that means he shouldn't even be going to Italy…'

'You are right,' she sighed. 'It's a struggle I won't ever overcome.'

'The notion that you were his best friend before doesn't erase the fact that you are his mother now. You need to choose, Anita.'

'I know. I thought I did. We have been going to Italy for five years now and still I'm not ready…' And Anita placed a pot full of pasta in the sink with the same frustration that resounded in her voice.

'You won't lose him. We won't lose him. You are his Praetorian. He will always be yours to love…' Eros replied, his eyes fixed on hers. 'To be honest, I can't wait to stop pretending I'm eating this food,' he added, smiling.

‘I can’t wait to stop pretending I’m good at cooking Italian food too,’ she remarked, sarcastic. ‘No matter how many books I’ve read on the topic, I just can’t. And tomorrow I’ll be reminded how their food tastes way better. Like every time we go…’

‘We are having pasta?’ Daniel asked as he moved to the table, picking up the work Eros had left unfinished. ‘You know, Ma, you can’t…’

‘Beat them…’ Anita interrupted, mocking him. ‘I know. God forbid you love the Irish more than the Italians.’

‘Are we going to see Mrs. Rita-Louise tomorrow?’ And a sparkle flickered in Daniel’s eyes.

‘Sure,’ Eros replied; a soft touch found his loved one, silently telling her again, it will all be OK. ‘And the girl you like so much from the town, Eléna. Last year you spent the whole month together. I thought we wouldn’t take you out of that place.’

‘I can’t wait. I hope everything is just as we left it, last year…’

Daniel’s hope had a solid ground. In a place where time seemed to be constantly under my brother’s spell, the entire Sicilian village and its surroundings were exactly as he had left them. People carried the same life, day in and day out. The long grey beaches crowded with people on their holidays, the glittering sea shone at the same rhythm with the gathering of the masses moving about, up and down the promenade, in and out of little souvenir shops.

In the middle of a tiny street, among a multitude of tiny tables, Daniel and Eléna kept hugging for a few minutes. They chatted and hugged in quick succession. After being a year apart they had so much to say that a month together would not fit the amount of news they wanted to share.

Just around the corner, sitting further away to give him space but close enough to watch his every move, Anita and Eros sat on two wobbling chairs, right next to a pile of magnets stand. In between customers and waiters alike, Anita blended seamlessly while Eros looked out of place. His Human features brought by magic paled against the roasting sun, almost revealing his transparent true form. In contrast, Anita already had some colour in her cheeks. Under her large, yellow hat, she wore black sunglasses. As she heard Daniel's laughs and chatter, the memory of their long past adventure in Rome brought a wave of nostalgia.

'Hands off the merchandise,' he had said as they moved among a sea of fake brands.

A few minutes after they arrived in Taormina, Anita and her son had almost replayed the exact same scene. She wanted that yellow hat and Daniel had made a strange similar comment.

'Is it you, or it's her?' Eros asked, interrupting her trail of thoughts.

'No, this time is me. This is a memory that belongs to me, not Cherish. I wish I could let it all out, you know? It's not the secret that torments me, it's the laughs and tears I can't share. Things we lived together and I can't recall with him…'

'For now. Soon you might. Thank you,' Eros said to the waiter who had just handed him a glass of prosecco.

'No, eh?' Anita asked him as he quickly passed the drink to her, an expression of discomfort crossing his face.

A few seconds later, Daniel and Eléna joined them at the table and the conversation, filled with gossip and updates, extended to the entire group. After years of studying the language, Anita had finally mastered a good level of Italian. Eros, gifted with the knowledge of a supreme being, had raised Daniel with the wisdom he needed to fulfil his destiny. After a few drinks and an ice cream for the two teenagers, the four walked down towards the old town centre, near the harbour. To the right side, the sea and its scent conquered half the street. To the left, a long series of small white houses with tall heads and a prominent front garden held the partition between the shoreline and the mountains.

They stopped in front of the third one where an old lady sat quietly on a chair, under the shade of a bright blue beach umbrella. A glass filled with iced tea dripped like a carbon copy of the lady's forehead.

'Signora Rita-Louise?' Daniel said as he ran through the front garden. A large smile appeared on her face as her arms opened up in a big hug.

'Oh my God you have grown so much!' she said as she extended her hands to the other guests. 'I wasn't expecting you before July…'

'We were supposed to, but Eros can't stand the heat, you know…' Anita replied, sitting next to her. To that remark, he smiled. *I lived in this world for millennia, faced way worse than a scorching star and here I am, living like one of them. My brother Prometheus would be proud*. And he looked back at Anita and Daniel, his heart filled with love.

'Oh, I understand,' Rita-Louise replied. 'This is why I'd rather sit here in the shade and close to the sea. The breeze gives some comfort. Besides, it brings also memories…'

'Memories?' Daniel asked as he sat on the grass, next to her.

'Yes, I pretty much grew up by the harbour. You don't know this but my father was in the navy. He would go for months at a time but I was always thrilled to see him coming back. Oh, how many times I waited for him, just down there, past the promenade… It wasn't like it looks now, full of bars and restaurants. It was a simple port, a simpler life, back then.'

'Did he live here? In this house?' Daniel's curiosity and the charm of the storytelling was once again pulling him in.

'When he was young, yes. Then he moved further inland, close to the volcano. He had this big old house. How many times he begged me to go and live with him…but I loved it here. Here is where I grew up, here is where Victoria grew up. Oh, speaking of, look who's here!' And Rita-Louise raised her hand towards her daughter who had just walked in.

Her long ginger hair, a few freckles on her face, she was exactly like Anita remembered. In the few years they had been visiting they had never met her. Carrying the instinct and will of the one who held the keys to every memory, Anita was determined to rebuild for Daniel the life he had and he was meant to have. Even if in her heart she wanted him all for herself, her sharp mind brought her in agreement with Cherish's. However, seeing Victoria standing there, smiling, made her uneasy. All the things Anita had witnessed, the terrible behaviour of a woman who could not be a mother, the actions of the Harpy that controlled her every move, was too much to forget.

Eros stood up and shook Victoria's hand. With a smile and gentle manners he introduced the rest of the group. In his movements there was no trace of danger. Whatever evil had coexisted with Victoria, it felt long gone.

‘So you are the ones that rent the house down the road every summer?’ Victoria asked. ‘I’m so sorry I never managed to meet you. My life and work is in Rome, so I rarely come back. Just to check on my mother, here and then…’

At the sound of Rome, Anita stood up, stiff. Even if she wasn’t the Victoria they knew and the Harpies had been sent to oblivion, her memories held strong in that new reality. She could picture Carla’s ugly face and hear the stories she told when they questioned her about the old picture. She could still see Victoria speaking to the person who was now her son, telling him he wasn’t good enough, he was a sinner. The suspicion she could have entangled herself with the cult once more, in their new reality, took over and made her instinctively move.

‘Right, we better go, we still have to unpack,’ she said, sharp.

‘Ma, we just got here,’ Daniel objected. After briefly exchanging with Eléna a look of disappointment, he stood up and kissed Rita-Louise on the cheek.

That evening, after Daniel had left to go for a walk with his friend by the promenade, Anita and Eros prolonged their staying in the small terrace, at the house. The fresh air had finally removed the humidity of a long, hot day and the two kept looking at the sea, each lost in the shared contemplation of that beauty.

‘I know Time did the right thing by rewinding their lives, bringing them back to a better past, but…sometimes I wish he had done the same for all of us…' Anita confessed.

'It wasn't Time's decision alone, you know that,' Eros replied. 'Love wanted it too. This is his way to repay them all for their sacrifices. We all got what we wanted. He gave me the chance to stay behind, with you. Gave Daniel a mother… The best mother he could possibly have, if I may add.'

'True. Rita-Louise didn't have to raise an evil daughter, nor take care of a God in a child's body… I wonder…' Anita's words trailed off as Eros stood up to move to the edge of terrace where a stronger breeze carried the scent of the sea salt.

'You wonder…'

'I wonder if I should put an end to this idea of giving him back his memories. What would I do that for? I won't be doing the same to any of them.' And she pointed at the landscape ahead, where the faces of the many people Daniel had shared a life with virtually popped up in the dark scenery. 'He won't be able to tell them who they truly were. He will have to carry the same secret I'm carrying now…to do what then? To attempt another sacrifice?'

'The real question you should ask yourself, my dear, is another one: is telling him an act of love or not? I know you don't want him to do what Love asked. Yet, you still move the plan along. So, my question is: do you want to tell him because you have to or because you miss the Daniel he was?' That question found her unprepared. In the last eighteen years they had discussed that very topic many, many times but Eros had never come forwards with a similar, sharp statement.

'Of course I miss the Daniel he was,' she replied, almost offended. 'I miss who we were but we have become much more now. He is my son. I love him more than I love the memory of our friendship.'

'Then let it go…'

'I can't,' she immediately said. 'I won't let go…'

'Cherish?' Eros turned around and met Anita's eyes. As if he could scan her heart and soul in a blink, he moved closer and sat again next to her. 'Cherish, it's all over now. Our duty has changed. The Gods have built an unbreakable defence against Nothing. Love is spreading his magic on here and on Runae. Let it go…'

'We owe Daniel our lives. We owe Daniel the future we are living. How can I betray him by withholding his memories from him? This is not love, it's cruelty.' Anita stood up, the reins of her body and mind in Cherish's hands.

'The happiness we are giving him is love,' Eros replied.

'A happiness made of lies and deceit,' Cherish's sharp response came as a surprise to the one who had loved her for many lifetimes. But before he could respond, a bright light flashed beside them. 'Besides, we respond to Love's will before anything else. And he said Daniel must do it.'

'Do I have to do this every time?' Harmonia suddenly manifested, a big smile followed her question. 'There is no need to be upset…'

'Go away, I'm not in the mood for a therapy session,' Cherish blurted out. 'Deep down Anita feels the same as me. She is getting old, time is passing fast. She doesn't want to bring this secret to her grave.'

'She's only fifty-five, there is plenty of time…' Eros objected as the idea of spending the eternity without Anita pounded in his head, like it had many times before.

'I wasn't sure at first,' Iris interrupted, showing up out of nowhere. A sudden secret meeting between Awokens unfolded quickly. 'But Time was right in everything he said and did. He gave me the power to hold the house by the lake suspended between past and present. Thanks to him I preserved Siobhan, Noah. Yet none of us is questioning the life they have now…' she concluded, moving to the corner of the walls, her duality finding the right spot, adding a visual emphasis to the contrast she had just brought to the group's attention.

'Noah has kept his memories, his past and his role in everything we did…' Cherish replied, almost annoyed by the multiplying of Awokens now populating the house. 'Why would it be any different for Daniel?'

'Noah got what he wanted and deserved. So did Daniel,' Agapei interjected.

'Let her speak. Let her tell us what she wants,' Storgén added. 'After all, she is the one of the three that made all this possible…'

At his request, Cherish suddenly vanished, leaving Anita to face a decision of supreme importance. She gazed at the Awokens for a moment without saying a word. After her eyes met Eros's, she moved next to him and took his hand.

'When all this started, I had no idea what I was getting myself into. I followed Daniel because I trusted him. I entered Runae because Cherish was in me and I was with him and Noah. From that moment on, I felt I had no say. I was driven by my love for Daniel and by Cherish's will. But was I?' she asked almost as if she talked to herself. 'No, I wasn't. The me that wanted it, is the same me that wants it now. I asked to be Daniel's Praetorian if he ever came back. I asked to have him for as long as I could. A part of me still wants to keep him in the shadows of our secrets and yet, I want him to know. I brought him here. I let him meet the people he had a life with. It wasn't Cherish. It was me. I wanted it to… I've been making sure he is ready, when the time comes… Now that I feel getting close to that moment, I'm the one who's not ready.' After giving Eros a firm look, she added, 'I can love him and still want him to know. I might want him to know and still be scared…'

'This is because your love as a mother has surpassed the love you had for him as friend,' Philiat replied, smiling. 'And it's OK.'

'I think it's time that the girl with no name comes forward, my love. Let him see you for who you are. He will love you both as mother and as a friend. He'll understand.'

'Dad? Mum?' Daniel's voice reached them from the front door. I've brought ice cream…' and instantly the house emptied of all its ghosts.

When he walked outside all the Awokens had disappeared. Beside Anita and Eros, only the spectres of a difficult decision still filled the atmosphere. In the recesses of her mind, Anita kept doubting her decisions. She knew, deep down, she would pursue her choice of a full confession and, because of it, she kept moving ahead and worrying about it at the same time. After all those years, one thing hadn't changed: her mind and heart carried the heavy weight of two contrasting wills.

Chapter Sixteen

John

∞

For the next four years, the three kept spending their summer holidays in the south of Italy, enjoying the company of the old lady next door and Eléna. Eventually, Anita and Eros had decided to buy the house they had been renting and live there for six months at a time. Free from major commitments, they could prolong their stay as long as they pleased. Daniel, on the other hand, kept returning to Dublin at the end of every summer, before a new semester in college would start again.

The beginning of the final year had finally arrived and once again Eléna insisted that he stay a little longer. She sat on the large windowsill that looked out onto the terrace; a gentle breeze came through, lifting and moving her hair, revealing a sad expression on her face.

In between open suitcases and her complaints, he moved about in his room. His face and size that of a full grown man, his messy hair stook out in plain contrast.

In the background, an old radio chattered unheard. A pop song had just left the spot to the news when Eléna moved onto the large bed.

'Looks like we might have to rewrite the entire human history,' a male voice said. *'The site of Göbekli Tepe, in modern Türkiye, has been confirmed to be older than eleven thousand years, possibly even more...*

'At least you could have booked a flight after the beach bonfire and go there with me,' Eléna lamented. 'The guy from the Sunrise Bar, the one you like...he asked me about you the other day.'

'Liar...you would come up with any story to make me stay,' Daniel replied as he tried to fit five large books in his luggage.

'You read too much...' she mocked.

'I don't need to, your intentions are plain and clear.' He laughed.

'I meant the books! That suitcase is going to weigh more than you...and besides, I'm not lying. He's really into you.'

'Apparently multiple sites in around the same location might have the same age,' the voice on the radio continued. *'This comes after the recent claims that the pyramids, and so the Sphinx, bear the signs of a long-lasting*

rain erosion, an event that hasn't happened in that region for at least the last ten thousand years…'

'Sis, he is good-looking, I have to admit I like him but he's not my type…' *Sis*. That word meant a lot to her. She was a single child with a personality too big to facilitate the building of friendships. Yet, hers and Daniel's had gone beyond. They loved each other like brother and sister.

'Yeah, I know your type… overpowering, mad in the head. You have spent four years in art college and you couldn't find one? I think it's because you think you know what your type is but you don't. You should trust me… Oh, imagine! You would be moving here and living with that guy and I'd be getting free breakfast!'

'Now, the weather forecast. Seems like this scorching summer won't be leaving us any time soon. Next week temperatures will stay above average. Good news for the ones who were planning to extend their holidays!' And the news had concluded, replaced by a long sequence of ads.

'Did you hear?' Eléna said. 'See? We could be spending another week at the beach…'

Laughs and never-ending chats soon turned to tears when Daniel left the holiday home and got to the airport. There, Anita and Eros said the last goodbye before he would pass the security checks. In his mother's face something caught his attention. She looked sad, more than usual, but a strange sparkle shone in her eyes.

'Give me a call when you land, alright?' And she briefly hugged him and moved away.

'What's wrong with Mum?' Daniel asked Eros as the two hugged.

'I've been married to your mother for twenty-three years, and still I can't tell…' And Eros smiled. 'Now, son, enjoy your final year. Get the most out of it. And call your mother when you land! I love you.'

To add to Anita's strange behaviour, Daniel felt his father's arms squeezing stronger than usual, as if he wanted to tell him more than he had just done. Eros's hands moved on his dark hair and their foreheads touched. A shivering feeling rose from the ground up, shaking Daniel's legs as if he was about to collapse. In a mere second, his energies came back stronger than before, leaving him astonished. Unable to understand what had just happened, Daniel gazed around perplexed. After saying, 'I love you too,' he took his suitcase and moved towards the check-in queues.

'Are you OK?' Eros asked Anita as the two exited the airport.

'I am. And now it begins…' She sighed. 'Did you do it?'

'I did,' he replied laughing. 'It's who I am, after all… He is ready.'

Three hours later Daniel was still at the airport. The flight back to Ireland had been delayed and his patience had worn thin. After walking up and down the terminal he eventually moved back to the gate and sat on one of the hard, metallic chairs. No matter if he sat or lay down, he was uncomfortable. With his head on the wooden partition between the seats and a book held over his face, he read the same page over and over. He briefly gazed at the large clock displayed under the *delayed* sign and he sighed out loud.

'I know…' someone said. 'This wait is unbearable.'

'It feels like we are the only unlucky ones,' Daniel replied without even looking.

'There are a few more over there. Their Cork accent tells me they are on our same flight.'

At that statement, their gazes met. To Daniel's surprise the same guy from school he had briefly talked to what it felt like decades before, stared at him, smiling. His pale cheeks clashing against the blond hair and his magnetic eyes made Daniel weak. Whatever he had felt years before, it was still lurking in the shadow of his heart, ready to take over his emotions once again. And so his hands gave in and the large book fell right on his face, triggering a loud laugh.

'Are you OK, Daniel?' John asked, moving closer and leaving behind, on the floor, a large notebook and a few pencils.

'You remember my name?' he replied, ecstatic.

'Of course I do. We were in the same school for years. Do you remember mine?'

'John…' And Daniel's voice trembled. *What am I feeling?* he thought. *After all these years, he's as beautiful as he was in school. Of course I remember his name, he's been in my mind all this time…*

'*The Lives of the Forgotten Ones*, by Anita Byrne. What is it about? I never heard of this author,' John asked as he sat next to Daniel. 'Feels heavy…'

'It is. And so is my mother.' Daniel's smile conquered the large space, right into John's heart. For a moment, they kept quiet, staring into each other's eyes to the point of pure embarrassment. As if attraction and desire had come to rule their every move and feelings, they gave into the surging sense of belonging.

'Your mother?' John said, after collecting his items scattered on the floor.

'She wrote it. The book is about a forgotten history. A bit fictional but, I have to say, very good. It talks about ifs and maybes of a world that existed once and disappeared after an apocalyptic destruction. She draws a line across many things left around the world as a testament of a reality that allegedly we have forgotten.'

'Wow. It does sound interesting. What about you? Do you write too?'

'Not really. I struggle to put my thoughts together, sometimes, never mind writing them down…'

'Maybe I can help you. What are you thinking right now?' John's face was only a few inches away from his when a pencil appeared in between them. 'I can draw anything…'

A self portrait then, Daniel thought instantly. 'I remember you were very good,' he added embarrassed by his own thoughts. 'Show me what you think I'm thinking…'

John smiled and opened up his notebook on a fresh white page. After looking at Daniel a few times, he started to draw the simplest version of two men holding hands. Like a little boy's drawing, the two figures were merely lines and circles. Next to them a small doodle resembling a dog stood next to a few flowers. Once done, he moved it closer to Daniel and showed him his masterpiece.

'Here. That's you and me,' he said. The scent of his skin, so close to him, drove Daniel insane. The clear, playful way of John showing he was completely into him was overshadowed by his movements, his voice. 'What do you want to call the dog?' he added.

'Oh,' Daniel stuttered. 'We have a dog too… Let's see…can it be a she? I don't know, she stands beside some flowers…we can call her Daisy?'

'This is the pre-boarding announcement for A91 to Dublin. Boarding will begin in approximately ten minutes. Thank you for your patience.'

'This is us!' John let out. 'Should we ask if we can sit together?'

As Daniel nodded, happy, they both collected their belongings and moved towards the gate. In between the growing queue and the chattering of tired people, they walked close to one another. As if the few minutes they had spent together was enough to feel the certainty of their feelings, John took Daniel's hand and, after gazing into his blue eyes, he kissed him.

'I wanted to do it since that day in school…' he whispered.

Staggered by a mix of conflicting feelings, Daniel stood still, his eyes fixed on John's. *Is this happening for real? It does feel too much like one of my dreams, my visions. But he is really here… He kissed me, he likes me as much as I do… This is so strange… It's like I've known him my whole life. His lips felt like my own.*

Silently agreeing on a mutual liking and holding on to his hand, Daniel followed John through the queue and all the way into the airplane. Unknown to them, their relationship formed then and once again, against the odds, exactly as it had the first time. Their lives now different, their worlds built on different stories, they found each other as if that part of their destiny could not be changed.

As Iris had told him once, John was Daniel's choice only. Their love, their relationship emerged on its own, outside of the many scheming and planning of the Gods and the Awokens, independently. They had delayed Daniel's encounter with Noah by three years and right in those three years, Daniel had built the bond of a love that could not be overcome. John was his to have, his to follow. Right from the start and now once again, Daniel desired that life with him beyond comprehension.

On a half-empty plane, they defied the steward's instructions and sat together to continue their mutual digging into each other's lives until they arrived in Dublin. The change in scenery, the cold, misty rain and the grey landscape were the only thing that had changed. The two of them continued to tune into each other's beat, their hands searching for each other.

And so Daniel accepted John's invitation to spend the evening in his flat. When he walked into the apartment, the entire scene was a contradiction in terms. The small space was spotless and bright, yet dozens of canvases were scattered everywhere. A faint scent of fresh paint floated in the air.

Most of John's work was incomplete. Parts of the paintings bore the signs of a conflicted will, their colours abrupt and their pictures left unfinished. Some had lines and figures barely sketched with pencil, overlapped by blasts of colours randomly scattered. The largest painting in the room was placed on a stand, as if still emotionally attached to its creator's desire for accomplishment. A red line crossed it from top to bottom, right in the middle. On each side, two figures stretched their hands towards each other.

'John, your work is very good!' Daniel exclaimed, moving slowly around the room, trying to find a path among the paintings.

'Thank you!' John replied, placing his suitcases in the corner of the hall. 'I'm going through a phase at the moment. I'm stalling, really…struggling to find the right inspiration.' He moved beside Daniel, their eyes fixed on the large painting. John's lips moved close to Daniel's ear, his breath warm against Daniel's neck and cheek.

'It's like they're trying to reach each other but can't,' Daniel observed, his voice soft.

John nodded. 'Yeah, that's kind of the idea. It's about the struggle to connect, to bridge the gap between souls.'

Daniel turned to face John, their proximity creating an intimate bubble amidst the chaos of the room. 'Maybe the struggle is what makes the connection worth it,' he said gently.

John pulled Daniel by the arm and kissed him. In the space of a single heartbeat, his hands were already everywhere that mattered, searching for possession, led by the desire of being one with him.

Words were cut in half, sentences hung in the air as they laughed and smiled and kissed in a quick succession. They had so much to say still but the yearning for their flesh interrupted every attempt.

The large bed on which they plunged carelessly was too big for that confined space. The walls almost enclosing it in a square box kept them safe as they rolled on the sheets, anxious to head what their minds craved. Their breath, barely keeping up with the beating of their hearts, rose faster and faster. As they lay naked, one next to the other, they paused and resumed the frantic search of pleasure, staring into each other eyes, counting every move, measuring every inch of their skin.

'Is this madness?' John asked, his breathing skipping the rhythm.

'It is…' Daniel replied as he hovered over his back, kissing his neck, his shoulders, his sides. 'Does it make it less real?'

'I've been waiting to know you for so long, I feel we are skipping the best part…' And John turned around, his arms around Daniel's chest, his legs trapping his tightly.

'Or we are making up for the time we lost. Who says this is not our true beginning?'

The following morning, Daniel woke up to the sound of heavy rain ticking against a skylight. The darkness brought by the dense clouds had caused him to oversleep. As his eyes adjusted to the dim light, John's figure appeared, sitting on a stool, wearing only a pair of socks. Staring intently at his largest, unfinished project, he examined the recent addition he had made.

As Daniel got up and moved next to him, John turned around, revealing a white trail of paint across his nose and cheek. Even with the stark, enchanting contrast with his eyes, his hair, Daniel could not help himself and burst out laughing.

'What?' John asked, smiling.

'I thought this,' Daniel replied, brushing his fingertip against the paint on John's face, 'was supposed to go there…' He gazed at the canvas and fell silent in shock. The painting was finished. Every detail had been added sometime overnight.

Two men stood as reflections of one another, partitioning the painting into virtual halves. Their fingertips still touched where they had left them the day before, but now their forms, their muscles, their bodies were fully formed. Their other hands had been drawn too, each wearing a silver, shining ring on a finger.

Whether destiny was forcing the hand on me, on Daniel, on John, or if it was all meant to be, it's something I'm still not sure of. In that house, in their bodies, no Awokens moved, no mystical presence loomed. It was them and them alone who drove their magic as if it belonged to them only.

'Would it be too soon to say, this is us?' John asked.

'I don't know. I never trusted time to be the keeper of what is right or wrong. I believe some things are just right from the start, whether we wait to find out or not,' Daniel replied softly.

As if Daniel's words were prophetic in nature, their relationship developed fast, beyond expectations. The final year in college came and passed in a snap. Soon life became the one of two adults who try to build a future together, merge their dreams, hoping to achieve them all with just the power of love and companionship.

A year later they had already moved together into a small cottage in a town up north at the exact distance between Daniel's and John's work. Unaware of how close they walked the steps of their past life, they ended up living in Castlecross, only a few miles from where their true home once stood.

As the keeper of every emotion, every feeling, I am at a loss in understanding how Daniel retraced his life almost as if my curse, his curse, had never been broken. He was like he had reborn once again to repeat history, walk the same steps that would lead him to my liberation. Yet, his path was his alone. I had no part in the choices he made, and that has troubled me all this time. As if my power, true love's power, goes beyond who I am, beyond a God that can't master its own true full nature, he showed me, over and over again, that he reached an understanding that escapes me still. He wielded an entire new level of magic, a magic that confirmed to me he was the one, the only one who could carry the deed as I moved towards my final day in this level of existence.

I had set him free, we had given him the life he wanted and yet, he wanted the life he didn't know he had. It's funny how, even then, Daniel showed me his true character, his determination to live a life at its full, on his own terms. Even with the help of Anita, Eros and the other Awoken Ones, steering his path where he belonged, he still decided for his own and loved those he was destined to.

I truly believe Daniel, somehow, stole a piece of me, slowly, century after century. His soul controlled mine when we faced Nothing, leading me to survival, leading to humanity's safety. And after everything, his soul continued to control and protect his own life more than I could do.

Chapter Seventeen

The Ones We Were Before

∞

'Oh my God, Daniel, this place is huge!' Anita exclaimed as she entered the house he and John had just bought together. 'Look at this room here…it would be perfect for a tiny library.' And she moved inside, leaving the two boys smiling at her well-known obsession.

'Well, you can help us decorating it then, Mum,' John replied.

The sound of the word *Mum* filled her heart with joy. She was proud of all the things her son had achieved at only twenty-six and yet, John was the greatest of them all. He had given her back the life she had before the madness, before the loss and the Gods' war, bringing back the ones she was closest to.

As she peeked through an old, worn-out window, a feeling of sorrow flashed before her. The house the boys had bought was way older and smaller than the one they owned in their past life but the large garden all around resembled the one she'd spent so much time in, talking with the two of them, playing with Daisy on summer days.

Voices, laughs, chattering and clinks of glasses echoed in her mind.

'Why are you not asking your friends to come along any more?' Harry asked Anita, his hands hovering on his chest, a clear reference to what he was truly after.

'Oh come on, Harry…' Shannon moaned, looking at her boyfriend Mark with a look of disapproval.

'Or it could really be a ghost!' Theresa said. *'You know my Aunty Marge? She had one… I'd say even more than one, considering how mad she went in her later days!'*

Harry, Mark, Patrick, Theresa, were all people she had learnt to let go. Even Shannon and their constant disagreements were things she missed.

'Any chance she might be a Harpy?' she said as they sat in a park in Rome.

'Who?'

'Shannon!'

'Just because you don't like her doesn't turn her into one of them, you know…' Daniel replied, smiling.

'Yeah, but it would make me feel better!'

'Yeah, I know.'

Is any of this even real any more? she thought while a new memory popped up in her head.

'Did you have any other episodes?' she asked.

'Nothing. Since we came back, it has been quiet,' Daniel replied as he followed her outside the house, by her car.

'Good,' she said. *'Don't worry about John. He will come around.'* And she took her bag, ready to go. *'You know, there is something very strange in this house…'* And her eyes moved across the fields, the house, that strange world.

'Alright, time to go,' Eros said as he entered the house, bringing Anita back to reality. 'We need to be at the airport in three hours. We'll see you both in two weeks?' he asked, looking at Daniel and John.

'Yes, can't wait! John and I agreed on having our honeymoon there so we will be planning stuff with Eléna while we are there…'

'I still think you should get married there too. Rita-Louise is too old now to travel and I'm sure she'd love to attend the wedding,' Anita said.

'Ma, it's Italy...' Daniel said as they moved outside. 'Unless you want people to throw tomatoes at us instead of flowers and rice.' And he laughed.

'This is exactly what my next book is going to be about,' Anita said, excitement glittering in her eyes. 'How the history of a country that brought so much culture, openness and innovation could become such a rigid, bigoted place... Something has happened, and I'm going to tell the world!' But her words trailed off as Eros nudged her into the car, her audience uninterested in statements she had repeated over and over again.

Two weeks passed in a flash and soon Daniel and John landed in the roasting land of Sicily. The excitement of spending some time by the beach, tasting good food and enjoying the sun was tainted by the abrupt news of Rita-Louise passing.

The night before the boys arrived, she had departed the world of the living quietly, her face serene, her spirit at peace. When Daniel arrived home he dropped everything in the hall and ran next door.

Anita and Eros stood next to her casket, quiet. If their silence could easily be interpreted as a display of sorrow, in their minds the upcoming revelation silently played in their heads. Time had come not only to let Rita-Louise go but also their son.

'Are you sure it's natural?' Eros whispered inside Anita's heads.

'Yes,' Cherish replied, silent. *'There is no trace of Harpies here. This is the making of matter decay. Death has not walked near this place. He is still where we left him.'*

'I can't stop thinking her being trapped in that horrific place…' Anita said, as if talking to herself. 'I want to believe we destroyed all the books and his spell when we took Creation's artefact, but then…where is she now?'

As Daniel moved next to them, followed by John, tears appeared in his blue eyes. It was painful and yet strange for Daniel, feeling so close to someone who he didn't know well. Although he had spent many summer days with her, listening to her stories, drinking iced tea in the garden, she wasn't family. *Or was she?* he asked himself. *She felt very much like it… Where does everything go?* he wondered. *Every connection we make, every laugh we share, every tear we shed…where does it all go?*

'Daniel, love,' Anita said, interrupting his thoughts. Her face bore the marks of aging mixed with the signs of fear and struggle. For a moment, Daniel glanced at her, seeing an older version of his mother.

'There's something we need to talk about. Not now, after the funeral, perhaps?' she continued, her voice trembling slightly.

'What is it? Has something else happened?' he asked, worried.

'No, no, son,' Eros interjected as John approached them. 'It's all good. We just want to talk to you. You know, in light of events like this, one revaluates things…' But at those cryptic words, Daniel gazed at John, visibly confused.

The next day they all gathered for the funeral. After a brief, solemn ceremony, they walked all the way uphill to give their respects to Rita-Louise one more time. The sun shone bright on the large graveyard, bringing the unbearable heat of a scorching summer on their heads. A few people stood under the shade of large olive trees and yet they struggled in their sad composure. As the last farewell was whispered, the crowd of family members and long-lasting friends dispersed. Among the few left, Victoria stood silent, next to the tombstone.

Seeing her motionless, without any expression of any sort of feeling on her face, made Anita uneasy. She could not help herself seeing Athymos in her features, in her movements. The cold, gelid tone she had when spoke to Daniel in Rome, the evil power she unleashed on them as they fled the ancient city, were memories too vividly embedded in her scars. To her surprise and almost temptation to stop him, Daniel moved next to Victoria. After a moment of shared silence, the two started to talk.

'I got to know her only in these last few years. I understand she was a beautiful human being…' he said, staring at the ground now covered with fresh soil. In sharp contrast with the sadness lingering in his heart, the hot air had already turned it dry, almost red, as if pushing time against them.

'She was,' Victoria replied. 'She raised me on her own since she was very young and, believe me, I wasn't a well-behaved child. I had my demons to face, my own fears to test me. But I'm old enough now to feel like I've managed to silence them all. She probably knew I was ready to go on my own, now...' After gazing at Daniel, she continued, 'She spoke about you, you know? Many times. I think she saw in you the grandson she never had...'

'Did she?' Daniel said, his voice breaking up.

'You must be a very good man. She was particularly good at judging people's characters... Anyway, I'm going to go. Stay as long as you need. I'm sure we'll meet again...'

And as Victoria turned around and left, a feeling of oppression rose from the ground up. As if Victoria was followed by a silent, dark presence, Daniel caught a glimpse of an unnatural duality within her.

Her senses sharp, her duty the one of a mother and a Praetorian, Anita immediately tuned in with that shift in reality, perceiving the scent of an enemy she had been on the lookout for. Leaving Eros and John behind, she hurried next to her son.

'Something strange is happening...' he let out as she took his hands and gazed in his eyes.

'This can't be...' Anita blurted out, triggering Eros's attention. After briefly looking at John, he joined them.

'What is it?'

'She's still alive she's still with her…she's been here all this time? I can't be wrong, Eros… This is her trace!'

'Is everything OK?' John asked, worried. The two held Daniel's hands as if he needed immediate attention. On their son's face, a shadow had fallen. As if every inch of blood had dried out like the hot soil now covering the memories of Rita-Louise, he looked pale.

'Something is not right,' Daniel repeated. 'I'm not sure what I'm thinking… I don't understand. Victoria spoke to me and it was like I knew her, like I really, really knew her from way before?'

'What did she say?' Anita pushed, unafraid of being rude. 'Daniel! What did she say?'

'She said she had her demons to face…but she has learned to face them. And her mother was happy to go knowing she could, I don't know…be at peace with herself?' And Daniel pulled his hands away and brought them to his face. 'This is not, I don't understand… We met Rita-Louise here, years ago. But I can see her somewhere else, like we knew each other from before…'

'Eros?' Anita gasped as she stared at him. Whatever she hinted at, it wasn't clear for John who started to worry.

'We could be wrong…' Eros replied, looking all around as if searching for an invisible lead. 'Every past has been rewritten. She should not be here… Love should be containing them all…'

'Daniel doesn't carry his soul any more. Athymos doesn't respond to his presence 'cause he is not here. How did she surface? When?' Anita inquired as she gazed over the boys, right at the gates of the graveyard where Victoria had just disappeared.

'Can anyone explain what's going on?' John interjected.

'We kept our promise and so he must have too,' Anita continued without regard for John's question. 'He's supposed to hold them off until Noah had closed the gates, until Daniel was ready…'

'We knew it was risky, Anita.' Eros replied. 'We knew it was going to happen, eventually… This means only one thing: it's time. Whether Noah has succeeded already or not, we need to do it now. If she is out in the world, so are the others!'

'No! I'm not ready!' Anita suddenly shouted, taking the group by surprise.

A blinding light flashed from within her body, engulfing her in an ethereal, shining glow. As Cherish manifested in the open, Eros's magic resounded with it and his Human features dissolved like steam. Under the shocked gaze of John and Daniel, the two Awokens appeared in their true form, pushed by an unseen threat, ready to confess the difficult truth.

'Stay still,' Cherish said to the two boys. 'It will only take a moment...'

Embraced by magic, a white tome appeared in her hands, its pages flipping fast. After many years, the one who had kept Creation's artefact concealed under her protection placed her fingers on their foreheads, releasing an astonishing power inside their minds.

The graveyard, the many olive trees and the entire space around disappeared as the four were brought in between realities, in between existence and spirit, past and present. The glittering blue sea in Daniel's eyes turned into a stormy gold as vision of many lifetimes spent conjuring the one who had saved them all replayed in his mind.

Every memory, every tear, every act of love filled his soul and heart as if it was never gone. The remembrance of John merged with the one he had learnt to love again, past and present days becoming one. As if he could love him twice just by blending the different memories of him as one, he started to cry, desperately. The emotions connected to who he was, the things he had done, the secrets he kept and the sacrifice he had made flooded his heart and mind, bringing him to his knees.

Then the final understanding came as he gazed at Anita. His mother, his best friend, the keeper of his most tormented secrets, Cherish and their existence as the bearers of a supreme power rolled in his head.

'You are the girl without a name…' he whispered. 'You, you never said her name in your stories because I couldn't know it was you, it was your story, our story you told…'

Anita could not oppose a revelation she wasn't ready to disclose. She knew the time was near and yet she wasn't prepared. Knowing her hands had been forced by the unexpected presence of Athymos made her furious. She joined Daniel in her crying but her tears were of anger and fear. She had been tipping at the edge of a decision, allowing her son to have what he deserved, to get back the ones he once loved but without conceding more, without risking the bond of a mother and son, a Praetorian.

Without realizing it, she had acted exactly like Rita-Louise, preparing Daniel for a future she kept fighting against, holding on to the hope that he could just be a normal child, hers to love, only hers to care for.

As the magic moved across the intangible space, the Chomps' village appeared in John's mind. As if his memories were brought back in reverse, the latest moments he had with Daniel, right before releasing the last Awoken One to his owner, displayed vividly. He gazed at Eros and the nature of his being changed. He wasn't just his future father-in-law any more. He was the one that had kept Daniel and John together against the rising threat of a terrible destiny. He had kept them close to one another when love seemed too fragile to resist even a weak pull.

And then every other detail added to the rest. The house they lived in, the friends they had, the life they lived together. It was like growing older in the space of a second and looking back at what they had been.

In an instant, Daniel and John found each other in a hug that carried the immense joy of finding themselves reunited again.

'Daniel, baby…' John cried, 'I can't believe it…'

'I swear I'd die hundred times and I would still find a way back to you…'

They kissed and cried as if their hearts could beat three times faster. They gazed at Anita and they both moved at once. Their arms around her, the three merged like one unique, happy body. They kept staring at each other in disbelief, their thoughts hanging in the air as if they carried too much meaning to transform into simpler words.

Then, suddenly, Daniel froze.

'Noah!' he let out, fear quickly erasing every inch of happiness. 'Where is he?' And he looked at Anita, then Cherish and Eros.

'He is fine,' Anita replied, smiling. 'He's been busy…'

'Where is he?' Daniel repeated.

'He's with Revelia and Trusk,' Eros replied. 'I think now would be the right time to meet them?'

Chapter Eighteen

A New Old World

∞

The moment Anita and Love crossed the node back to Earth, sadness and excitement mixed in Noah's heart. He had been granted more than just his life. Time had gifted him with the power belonging to the Gods the moment the clepsydra moved in his hands.

Revelia observed silently while the entire planet shifted backwards and matter rewound to a past state. She gazed at Noah as he held the precious artefact and she briefly smiled. For her, it was almost cathartic seeing the relic in the hands of someone who had never wanted it nor desired any power. In strong contrast with Una who sought the full domain of every land in

Runae, extorting Time's power for herself, Noah instead felt overwhelmed with the honour.

'Something tells me you have a lot of work ahead of you,' Revelia hinted as she moved towards the shoreline. The warm sacred waters had seemingly stopped wobbling, a clear sign that Time's magic had come to an end. 'How do we cross the Aqualymphs' sea?' And she turned around, looking at Trusk. 'What is it?'

'I'm nof sure I sfill have if…' he replied. He raised his hands to evoke the Sháten Déil but no magic manifested. 'I had fhe feeling if was gone. When Fime did fhe magic, I felf my body lighfer, as if if was gone…' He looked back at his hands, a trail of sorrow moved across the space as Revelia moved closer and placed her hands on him.

'Your magic was never in the stone, Trusk. It was in your heart,' she said.

'You are everything to us,' Noah added, kneeling. 'Look me in the eyes, my friend. Don't cry. We are back home thanks to you. All we need now is your wings. Can you help us?'

Speechless, the Chomp moved in between Noah's arms. Their journey had proven to be longer and dangerous to a point of no return. Not long before, he and Anita were the only two left standing and now his friends had come back.

'I see two…oh, never mind,' a familiar voice spoke at their back.

'Aura?' Noah exclaimed, joy surging from within. 'I thought you were all dead! So this is what Time has done…this is what was happening to this place, just now.'

'I'm not sure he has granted the privilege of retaining our memories to everyone. but I do surely recall every single hoc, rhoc and yac,' Aura replied, almost anticipating Noah's next question. As her body took the hues of the green grass and the red soil, she continued, 'Yes, Time has done it again. He is still doing it… You are still doing it.' And she pointed at Time's artefact glowing bright in his hands.

'How do I make it stop? Do I make it stop?' he asked, confused. His eyes gazed at Revelia, Time's last words echoing in his head.

'I'm not…sure,' the Leonty replied. 'I don't think I'm allowed to see any future until you are done.'

'Me?' Noah was puzzled. 'I don't even know what I'm doing… I didn't even know I was doing it…'

'Something tells me everything will sort itself out once we cross to the other side. Shall we?' Aura's arms extended a familiar invitation. Although they could fly over the sea through the powerful wings of the Chomp, a sort of ceremonial respect was due. Aura, the protector of the node, was back and so hers was the honour and responsibility to lead them ahead.

They plunged into the waters like bullets, travelling fast across the azure depth. Towards the bottom of the sea, a myriad of Aqualymphs moved in every direction. Submerged constructions made of stones and corals erected on their own, fast. Guided by an invisible power, they extended in every direction, their tips and heads growing as if to conquer all the way to the surface. When the four reached the other side of the sea, another Aqualymph emerged in the open. Next to Aura a male of her kind smiled as they walked on land.

'Aura, my love. Queen Eah needs you at the Sacred Horn. She says the celebration song must be sounded by you only…'

'Yes, Mareen. Tell her I'll be there soon. I need to guide these three a little further. I'll be back shortly.' And her crystal hand brushed against his clear face, his essence made of water swaying as he dissolved back into the sea.

'So all the Aqualymphs are back?' Revelia asked as she attempted her magic once again. To her dissatisfaction, she couldn't see beyond the multiplying of minds quickly forming in their present.

'They are. Our queen is back. She has returned to us as the true, pure leader she was meant to be,' Aura replied as she invited them to walk uphill.

'Do you sfill have fhe Anún Déil?' Trusk asked.

'Our Flare is the only thing that hasn't returned. But I believe it's better this way.'

'It's safe to assume none of the stones are back then?' Noah added as his eyes set on the gigantic masterpiece ahead.

On top of the first hill leading to the Chomps' village, a spectacle made of green opened up. As if Noah had been suddenly teleported back home, his heart rejoiced at the sight of the landscape filled with the beauty and strength of nature. Anticipation of what appeared ahead took control over his body and he started to run. Exactly like the first time he had set foot in Runae, Noah sped through the lands, right into the Silent Forest.

'Noah!' Revelia shouted from behind. 'Slow down!'

'Let's meet at the turn of the Gochi River,' Aura said, smiling. 'Go, my friends.'

'Are fhey really back?' Trusk asked her as his feet rose from the ground and pulled the Leonty up in the air. Gliding through the forest, he quickly reached Noah and lifted him as he propelled ahead. In the space of a few minutes, they reached the Chomps' village.

At the edge of a long-gone dome, Aura awaited their arrival. Her body hung in between magic and physical matter, yet happiness could be clearly seen on her face. Hundreds and hundreds of little homes scattered across the fields, their shape and size reflecting the nature of their inhabitants.

'It's like we never left!' Noah let out, in disbelief.

'Fafher?' Trusk's eyes widened as he gazed at the heart of the village where Treekan hurried his steps to help a few Chomps that had just appeared out of nowhere.

They were coming back from the depths of oblivion and a lost past in a quick sequence. Everywhere more sleepyheads appeared at every tick of every second, disoriented and confused. By the time Treekan was done in taming the worries of the newly arrived, more Chomps appeared all around.

For every pop he heard, his heart jumped. For every fellow returning from extinction, the hope it could be Trusk rose a little. When his son's voice shouted from downhill, he almost fainted. The three companions hurried uphill, followed by Aura, their steps unable to keep up with their happiness.

'Trusk!' Treekan cried as the two met midair, hugging and spinning at the speed of their renewed joy. 'My son, I thought you'd never come back!'

'Fafher, you remember? You remember everyfhing?'

'I do, of course I do! Oh, Revelia, my friend…' Treekan added as the Leonty extended her arms in a hug filled with gratitude and delight.

'You stubborn little head, I knew I'd see you again,' she said. 'Look who's here…' And she moved aside, revealing Noah's presence, a wide smile bringing the happiness of their long-craved reunion.

For a few moment the returning of all the other Chomps went forgotten. The group stood together, crying and recounting all the things that had happened since they the moment they had departed. Eventually Aura moved closer and spoke.

'I can tell there is no past nor future this bright in the Ancient Mirrors. We get to live the present we sought and fought so hard for. There is so much I'd like to say to you… All the things I've seen since the evil entered our lands.' And a shadow fell on her crystal face, as if tainting her joy. 'Still, my memories come to you for a reason way different than sorrow.'

'What is it, Aura?' Noah asked.

'You and Time are bringing back everything that existed. Although you carry his magic now, he is the one who initiated it and determined the when, the who. I believe we are going back to ancient times, before the Great Flare was unearthed, before the Humans moved against the Leonty…'

'So *everyone* is coming back?' Revelia asked, terror triggering the red flash of premonition.

'I'm confident they are…' Aura smiled. As if her words carried no worry, she seemed pleased with the unfolding magic.

Suddenly her body shifted. As if it had disappeared and reappeared in a short sequence, her form flickered. Her features remained unchanged yet her face looked strangely younger. Next to Trusk, the old Treekan had transformed into a younger version of himself, the signs of aging wiped out of his face.

'Aura?' he cried. As if his sudden change wasn't the only surprise he'd bring, he rushed towards the Aqualymph and hugged her. 'I thought I had lost you,' he wept. 'How is this possible?'

But before she could answer, the Chomp dissolved into thin air, leaving the others astonished. Trusk's mouth open in shock, he could not understand the magic they were witnessing.

'Where is he gone?' Revelia asked. 'What's happening?'

'They past is happening. Exactly what has happened already in the sea, is happening on land,' Aura said. 'You, Noah and Trusk are the only ones out of sync with Time's magic. Well, I am too by the grace of our God. I'd say he granted me what he's granted you…'

'You're saying we are still going back in time?' Noah gazed around. The entire Chomps' village changed and shaped again. Wings kept appearing and disappearing in a fast sequence, almost making him sick. 'We are literally going back as we speak!'

'How far are we going?' Revelia asked her eyes fixed on the one who held the precious relic.

'Don't look at me… I haven't—' But Noah suddenly stopped.

He looked at the artefact shining brightly as if questioning it directly. Time's magic flooded around him, invisible, yet a glance of power flashed around his wrists and arms. As he closed his eyes the vast knowledge stored within his fingers invaded his mind, his head. Time's will became his, the God's great plan revealed it as if Noah himself had conceived it.

'Time is recreating every piece of this world, bringing back lives and matter as if they were never gone. He is…we are rebuilding Runae as if evil had never entered these lands.'

'But…' Revelia blurted out. 'But we can't change the past. We would be changing everything we have done to get this far…'

'We are not changing the past. We are creating a new present made of all the lives he's bringing back. We are here to make sure his evil army won't infect this planet ever again.'

'So this is it…' the Leonty said. 'As they battle Nothing for the eternity…'

'So we will, here in this world and in mine…'

'Whaf abouf Mofher and Fafher?' Trusk asked, his eyes still glittering under the influence of a heavy heart.

'Oh they will come back.' Noah smiled. 'Like they are meant to. We will only have to be patient enough and wait for their time to come. In the meantime, there is a lot we have to do.'

'And I'll be by your side,' Aura added. 'But for now, I have to return to the sea. I'll see you very soon.' And the Aqualymph floated towards the Gochi River, her shape turning into steam as she plunged into the waters.

'Revelia, Trusk,' Noah resumed. 'You'll have to guide me in what comes next. Soon the magic will finish its course. We have to make sure to be where we need to be, when the time comes…'

'You are already talking like him.' Revelia smiled. 'A few moments wielding his power and you are already speaking in riddles.'

'Where did they find the Flares?' Noah asked as they started to walk towards the large building at the edge of the Chomps' village.

'For what we know, the Mother Flare was brought to the surface by Time and the Valahan Mogs from the depths of the Mogs Mountains.' And her eyes flashed red once more. Whatever Noah's plan was, she could not help but try to see if for herself. After looking at Trusk, she turned her gaze towards the far, towering mountains keeping the Chomps' land and the Steppes apart. 'Something tells me Trusk will be our free pass inside their homes.'

And so the three walked past the narrow path to the west side of the hills and moved towards the rifts of the rocky grounds where the soft grass gave way to the rising mountains and the shadows of the tall Mogs brought the sharp darkness of a sudden night. There, attuned with the power Noah carried along, an extensive sequence of caves started to form. Hundreds of homes nestled in the side of the mountain scattered all around. Each one was guarded by a heavy door, and a flickering flame, burning inside a small lamp, brightened their rocky contour.

'This is an absolute spectacle,' Revelia let out as she gazed all the way to the summit.

'Is so differenf fhan whaf if was lasf fime we were here…' Trusk added.

As they entered the depths of the canyon in between the mountains, where the road split in two, a large wall stood as the entrance inside the large Mog. Before the Leonty and the Chomp could question where to head next, Noah stretched his hands forward, turned the green clepsydra upside down and waited for a few moments. As the viscous liquid moved, a few drops left the magic of the artefact and dripped on the ground.

An instant whirl rose from the hard soil and, with it, three tall, hairy Valahans formed out of nowhere. Their forms brought back from the land of the dead, they slowly appeared beside Noah. As their eyes met his, they quickly moved back, in shock.

'What's the meaning of all this?' Vasheer exclaimed as his eyes darted to his sons. 'A Human, a Chomp, and a Leonty, here, in my house?'

'Brother?' Varuk let out, bewildered. 'I thought I had lost you!' And he rushed to hug Voishan whose expression resembled the one of his father. Confused and lost by the sudden magic, he stood still, silent.

'Varuk.' Noah spoke. 'I brought you back from a time that goes over your brother's rhocs but before yours and your father's final moments. It's important for you to retain the knowledge you had after Voishan passed away.'

'Who are you? What magic is this?' the King's son asked as he moved a few steps back, worried. Whatever power he witnessed, it closely resembled Time's.

'I'm Noah. There is so much we need to explain to you but, for now, be happy to know Time has sent us here. We found a way to bring back your people and every lost soul in your world.'

'Whatever trouble you faced has been erased,' Revelia continued. 'Your families and your homes are coming back... Look!' And she pointed at the majestic landscape. Every mark, every spell and intricate decorations placed in protection of their homes shone under the light of Time's magic. Everywhere Valahans appeared as if just roused from their slumber, coming out from their homes to breath the fresh air of the new morning.

'What happened to the enemy? We were under attack... Father and I were trapped in the caves...' Varuk asked as he teared up with joy.

'This reality knows the enemy no more,' Revelia replied.

'And yet, we must be sure it stays this way.' Noah added. 'Varuk, Vasheer, Voishan, the Mother Flare is back in the depths of the mountains. We need your power to get it back in the open. We must place it as protection in the Cloudy Mountains.'

'That's where they came from!' Voishan objected. 'Why would you bring it to them?

'You are not the first Human who tried to get his hands on the stones,' Varuk interjected. On his face, the firm look of suspicion and fear clearly spoke of regrets. He had trusted a young king and his Aver before paying a dear price because of it.

'If the Flares were used to harm others, to destroy this world, it won't be the case any more. We will shine the one Flare as a beacon of protection right where the enemy entered this planet. We need to move fast,' Noah replied.

'You look familiar,' Voishan said to Trusk as if he hadn't paid any attention to Noah's words. 'Your face, your eyes,' he continued, moving towards the Chomp. 'You are Kasthor's exact copy…'

'Kasfhor was my grandfafher. Did you know him? Did you know Faróel too?'

At Trusk's question, Voishan smiled. As he finally caught a glimpse of what had truly happened, he turned around towards his loved ones and said, 'They really come from yacs ahead… We should do what they say, brother.'

And so, after a long debate between themselves, the tall miners decided to trust and guide the three strangers through layers of rocks and metal, all the way to the same place where they had helped Time extract the precious stone. As if repeating a similar version of their past, they removed the Flare out of the abyss but, this time, there was no partition nor splitting of any power among the kinds of Runae.

After leaving Vasheer behind to take care of the many Valahans coming back to life, the group walked through the steppes and across the Leonty's hills, all the way to the peak of the Cloudy Mountains where the stone was going to act as barrier between good and evil.

Chapter Nineteen

The First Act of Evil

∞

Trusk had just returned to the peak of the Cloudy Mountains, with two Valahans clinging to his hips, when Noah and Revelia moved to the centre of the vast plateau. Among shards of ice and sharp rocks jutting from the mountain's tip, they appeared as if encircled by the gaping maw of a beast.

A fierce, cold wind howled through the silent place, lifting snow from its resting spot, creating a swirling, white mist. As Noah and Revelia shielded their faces, struggling to see, they moved forward, slowly reaching the centre of the icy expanse.

Following their footprints, Trusk, Varuk, and Voishan walked side by side. The Valahans' long beards had quickly turned white, their teeth chattering and their powerful limbs trembling with uncontrollable shivers.

'Th…this is…' Varuk attempted to speak, but his broken words were swallowed by the raging storm.

'D…do y…ou hear?' Trusk stuttered, his eyes squinting into thin lines against the freezing, dense fog.

Amidst the thrilling whistles of the mountain, another sound murmured within the wind. A deep, resonant noise echoed from the rocks, as if descending from the low, heavy clouds and bouncing back off the white ground.

'What is it that we are looking for?' Revelia shouted. Even if a few steps away from Noah, she could not hear her own voice.

'I'm not sure yet…'

'Can't you do something?' Varuk let out as he moved closer. 'We are g…going to freeze to death. 'We…we are cr…creatures made of heat and ff…ir…re.'

'Hold on,' Noah said as he raised his hands in the air, a green glow radiating through his fingers. As he brought time to a halt, the gusts turned into a mere breeze and eventually the wind stopped. 'We are in the right place but not there yet,' he added.

'What does it mean?' Voishan asked as he gazed around, trying to understand why that place held such significance. All around he saw no presence of any evil, no signs of any diabolic hand.

'Trusk, can you bring up the stone? You were able to carry it all this way…' Noah asked, ignoring the Valahan's request.

'My wings can barely move,' the Chomp objected, worried. 'I can sfill fry…' and he walked back and plunged into the empty space, disappearing in a blink.

'Nothing's followers know this is their way in. After the destruction of Runae, their access to the planet was also lost. Now that we've restored everything, they'll be aware the way in is open again,' Noah explained. 'Even if he's been held off from advancing, his army is still free to move and attack anywhere they can reach. We must stop them from passing through. I'm not sure what kind of power we'll face, but if Time believes we can trap it here indefinitely, then so should we.'

As the white mist quickly dissipated, a large well made of dark stones appeared at the centre of the plateau, just a few steps away from the group. Revelia moved slowly towards it, counting her steps, her eyes fixed on the strange structure.

'What is this thing?' she asked.

'It's a Human well,' Varuk replied. 'The crown city is full of those, though smaller than this one. It's used to extract water from underground…'

'A Human structure up here?' Voishan voiced their doubts loudly.

Noah moved close enough to peer inside the dark hole. Expecting a sudden evil manifestation, he placed his hands on the black stones and slowly bent forward. As if a knowledge of cosmic proportions had risen from within the well, an astonishing array of images, events, and emotions played in his head. The longer he stood there, the greater his shock in discovering a past that went beyond what he knew, beyond what the clepsydra had granted him access to.

Six figures walked around, inspecting the exact same spot where Noah now stood. They moved as if hunting for something invisible to their eyes, something eluding their heightened senses. A seventh figure, a woman, had just reached the summit of the mountain. Her breath came in hastened gasps, and she was on the verge of fainting.

'So we travelled all this way to die in this empty, freezing land?' She wore layers of heavy clothes, but her eyes and hands, exposed to the cold wind and exhausted from the long climb, had turned stiff.

'This is the place I've seen, Meeriah. You've seen it too. Stop doubting our visions!' another woman replied. Though her face was mostly covered by thick fabric, her resolute expression still shone through. 'I must know what to do to fix this…'

'King Lohan is the only one to blame for not producing an heir, Shahara,' Meeriah replied. 'We consulted the Radhal Daíuh, the ancient stones… Even the

Whispering Forest had no solution for your problem. Why would here be any different? Are you going to make us walk to the end of Runae to satisfy this madness?'

'We know it's not you, sister,' another woman added as they walked on the black, flat rocks paving the entire plateau. Her large, black eyes showed the same tiredness they all shared. 'We've walked from east to west, from the deep south to here when we could have just run. Listen to reason, Shahara. Let's leave the king and the kingdom and flee. He won't find you…we can hide in the Whispering Forest if we have to.'

'I'm a queen, Tarash, not a fugitive,' Shahara responded, exhausted. 'I'm not going to lose it all because he has no way to have a child. I'll use any spell I can, anything the Fárahal's power can grant me!'

'What is this whisper I hear?' Meeriah asked, startled by a sudden whistle.

'It's the wind, my lady,' a young man replied, fear mounting as he gazed at a dark mass of clouds descending rapidly over their heads. 'I think we should head back…'

'No,' Shahara replied. 'This is the place I've seen… This is where I get to have my wish granted. Sisters,' she declared resolutely, 'we do the rite right here.'

Meeriah and the other woman moved next to Shahara. As she pulled back her heavy hood, a golden tiara shone in the dark surroundings. From within their robes, they revealed a few items they had long been carrying, waiting for the right moment. A long knife made of gold and white ivory flickered as Meeriah extracted it from its fold and placed it on the ground. Next to it, Shahara kneeled and opened a small, old book. Its pages were brown, its binding made of green ligaments, worn by time.

The third sister followed suit and placed six small stones next to it: a green, a red, a black, a brown, an orange, and a white diamond, positioned around the knife as if a circular ritual was about to begin.

'Here are the stones, sister. Whatever power we foresaw, it revealed itself to us as six gems placed in a circle. Make sure you place your crown in the middle…' As a glimpse of terror flashed across her visage, she took a few steps back.

'The Witches of Fárahal gather to summon the ancient secrets of our world,' Shahara intoned, her hands stretched over the scattered items as she read from the old book. 'The unknown power in the bloodstream of Runae rises to bring new life. I am Shahara, queen of the Humans, granddaughter of the first Souls Whisperer, the Gifted of Visions. I hereby conjure the power that was never found, the buried secret of our world. I give you my future so you can grant the one I seek.'

Shahara took the knife and pressed it against her left wrist. As blood surfaced and began to pour, she removed her tiara and placed it among the stones.

Keeping her left hand over the precious crown, she let her warm blood cover it, slowly forming a red stream all around. Drawn by power and magic, it split in six directions, reaching each stone.

With the ritual prayer concluded, they waited. To their surprise, nothing happened. The darkness enveloped them in a foggy silence. No magic nor supernatural presence manifested.

'Is it not working?' one of the women said.

'I told you, Shahara,' Meeriah mocked, her frustration clear. 'You are a Witch of Fárahal, yet you ask for a Human life to be granted to you…'

'Very well then, let's do it,' the queen replied sharply.

Meeriah gazed at the young man standing several feet away, muted by the strange ritual he observed. He knew of the witches' great power from the legends he had heard as a young boy, but seeing it with his own eyes terrified him. Overwhelmed and in shock, he stood frozen. Meeriah snapped her fingers and moved them in a circular motion. The ligaments holding the book together expanded and extended towards the man in a flash. Dragged by powerful magic, he was pulled next to her. In a swift move, she snatched the knife from the queen's hands and cut his throat in an instant.

'We better be sure,' she smiled, a wicked expression imprinted on her face.

The man convulsed for a few moments, twitching in the horror of a quick death. His blood mixed with Shahara's, reaching the stones one by one. This time, the ground quivered, cracking and breaking apart. The black stones of the pavement rolled on their own, splitting into numerous bricks. As the ritual unfolded, the fierce wind resumed, and where the fissure stood, a large well formed.

The red, crimson hues of the warm blood turned black as it expanded, filling the interior of the newly shaped structure. It wobbled and moved as if someone was gasping for air from underneath.

'Finally…' a voice moaned. 'The supreme act of evil finally enters this world, granting me access.'

'I am Shahara, Queen of the Humans. The first one who has ever completed the rite. I must be granted my wish,' she said, unafraid. While everyone else moved away, fear squeezing their hearts, she stood firm, her hands clenched, blood covering her pink, delicate visage.

'Look inside, Queen…and I'll grant you even more than your heart desires…'

There, where her eyes gazed at the dark fluid and her hands held the well, Noah stood as if an exact replica of the indomitable queen. He came back to reality with the heavy awareness of the evil origins, shocked and disturbed.

He released his grip on the wicked structure and staggered as he moved away. The realization of the evil's beginning mingled with the vast knowledge Time had granted him. The Witches of Fárahal had found a spell powerful enough to channel the magic of Creation's buried stone across the mountains, into an entry point. Like the Aver, the evil Harpy who had used the Flares to open the passage for Nothing's return, they had extracted the Mother's stone magic through the cracks and passages under the planet's crust.

There, where the void had found its spot for Nothing's army to invade, it had left whispers in its wake, voices traveling all the way to the Mogs Mountains. Voices that Vasheer and Queen Eah would soon hear, their enchantment leading to the demise of the entire cosmos.

'So this is why Time didn't bring the Humans back the first time?' Revelia asked, pondering Noah's recounting of his vision.

'King Romohan was the son of evil,' Varuk said to his brother. 'All those rumours about his father sending the witches away in exile...and his queen was one of them. The worst of them all!'

'Their spell required the power of the Flares to open the passage, so the evil could grant them what they wanted. But the stone was inside the Mog, within our kingdom,' Voishan added. 'They would have never found it. We would have never let them in!'

'So when Time helped us unearth the Mother Flare…' Varuk's words trailed off as his mind filled with impossible conjectures.

'He wanted to take it away from them. Because the enemy fed from it,' Noah replied. 'Through the invisible passages all the way to your mountain, they kept absorbing its energy. Time wanted the stone to be used for protection instead.'

'Whaf are we going fo do now?' Revelia asked, glancing over his shoulder. Something sinister stirred in the air, electrifying the feathers on his wings.

'We close this passage for good. We won't be giving the Flares to anyone. We will use Time's magic and Creation's stone to seal this godforsaken place. Revelia, it's important you guide me. We need to see the exact moment when they'll rise from their evil abyss.'

The clepsydra moved on its own, spinning before the gathering. Noah's eyes closed as he took Revelia's hands. As if his recent vision replayed in their reality, the ground started to shake, displacing thick snow and breaking the plateau's foundations. As the white coat fell away from the well, the dark, ethereal liquid inside reappeared, bubbling and swirling in a continuous, circular motion. Its centre rose into a spinning tip as voices started to emerge, spilling from the structure. A dense, black mist moved on the quivering ground, lifting into the air to meet the descending clouds.

'Someone else has come here before, to ask for it…' A voice rose above all others. 'You carry great power with you…but I can give you more,' Nothing moaned.

'How is the fight going?' Noah mocked, opening his eyes and gazing at the well. 'You can't defeat them, so you hope to sneak back here, deceiving the Gods, convincing them to abandon their position to come and rescue the people and the world they love?'

'Who are you?' Nothing echoed in the space, his voice shaking the ground like an earthquake. Rocks broke off from the mountain peaks, rolling perilously close to the two Valahans. Their eyes widened in terror, witnessing the surge of the greatest power of all.

'I'm Love's carrier, the one who brought him back to life, the one that now wields the power of his brother, Time!' Noah replied, standing firm against the crumbling ground. 'You want to conquer this world? Send them! Send your vile creatures here and show me how you win this fight!'

The well exploded in a loud blast, pushing the group away and scattering them around. Voishan slid on the snow and was rolling towards a large fissure when his brother's hand grabbed his wrist. In the struggle between life and death, Varuk started to slip, his eyes fixed on Voishan who swung over the empty crater. As the two plunged into the mouth of the mountain, Trusk darted through the air and lifted them to safety.

The past repeated itself as a Chomp came to their rescue, snapping them away from certain death. He gently released them on safe ground, but his eyes widened in terror. The large stone he had carried from the Mog had just fallen into a wide opening and disappeared. Without hesitation, he dashed across the distance and dived into the void.

'He's coming!' Revelia shouted, tightening her grip on Noah's hands. The fire in her eyes was as bright as her will. She had struggled with her magic for a long time, but she could not fail him, fail them now. Her rage and frustration mixed with the joy she felt when she had come back to life, when she had found her friends again. She clenched her hands firmly on Noah and added, 'Now!'

The entire mountain split in two, a gigantic fracture cracking all the way to the edge of the cliff. A large figure emerged from within, its form shaping into a deformed giant when Noah called for Trusk.

Even though the Mother Flare was gone from sight along with the Chomp, Noah's trust was absolute. In their long planning, trying, dying, and coming back to life for the sake of an ultimate victory, the one who had saved them many times before sprang like a bullet from the darkness below. The large stone reacted against the evil, pulsating and glowing in quick succession until it met the power of Noah's artefact.

A second explosion struck the space, a green wave dispersing in the air. There, the evil found itself surrounded by six bright Flares, spinning around its core. Over their magic, the spell of frozen time brought the green shades of victory. There, trapped in a never-ending moment, Noah had brought the long-sought revenge.

The same sentence Nothing had inflicted on Time, Noah imposed on the diabolic army, enclosing them in an unbreakable, eternal moment.

The five companions gazed at the incredible spectacle displayed before their eyes. The deformed shape of the enemy contorted and convulsed until it halted. The Flares and Time's magic, resplendent with supreme power, shone as bright as the large Erion. A long silence followed suit as they all stood still, staring at the mystical prison the enemy was caged into, their hearts and minds finally tasting the sweet taste of victory.

Conscious of their success, they hugged each other, smiling and crying at the same time.

'Will it hold?' Varuk asked. The fear of giving into a premature joy sneaked into the tone of his voice.

'It will,' Noah replied, resolute. 'It must. We'll make sure these evil doors will stay shut for eternity.' After a brief pause, he added, 'It's time to go to the crown city. We have an entire kingdom to rescue.'

Chapter Twenty

The King of Runae

∞

Aura waited a few moments as the node flickered, and its circle of magic completed, allowing three Humans to walk in. Skipping the ceremonial words, she smiled warmly at the sight of Daniel, Anita, and John.

'Aura?' Daniel exclaimed, rushing towards the shoreline. Instinctively raising his arms to hug her, he suddenly stopped, realizing her transparent body hadn't fully formed yet.

'I spent an eternity watching over this spot, and there have been more people coming and going in the last yac than ever,' she said, smiling as she slowly extended her hands to Daniel. 'Oh, you carry his power still…' she remarked, gazing at Anita.

'It's a long story,' Anita replied.

'I'm sure you don't mind if I hold on to my duty and ask the others to reveal themselves for a moment?' Aura interrupted.

At her words, Eros and Cherish manifested from behind the other three, their features resembling those of the Aqualymph's. As they took full shape, Anita continued, 'Time has come, Aura. We are ready to finish what we started.' Though her words were resolute, a hint of uncertainty lingered in her voice.

'Is Noah alright?' Daniel asked.

After everything they had gone through and the magic he had witnessed, John's reaction to Daniel's question had drastically changed. They had found each other against the odds, rebuilt a life together as if nothing else mattered. Even with their fate challenged once more by the mission Noah and Daniel shared, it was no longer a threat. He moved closer to Aura and asked, 'Is Reela back? Are the Chomps back?'

'Everything is exactly how and where it is supposed to be. Reela was born ten rhocs ago. I doubt she'll know who you are, but she is fine. In a few yacs, she and Treekan will rebuild a life together, just like you two did… Everything is exactly how and where it is supposed to be,' Aura repeated as she raised her hands and invited them to follow her.

'To the hills?' Daniel's heart started to beat fast at the idea of seeing the Chomps again.

'Not this time. We cross the sea to the left, past the outskirts, to the King's Thousand Steps. We go to see the king. Isn't that why you came?' Aura replied.

Before Daniel could question her statement, Aura led them into the waters, sprinting through the Aqualymphs' Sea. Carried by the power of the aldúrin, they swam through the deep sacred waters inside a large, clear bubble. As they emerged on the other side, a vast sandy beach welcomed them back to land. To the left and to the right, a sharp line ran between yellow and blue hues, the sand and the sea holding the partition between the two worlds.

'These grounds have seen many horrors,' Aura began as they exited the magic carriage. 'I can still see the Leonty's soul floating over the waters…' She turned sad for a brief moment. 'I know this past exists no longer, but I carry a great weight in my heart, even greater because I'm one of the few who remembers…' At those words, Anita's emotions surged vividly once again.

'Who's actually back, Aura?' Daniel asked. The Aqualymph's words hinted at the past being reforged. His opinion on the Crimson Queen's destiny hadn't changed. Somehow, he hoped Aura could confirm a divine, benevolent justice had reached Una too.

'Everyone,' she replied. 'Now, you reach the first steps just over there. Someone is waiting for you.'

'You're not coming with us this time either?' Anita asked.

'There is no need. You are safe here. Everything is exactly how it's supposed to be.' Aura turned around, smiled, and dissolved into the sacred waters.

The group stared at the grandeur of the crown city. The last time they had walked those lands, it was all in ruins, the Witches of Fárahal's ghosts filling the air with dangerous spells, taking Anita's soul prisoner in exchange for freedom. Now, the white buildings, towers, walls, and gates spoke of a renewed, good magic. They sped ahead and reached the king's steps.

There, a Human waited for their arrival. His body and head covered by a white cloak, he pulled down the hood as they approached, revealing a dark, bronze complexion and sandy, almost white hair. His eyes brought the peace of a welcoming gaze. He opened his arms and spoke.

'We were expecting you. Revelia saw you crossing the node. Allow me to introduce myself. I'm Kareesto, commander of the crown city's affairs. Let me escort you to the king.'

'Please tell me we are not walking all the way up…' Anita let out. 'Look how many steps!'

As if her prayers had been instantly heard, a flying being darted from their side. Clashing straight against Daniel, Trusk pulled him a few feet off the ground and together they rolled on the sand. Cries and laughs mingled together as the two hugged tight, the joy almost making their hearts explode.

'You were gone,' Trusk cried. 'I missed you so, so much!'

'I know, little one, I missed you too,' Daniel replied, his hands moving through the Chomp's messy hair.

'Mofher and Fafher are back, but fhey are so young... Fafher looks like me!' the Chomp exclaimed, as Treekan descended from the sky alongside Faróel and Kasthor.

In a few flaps of their wings, the Chomps carried the Humans to the summit of the crown city, flying over the white walls and all the way to the king's abode. As they entered the palace, they saw Humans, Valahans, and Leonty seamlessly blending together as if they were one busy, harmonious body.

They ran up the stairs, following the hasty Chomp whose excitement grew with every step. He guided them to the large throne room, pushed the massive doors open with a gigantic smile, and flew to the corner of the chamber, disappearing behind a white stony chair.

The anticipation of what was about to happen made Daniel weak. He entered the room as Noah appeared from behind the throne. A crown made of silver and gold adorned his head, with shining golden stems and leaves running across his forehead. They rushed towards each other, feeling as if only a moment had passed despite the eternity that had kept them apart.

Their wet cheeks touched and rubbed against each other as they embraced.

They stood silent for a minute, sobbing and exchanging gazes that carried the understanding of a lifetime. Revelia's gentle walk took Daniel by surprise as she joined them. A new wave of joy took over him as he extended his hand towards her, bringing her into their circle of love and trust. A moment later, Anita and Trusk found themselves surrounded by friendly hands, tears, and smiles.

'What…' Daniel spoke, trying to withhold a sudden laugh. 'What are you wearing?'

'Oh,' Noah replied, looking embarrassed. 'This? Oh, I wear it just for show. You know… We have been rebuilding and shaping their destiny as best as we can, but some traditions are hard for these people to let go…'

'And it looks heavy too by the look of it,' John added as he hugged Noah.

'So he got you back,' Noah replied, taking the crown off his head. 'I knew he would… He was never going to leave you behind.' He turned his gaze to Daniel. 'I understand what you meant, what you have been telling me since the beginning. We were destined to be together in all this. We were destined to walk together, side by side like…brothers.'

'I do love you, Noah. I always will,' Daniel said, his hands moving to Noah's face as he stared into his eyes again.

'If I think about it, now that I know how this played out, I was always meant to come here, protect this place, watch in place of Time, becoming…him. And you, with what comes next, you were always meant to be Love. As it's true you are the one that moved beyond, by his side. The one who controlled him, conquered his heart. You and me, like them, will be forever linked together.'

'Yes, yes, yes, touching, very touching,' Varuk said, crossing the room accompanied by Voishan. 'But we have to finish getting ready for your departure. There is so much to do here…'

'Daniel, John, Anita, these are Varuk and Voishan, sons of the King of all Valahans,' Noah introduced.

'The Valahan Mogs...' Daniel blurted out in surprise, as images of a long, perilous journey through the deadly mountains replayed in his mind.

'Not anymore,' Revelia replied, placing a hand on Varuk's shoulder. 'That name, like that past, is gone...'

'They helped us close the gates of this world. They will be staying behind as I and the others join you in our final steps,' Noah continued.

'The others?' Anita asked, wondering who else would come along beside Revelia and Trusk.

'We need as much help as we can get. We need magic beyond what we have already.' Noah stepped aside, revealing someone whose presence was both unexpected and terrifying.

She walked slowly, her steps soft on the white pavements. Like every Leonty, her movements were feline in nature, a sharp contrast with the heavy shock her face triggered in their hearts. She looked like a younger version of the one they had faced and defeated, yet almost identical to the Una they had seen in the mirror they had taken from her tower.

'This can't be…' Anita exclaimed.

Daniel moved at once. In his heart, he always knew there had to be a way to redeem her. He stopped a few inches from Una, whose look carried the magic of scrutiny. Her eyes ablaze, her expression firm, she gazed at Daniel with vivid interest. At their back, Anita instinctively moved to his rescue but Revelia stopped her, nodding a silent, *'It's OK.'*

'Your mind is way too vast for me to reach,' Una whispered. 'I was given the knowledge of what I would become if I had lost my mother, my father, the peace of a good heart. I know it's strange to apologize for something I haven't done, but I know I could have, if my past had been the one Noah showed me.'

'So you know…' Daniel replied. 'You saw what happened. You saw what you did and what we did…'

'I do, and I'm truly sorry. Yet, I fail to feel close to the queen he described. My powers are not shaped by evil and anger today. I was raised with love and care by everyone I met. I can't even comprehend what that life was.'

'You and I are very much alike, you know?' Daniel added. He took her hands and moved them to his chest. 'My heart knew you weren't given a chance to be anything else. You and I were driven by powers way beyond our comprehension. And now we both stand here with the understanding of many lifetimes. We lived more than once, we know more than one past, more than one present. We were both rescued by a magic that knows no challenge.'

'Love…' she let out as she gazed at the far side of the room, where Vertatis stood, quietly observing her beloved daughter.

'Does she know too?'

'No, she doesn't, and it's better this way. Noah has rebuilt this present in a very peculiar way. He prevented the Humans from attacking us, yet he made sure my mother and my father would meet so I would come along. I believe he wanted to redeem me, as you did—I can read it in your mind.' She smiled. 'But he also needs me, now that we face the last enemy standing.'

'I'm glad we have you.'

'Well, you may be, but I can read your mother's thoughts, or is she your friend? I can't really read her mind properly. I see she is still…hesitant.' Una concluded as she moved towards Anita.

To the Leonty, she might have struggled to accept her redemption, but what she couldn't see was that Anita wasn't too keen to forget or forgive. As Cherish had gifted her with the love for history and memories, Anita was naturally reluctant to any revision, either in facts or feelings. Yet, she had learned to accept a magic that went beyond her certainties, and as Una approached, Anita lifted her hand as if to say, *'Hi, nice to meet you.'*

The group stood silent for a moment while the inhabitants of Runae tried to understand what that gesture meant. After Daniel, Noah, and John burst out laughing, Anita followed suit, finally releasing the tension.

'I think it's time we move forwards with our plan,' Revelia interrupted.

She stood next to Una as if their relationship had never been shaped by evil and deceit. The time when the Crimson Queen had made her believe she was her sister, exploiting her power for her gain, was now replaced by a reality made of true bonds of friendship. 'I don't see any threat ahead, here in Runae, but as I check each one of our futures, it's clear we need to move.'

'Let me call the others,' Una said. 'We'll leave once we have gathered them all. Noah,' she added, 'many of them don't know what evil they were prevented from facing. You better have a good speech ready.' And the Leonty left the room, accompanied by her father.

Soon enough, the group stood right outside the palace, surrounded by many friends and allies. The great fountain at the centre of the courtyard was filled with water, allowing Aura and Queen Eah to join the announcement. A few steps away, Revelia and Una kept close to a few Leonty. As Noah began to speak, Daniel gazed at them, recognizing Demetra and Trasfigea among the few. Some others he had no recollection of listened carefully to the words of their king.

'Chomps, Leonty, Valahans, Garughals, Aqualymphs, Humans, my friends, I've asked you to be here as the time has come for me to join the others in our final battle against an enemy that does not give up. As you were born and time passed by, I revealed to you a truth that was painful at first, but necessary for our survival. But you understood… You saw with the eyes of a mystical revelation what we prevented from happening. You swore to secrecy, forever withholding the past we erased from the people you love. And because of them, we must finish what we started. We need you, all of you, to make this possible. Queen Eah,' Noah called.

'The sea is ready, my king. We'll stop anyone from crossing the node. No exceptions allowed, no words of deceptions this time. Except for those who stand here, we'll destroy anyone that tries to enter Runae!'

'If we fail our duty,' Aura added, 'I'll sound the Sacred Horn in warning for everybody else.'

'The strongest Valahans will be watching over the Cloudy Mountains. Even if the enemy can't enter from there any more, it's safe to assume that's where any intruder would head. But we will be standing in protection of the stones!' Varuk stated.

Noah nodded, looking at each group with gratitude and determination. 'We have one final battle to fight, one last stand to make. We do this for those we love, for the peace we have worked so hard to achieve. Let us be victorious, together.'

'And if any of them walks on land, we'll hear them,' Garúth added. 'We have a few forests we can count on. We'll trap them there indefinitely.'

'Thank you all, my friends,' Noah concluded. 'If any of you need guidance and support, Kasthor and Faróel will be here, in the crown city. Kareesto will take care of anything you may need. For now, I only say, thank you.'

As the king's speech ended, the gathering dispersed. The two Aqualymphs held off, waiting for a last exchange with Noah. Daniel, Anita, and Trusk followed him as he approached the large fountain.

'Did you decide?' Aura asked.

'Yes. Time did it for our and your protection. We should do the same. Queen Eah, please, would you do me the honour?'

Noah stretched his hand to meet that of the Aqualymph. As their fingertips touched, the clepsydra appeared out of nowhere, glowing. Tuned with the magic held by Queen Eah, her red crown shone bright as if the power of the sacred water descended from her head to her arm and hand.

Several pendants formed in the air, spinning with a green hue. As they formed, they scattered around, looking for those who needed protection, giving them the right to walk back into Runae when needed. Reaching each one's neck, a string of magic embraced their features and eventually disappeared. Inside their bodies and hearts, the precious relics lay hidden.

'I know here is safer than it has ever been,' Daniel said to John as they approached the shoreline. The others had already crossed the sea, but they had stayed behind. As Daniel prepared for what came next, he was resolute in avoiding repeating the same mistakes. 'I won't leave you here, this time. No matter what Noah's and Time's magic has done to this place, I must have you with me. I'm not losing you again, not even for a second.'

'Why do I hear a but?' John asked.

'I'm back, we are back, and so our memories are back for a reason. We are going to end this once and for all, but I know what must be done. If I fail…'

'You won't,' John said, taking Daniel's hand and moving closer. Their lips met, sealing their promise, their determination to spend the rest of their lives together. They were granted a second chance, and there was no space for doubts. 'You gave me magic, this incredible truth, things that I would have never imagined possible. You got me back, you got us back. There is no way I'll lose you and you won't lose me. Now,' John concluded as he gently wiped Daniel's tears, 'guide me through this once more. I'll follow you to the end.'

So the moment arrived. The two entered the sea and reappeared on the island faster than the blink of an eye. The group gathered together and, under Aura's resolute watch, they crossed the node and disappeared.

Chapter Twenty One

A Destiny Fulfilled

∞

Once again, places exchanged, reality reshaped without any major difference. Though much larger, they left one island only to land on another that looked almost the same. From the tiny spot in the middle of the Aqualymphs' Sea, they emerged on Crossing Island in a snap. Day had surrendered to a dark night when they appeared on the other side. As the last one stepped onto the verdant grass, the portal flashed and glowed as if encased in glass. It emitted the clear sound of locks clicking into place, then dissolved.

'It's not a coincidence we're here, is it?' Daniel asked, his eyes fixed on Anita. Beside her, the two Awokens had materialized out of thin air.

'I've always wanted to ask you,' she began, her voice tinged with curiosity. 'Were you really here? Did you really come to us before we entered hell to rescue Noah?'

Daniel looked around in silence. After a few moments, he replied, 'I think I was... My time with Love is fragmented. I see shards of moments. I felt, and still feel, every instant as if I never left, but I struggle to remember all the details.'

'Well, what lies ahead is hard to forget,' Revelia interjected. 'Leonty, follow me,' she added, moving inland towards the cluster of trees at the island's centre.

'Not this time, Trusk,' Daniel said, holding the Chomp in place. 'I need you to stay behind.'

'Whaf? Why?'

'I need you to protect the most important thing in my life,' he said, glancing at John. 'He has no magic, no power to defend himself. Can you do this for me?'

'Of course I can, I'm a Chomp! I'd do anyfhing for you.' The simple gesture of Trusk taking John's hand sent a wave of comfort through Daniel.

'Stay with him at all times,' Daniel warned John. 'It's imperative that you stay together. I don't know how many Harpies we'll face. Some might leave the fight to attack you, like cowards. Anything to distract us.'

The vision of Algos using Strife to attack the Awokens from within their ranks loomed clearly in Daniel's mind. He shared an eternity of memories with me. He knew everything I knew, and he felt everything I had felt.

Daniel and John exchanged a soft kiss as they hugged.

'You want to know how I knew I loved you more than anything and anybody else?' Daniel asked. 'Because all my worries, the horrors of my past, were silenced by you. Your presence in my life…simply walking next to me…your smiles, the life we built together—these things made me forget. Damn, you almost made me forget I was meant to do all this. Even with all this magic, this pain, centuries of dreams, you tamed them all, at least for a good while.'

'Why are you telling me this? You're not…' John's voice cracked as he started to tear up.

'No, I won't. We are meant to be together. We found each other again, despite the odds. I'll find you, no matter where I go, no matter who I'll be. I'll find you, and you will find me.'

And so they parted, their minds still intertwined in the same resolve. Whatever they were going to face, they would not lose each other ever again.

When Revelia reached the large hole in the ground, nestled in the heart of the woods, she stopped and knelt, hovering her hand over the edge of the cavity. With the mystic power of her mind, she could perceive my presence, she could feel me surging from the void.

'This is where we emerged from. He is here,' she said to Daniel and Noah as they joined Leonty. 'He's been here all this time…'

'He's waiting for you,' Demetra said to Daniel. 'His mind…his will is as large as the universe.'

A red glow pierced the darkness. A white shell followed suit as Eros manifested among them, the artefact floating slowly in his hands. Six more Awokens appeared in quick succession, completing the gathering of the Seven.

A white mist rose above the ground, gliding over the field as I silently moved among the group. The light I brought with me intensified tenfold, almost blinding those who had come. Eventually, I slowly formed amidst the crowd and spoke.

'I see you have succeeded… I gather you managed to block Nothing's army from entering Runae. Well, very well. Everything has worked as we planned. We enter Death's domain together, but the journey below is difficult, even for beings like you. I'm holding Death trapped here, but at a great cost. Many are the Harpies that I keep confined; some have started to escape my gaze and roam free in this world. Thanks to the

Awokens, we have kept them subdued, but we must take him down if we want to defeat his army once and for all. They will not return if he is gone.'

'Time's plan is going to work,' Noah said. 'But we have to make sure our magic, their magic,' he added, glancing at the Leonty, 'will work against them.'

'Death has no connection with the artefact any more.' Cherish spoke, anticipating me. 'They can't detect our power like they did with the Chomp's dome. He won't see us.'

'She's right,' Revelia added. 'They won't.'

'Let's go,' I said, sharply. The Awokens instantly disappeared as the others joined hands, ready to plunge into the abyss. 'Daniel, you stay with me,' I concluded.

The group jumped without hesitation, diving into the darkest pit of hell. As they plunged into the endless abyss, the dark night transformed into a complete black void. Noah's clepsydra glowed green against the emptiness, casting a light towards the fast-approaching end. Like a beacon of hope, he followed its trail, trusting Time's magic as they sped like tiny bullets through Death's kingdom.

The artefact pulsed three times, and the relics they carried around their necks followed suit as they suddenly stopped, inches from the ground. Bringing time to a halt, Noah released it again, slowly, until they glided safely onto the black stones. Far above, I stood silent, secretly listening, waiting for the sign of their safe arrival.

'They made it,' I said. 'Now, it's time for us to agree on a part of the plan my brother and I kept to ourselves.'

Daniel kept quiet, his gaze fixed on mine. Our eyes locked, and he attuned his mind to mine once again.

'You might know by now why we did what we did. Why the Gods moved against Nothing while I stayed behind… Yes, we had to ensure Creation's making would survive, something we had to protect at all costs. And yet, we had no time. We spent too long trying to return, trying to emerge from our cursed slumber. And in all that time, Nothing's core was almost cleansed of our essence, our creative magic. His armies had grown so vast, we found ourselves at a loss. Even if, thanks to you, I came back and joined my siblings, it was still too late.'

'So you stayed to fight here what they are fighting there…' Daniel interjected.

'Like Time said before, there was no other way. If Mother and my siblings hadn't stopped him right then, everything we created in the universe would be gone, right in his destructive hands. Yet, we couldn't leave Earth and Runae under his army's attacks. We were going to lose, no matter whom we chose to face. So, Time showed me the only opportunity we had, the only future where we could spare the two worlds and let them survive.'

'What was it? Tell me...'

'He saw everything. He saw us losing because we couldn't find a way through. But then, a whisper, a prophecy glimpsed in his mind as he heard a witch woman speaking of someone who wasn't even there... There was a chance, perhaps? He inspected it, folding days, years, centuries to find all the pieces, all the things we had to do to grasp that one possibility. And so, Time let everything happen as it was meant to, intervening only a little, steering the flow of time just enough for our present to happen. He let the Witches open the portal so Shahara could say the words. He broke the stone into six Flares so Una could rise, so the Chomps could survive. He let Nothing take him neither too early nor too late, but just as he struck me and my sister. Time knew he would then run, leaving him in the custody of the Crimson Queen. And then, as it had to happen, my destiny and my brother's merged when you and Noah walked through the gates. Every little detail was meticulously planned so we could be here, right now.'

'Did you know? How much did you know?'

'I didn't. My brother knew me as much as I knew him. He knew my true essence would lead me to you all, blinding me to Nothing's attack for the sake of your survival. In every version of the future he sought, he saw me failing, over and over, except in one—the one where you would lead me to protect the others as they found Creation's artefact. So he waited. He waited to reveal everything to me only when the time was right.

And I saw the truth with my own eyes. I finally saw how we were going to win this.'

'So we found Time,' Daniel continued, as if his mind were fully fused with mine. 'And we found Soul and Health. We found all the artefacts and Creation's relic too. Once they were all free... they moved against Nothing, leaving us the duty to win the battle in our worlds.'

'We knew I wouldn't be able to face them in two different worlds, so my brother gave Noah his artefact and a great portion of his power. Here, I waited for him to close the gates, Nothing's access to Runae. Meanwhile, Anita raised you as the beautiful Human being you are...so you would also be ready to do what we are about to do.'

'You are going to leave us?' Daniel whispered, as if talking to himself. 'Of course you are... The Gods were never meant to resist him without you. They have been holding the spot, waiting for you to join them...'

'The ticking of time is something my brother owns within his soul. You need to understand, Daniel, this moment, right now, is the last stretch of a long wait we can't hold any longer. I must do this. But not before you get to be me...' My artefact shone brighter than before, engulfing Daniel with the soft light of my magic. His feet lifted from the ground as I empowered him with a new life, a new strength.

'This was your destiny all along, my dear Daniel. You were the one. Thank you for showing me what our true power is for. Thank you for saving us all. Now,' I concluded, 'we finish this once and for all.'

'I'm ready!'

I entered his body, penetrating his flesh and bones, reaching deep into his heart. Every inch of power he could sustain through Human means filled his soul, uniting us as one being once again. He glided back to the ground, and as his feet touched down, he leaped forward, plunging into the mouth of the evil. In mere seconds, he reached the others in the dark below, where they moved slowly through the darkness.

Leading the group through the narrow path, Noah shed a green light onto the road ahead. The surroundings seemed to teeter between survival and collapse. The sound of rolling stones against the gelid walls carried the chilling vibe of a kingdom in demise. Yet, the group stayed vigilant, confident that the enemy was anything but weak.

As they entered a small room, they found the same chair where Revelia had been taken prisoner now stood empty. The chains and Death's spell were gone, and the pedestal on which Creation's book once stood was knocked down onto the black pavement. Only a few feet away, the dark, ethereal doors wobbled with a familiar evil. Despite their accomplishments in taking the artefact and breaking the link between my mother and

Death, his evil magic still permeated the space, bringing a heavy feeling of misery and despair.

'After Nothing parted my soul in two,' I began, speaking through Daniel, 'and I entered the never-ending loop of death and birth, my Awokens continued the fight as best as they could. All around the world, they kept scouting, searching for places where the evil surged, just like this island. We had done it before, fighting the Harpies, and they kept doing it for centuries. In each location, they used the remnants of their magic to guide Humans to erect monuments for the protection of the gates, fusing their essence with stones, pillars, and soil. There, they initiated the spell of protection, hoping, waiting for a time I would come back. But the more openings Death created, the less magic we held. One by one, all Awokens were consumed by a fight they could not win. Many of those spots are still under our protection, my protection, but…as I do what I must, we need to eradicate this evil from this world…'

'If Athymos is back with Victoria, it's safe to assume others are out there, festering in the world. They have found another way out,' Anita replied.

'OK then. We do what we agreed on,' Noah said.

'No,' Revelia immediately countered, her gaze fixed on Daniel, on me. 'Are you insane?'

'It will work. After all, we have Una, Demetra, Trasfigea, and all of you. It will work, trust me,' Daniel and I replied.

'This wasn't the plan,' Revelia objected. 'Why would you risk it now?'

'What is it?' Anita pulled Daniel by the arm, fear quickly mounting.

'Like you said, there are Harpies out there. Remember what Death did when we faced him up on the surface? He called them all. Even Athymos, the one who would not take sides, responded to his call…' I replied. 'We need him to fear us as much as he feared us then. If he feels threatened, he will call them all here.'

'We can do this,' Una firmly added. Her face bore the determination of a resolute queen, echoing a different past yet the same strong will.

Mine and Daniel's plan was audacious, a gamble against the looming darkness. The weight of our resolve filled the air, every heart beating with the rhythm of impending battle. We were on the precipice, ready to plunge into the unknown, united by purpose and bound by fate.

Chapter Twenty Two

The Gate to Victory

∞

A group of Harpies moved silently through the grand hall; their steps carried softly against the stone floor as they inspected the dark archways. Just as they were about to enter one of the rooms, another Harpy appeared, her malevolent grin radiating power and malice.

'What are you all doing here?' Desolos questioned.

'We heard voices coming from these rooms,' one in the gathering replied. 'After what happened last time someone entered our home, we weren't going to stay put.'

'What voices? I heard nothing...' Desolos's deformed expression shifted, her gaze fixed on her brethren as she began to inspect the group carefully.

'Her core is empty but her mind is strong...' a Leonty whispered. Her voice, like their appearances, was muffled by the powerful and deceiving manipulation of minds.

'Has our master decided?' another Harpy in the group questioned. *'What?'* Anita added, her voice echoing in the secret of their magic. Responding to Daniel and Noah's look, she continued, *'She must know!'*

'What's going on here?' Another dangerous Harpy had just walked in.

'Of all the ones we could face, it had to be him!' Noah whispered, his voice unheard by Desolos and Strife.

'One of ours in their hands is something I will never learn to accept,' I said through Daniel.

'His mind is cracked, shattered in many pieces...' Demetra added. *'It's hard to even read it...'*

'These ones were roaming around when they are supposed to be down below,' Desolos replied.

'Death is sending a few of us through the ancient opening in Gope. The Humans have unearthed the site, breaking the seal, it would be a chance for some of us to escape through there,' Strife said, staring at two of the Harpies in the group. To him, something looked out of place. 'Move! Desolos, you too...'

The group followed Strife through the first archway to the right, entering the emptiness of another large room. Desolos watched them closely, her suspicion evident. Thousands of bookshelves lined the room in hundreds of rows. Blue flames flickered here and there, releasing the same deadly spell Anita and Revelia had witnessed before.

'I thought we had erased this magic when we took the first book,' Revelia said, in shock.

'Death's power must be holding them in place. I'd say this is why he hasn't left hell yet. Without the book, he is the only reason why everything still stands,' said the Harpy cloaking Anita's features, staring at the numbers on top of the bookshelves.

'You, move!' Desolos pushed. 'What's wrong with you?' she inquired as Anita inadvertently parted from the others.

They soon left the room and entered a narrow pathway, descending into the abyss. Stairs appeared everywhere, and towering walls rose from an invisible depth below, pierced by hundreds of holes. In each one, blue hues flickered, marking the countless souls of the dead.

Halfway through their descent, Strife turned left and entered a gigantic space. The paved ground mixed red and black colours, the mark of death as if fused with dried blood. A long sequence of tall columns spiked to a high, rocky ceiling. Towards the far end of the room, two smaller columns framed a stony chair. Around it, a large number of Harpies kneeled, while two more stood next to the largest of them all. Sitting on his throne, Death inquired, 'What about the passage in the desert?'

'My master, the seals placed by them are too strong. The large structures would not be a problem for us, but their spell is. The Humans have never entered the chamber where the magic resides… Those seals remain unbroken.'

'Useless Humans!' Death thundered. 'They had thousands of years to break through the pyramids and still can't find a stupid room.'

'They did remove the pillars in Gope, my master. A few of us have used it already to get out.' Mespherya's voice rose from the collective evil.

'What about that island?' Death asked, standing up.

'The statues are all there, holding the Awokens' magic. Last time you sent us there, we managed to knock a few down, but it wasn't enough…the gates are still closed.'

'So we have one passage only…'

As Death's words echoed through the chamber, the group knew the time to act was imminent. Daniel, empowered by my essence, felt a surge of resolve. He glanced at his companions, their faces set with determination. This was the moment they had been preparing for—the final stand against the darkness.

Death was furious. He moved around, measuring his steps, desperately trying to find a way through, when his gaze moved on to the small group of Harpies who stood way back from the other. He raised his right arm and fiercely whipped it back, pulling Anita and Una all the way to the throne, making them crash onto the black stones.

Before I could intervene, moving against the enemy ahead of time, Revelia stopped me.

'It's fine. It's all fine, Daniel.'

'So you believe you are exonerated from responding to my call?' he thundered as he lifted the two up in the air. Despite their struggle and the terror filling the Leonty's mind, Trasfigea and Illusiō stood firm, their eyes secretly shining like rubies, holding on to the extensive magic that covered them all. 'Why weren't you here?' And Death flung them back again, among the other Harpies.

If Una had risen back on her feet swiftly, Anita didn't. She was hurt, her arms and legs so sore she started to sweat, trying to restrain herself from screaming.

'These is something strange with these few,' Desolos said as her words travelled like the hiss of a snake. 'Lëogan, you might want to check for yourself?'

The supreme Harpy of lies and deceits moved slowly towards the two. His wicked, empty eye sockets fixed on Una as she found herself only a few inches away from the one she knew she had confronted before.

'You heard our master…why weren't you here?' he said as he floated around her. 'I don't know exactly what's happening but I'm sure something is going on here…'

'Fine, if this one doesn't talk, maybe one of the others will.' Algos moved away from the evil pack and her jaw dislocated, opening to release a terrifying whistle.

Trasfigea and the others fell on their knees, their hands on their ears. Consumed by the shrilling pain, the magic started to falter and our cover vanished in a blink. Exposed, surrounded by a countless number of Harpies, Noah and Daniel moved next to each other, prepared to fight. And yet, the enemy hadn't moved. They were all frozen in their positions, oblivious to the discovery.

There, Una's power spread like a raging fire. Her eyes so bright, she could illuminate the entire hell in a crimson light. The many, powerful minds were all hers to shape, hers to control. As if the spectres of her past, the lost Aqualymphs, had switched place with the evil of our world, she tamed their wills and, above them all, she infiltrated Death's mind into his fractured, malevolent core.

Daniel and Noah ran towards Anita, their hands on her face, her arms. Eros spun off Daniel's body, worried. With the many obscure entities around them, they were free to move thanks to the one who could make their minds dull, controlling them like dark marionettes.

'My love,' Eros said, panicking. 'Are you OK?'

'I think I broke something,' she moaned as she got up on her feet. 'I can barely feel my left hand…'

'So I'm destined to face this vile being in any present I'm gifted with,' Una said, raging with anger. A version of the terrible Crimson Queen carried through. The things Noah had showed her, the evil actions of that same Harpy, spilled into her being as if real memories.

'Una!' I thundered, as I emerged from Daniel's body, followed by an army of Awokens.

Her focus temporarily shifted from the collective enemy to one Harpy only, releasing Death and all his soldiers from the enchantment. The large Harpy thundered like an angry beast, evoking all the power he could master. Before he could move against us, he watched Una's magic pierce through Lëogan's corrupted mind, burning him from inside.

His ghostly body twitched as he gazed at her, locked in her spell. The last shred of thought was the one of the queen he had forged into a terrible evil moving against him once more. His matter pulsed rapidly and eventually exploded.

A dark cloud extended all around, enveloping us in the magic Umbra had released from behind the ranks. As it crawled on the ground, it reached the Harpies, one by one. As one of them appeared among us, Noah, Daniel and I swung our arms in the air, breaking their essences apart.

Eros left Anita to the care of Una and he joined the Seven in a blinding attack. They moved like a bright spear through darkness, erasing any Harpy they met on their way to their master.

'You!' Death shouted. 'You can't defeat me!' And his arms extended towards his slaves, dragging them within his deformed body. As he grew large and terrifying, Daniel and Noah emerged from Umbra's spell right in front of our enemy. And with them I rose from within my host, large and bright like our sun.

'This is your end,' I let out. 'You will regret not having all your soldiers here, with you!'

'Oh but they are…' Death laughed as his form expanded, making the ground quiver. A few Harpies appeared from within the pavement, some emerged from the walls. Every Harpy sent into the world was called back to fight alongside their king.

'Daniel!' Revelia screamed from across the room. 'She is coming, on the surface, by the node!'

'John! Trusk!' Daniel replied, gazing at Noah. The terror flashed in his eyes when Noah took his hands.

'Hold on,' I said, as I held my finger up, telling Daniel to wait, just one more moment.

'This world is mine!' Death's voice echoed in the expanse, bouncing off the ground, the ceiling, the walls.

Everywhere shook violently while the ones who had come to face him in our final battle ran away, tracing their steps back. Behind them, Una walked slowly, helping Anita to stand.

Right below the large Harpy, a crater opened up, finally revealing the place where lay the entrance to our world, the granted passage through which Nothing had sent them to bring devastation and sorrow on Earth. There he drew power from his master, the King of Emptiness. There I had to push him through it, casting him away as I followed him through. There, where Nothing had infiltrated my protected world for the first time, I would reverse his evil, using it to enter his wicked core instead.

'Awokens!' I roared. 'We close this gate and push the enemy away from our beloved world. Seven, take them all to safety!'

Agapei, Xena, Prometheus, Storgén, Philiat, and Pragma instantly dissolved, reappearing at the back of the fugitives. They lifted them up, raising them all the way back to the top of the staircases. Next to me, Daniel and Noah, Eros and Cherish stood close, their resolve attuned with ours.

'My home will be your tombstone, yours and theirs!' Death's vast power extended through every inch, every particle of his kingdom. As if he could live through it, arms and hands emerged and extended towards the group desperately trying to reach the dark doors.

'No!' Demetra shouted, seeing Trasfigea falling under the grasp of the rising Harpies. Umbra's dark power slid on the surface, rising among the countless bookshelves, surrounding the Leonty and the enemy in a blinding fog. There, Xena's soft hands lifted her off the ground and Xena sprinted forward.

Not far behind, with excruciating pain running all over her body, Anita fainted in Una's arms, her weight forcing her onto the floor. An evil ensemble encircled the two, the faces of the most terrifying Harpies forming before their eyes. Una gazed at the whirlpool of darkness moving against them, and her eyes blazed like two red stars.

'You won't touch us.' She spoke through her clenched teeth.

But the number of wicked soldiers multiplied with every second, too many to count, too many to enslave under her power. She couldn't see them, the many turning from a collective will to myriads of fragmented minds.

As Anita came back to her senses, her eyes struggling to focus in the dark, she gulped. Death appeared right between them and his army. His obscure form moved against his own kind as he commanded them to retrieve and join him in battle against Daniel, Noah, and me.

Without hesitation, they moved at once, deceived by the power of the one who lay just a few steps away. Illusiō swiftly moved towards Una and helped Anita to stand back on her feet. Their run resumed, quickly reaching the grand hall and the dark doors through which they could escape to freedom. One by one they crossed the evil gate and arrived at the bottom of the pit.

Lifted once again by the Awokens, they reached the surface and emerged into the quiet island. As they left the woods and moved to the node, the antithesis of everything they represented welcomed them in a new fight.

'I'm tired of your games!' Athymos's voice reverberated across Crossing Island. 'You won't escape me!' She released a dart of petrifying magic against Trusk, whose movements in the air were erratic, scattered as if he were struggling to fly.

As the group emerged from the greenwood, Trusk glided and moved between them. 'Fhis one is mad! And powerful!' he panted. 'Look whaf she did fo me…' He turned around, revealing a shocking set of wings: one made of feathers, the other of grey stone.

'Oh no, Trusk!' Revelia gasped. 'Wait a moment… Where is John?'

'Me and John flew fo fhe ofher side of fhe lake buf she wouldn'f give up, so I made her follow me back here. And fhen she hif me!'

Another flash of evil magic darted towards the group. Athymos's large figure moved unchallenged, her dark forms clashing against the early hours of the morning. Shielding the gathering of friends and allies, Storgén and Prometheus raised their bright power against her.

Athymos approached, her presence casting a shadow over the dawn's first light. As if her essence could hold the remnants of the night within her grasp, she obscured the rising sun's rays as she walked right in front of them.

'Stand back!' Philiat shouted, his voice a beacon of authority and hope. His bright aura intensified, clashing against Athymos's dark magic. Pragma joined him, their combined power creating a radiant barrier that pushed back the encroaching darkness.

'We have been watching you for centuries, taming your power. You think we can't do it again?' Philiat said.

'We have witnessed your madness, the horrible things you have done, stripping people of the only thing that makes them Humans. We won't forget how you moved Victoria against her son, turning her into a feelingless creature. Your days are over!' Pragma added.

Athymos sneered, her eyes glinting with malevolence. 'Your words mean nothing to me… You haven't learnt? I am the embodiment of muted emptiness. I feel no pain, no fear. Your feeble cries are meaningless.'

She lifted her contorted arms in the air, triggering an astonishing power from the ground up, lifting the group and scattering them around. Advancing slowly, the attacks of the Awokens missed her as if she were made of thin air. She stopped right where Anita lay, writhing in pain. For the third time, Anita was confronted by the spectre of Victoria, by the dark will of a Harpy who had tormented her son and her best friend for their entire lives.

'I saw you...' Athymos whispered, her voice a venomous hiss. 'I saw you as you walked in my world, pretending to be a better mother... Stupid creature. That day you escaped me, you only made it worse. All these...emotions you collected like precious relics...the years you extended so you could have him for yourself, collecting even stronger feelings... Your stupidity is what kills you now!'

Anita's eyes widened with fear and anger. 'You don't understand... You'll never understand the strength of love.'

Athymos laughed, a cold, mocking sound. 'Love? Love is a weakness. It's why you're here, lying at my feet, broken. Love is what made you lose, by my hand.'

Chapter Twenty Three

The Power of Love

∞

Death's power stormed around us, a tempest of darkness and malevolence. His Harpies swarmed, loyal to their master, amplifying his will until it pressed down on us like the weight of an entire world. In that final moment, the end of our eternal battle seemed inevitable. I stood with the carriers of my magic, side by side, the power of the Gods' artefacts coursing through us. Together, we pushed back against the waves of emptiness he hurled our way, inching closer to the abyss.

'There is no hope in opposing me.' Death's voice echoed, deep and resonant. His presence was so vast, it felt as if the very fabric of reality trembled at his words.

The ground beneath us began to crumble, transforming hell into a collapsing tomb. The floor gave way, revealing a yawning chasm that exposed the entrance I had sought for so long. As we floated amidst the dust and debris, the long-hidden secret was finally within reach.

Rocks and stones shot towards us like bullets. On either side, Cherish and Eros summoned the remaining artefacts. Soul's shining tiara appeared on our left, and Mother's book on our right. We were ready to strike as Health's sceptre formed in my hands, when a piercing whistle of danger rang in our minds—Athymos was about to attack on the surface.

In an instant, Cherish and Eros vanished, reappearing behind the Harpy whose arms were raised to strike.

'Hands off!' they shouted in unison, pressing against her back and taking her by surprise.

The Harpy turned into intangible smoke, reforming a few feet away. She twirled her hands, dark strings of magic rising from the ground. Eros swiftly pulled Anita away, as Cherish shielded them both, advancing against the Harpy with unwavering resolve.

'You didn't touch her before, you won't touch her now!' Cherish cried out.

Athymos ignored her, pressing forwards with relentless power. Her arm stretched towards Cherish, fingers outstretched, dark energy crackling. The moment her hand touched Cherish's face, the Awoken began to turn to stone, paralyzed by the Harpy's true nature.

With Athymos focused on Cherish, she failed to notice the Seven forming a circle around her. They glowed with a bright light, their collective power fusing into an unbreakable prison.

The Harpy convulsed, pushing and pressing against the Awokens, trying to shatter their bond. The more she attacked, the more they bounced back, desperate to contain her fury.

With a final, desperate push, Athymos plunged into the gorge, dragging the Seven with her. Anita's heart sank as she watched Eros, clinging to the edge. Their eyes met, an unspoken exchange of undying love passing between them. Then, he was gone, swallowed by the darkness below.

The moment the Seven and Cherish entered Death's domain, their presence resonated clearly in my mind. With them, they had dragged the last remaining Harpy into the abyss. In the vastness of nothingness, Daniel, Noah, and I seemed like minuscule dots against the omnipresence of Death.

I raised my core to its limit and looked at Daniel and Noah. 'This is the moment we've been waiting for, for all eternity. We move against them now. When I tell you to let go, you will let go. Is that clear?'

'Love…' Daniel began, sorrow turning into tears.

'Is it clear?' I repeated, my voice unwavering.

'Yes!' they both answered.

The Seven clashed against the dark storm, penetrating its countless bodies, dragging Athymos into the fold. They infused me with the pure power of Love we represented, and we sprinted forward, right into Death's embrace. Hand in hand, Daniel, Noah and I reached the heart of the evil. Noah's clepsydra shone in the air, halting every Harpy in their movements, allowing me to pierce through. Wielding Health's sceptre as my pointy weapon, I shredded Death's matter, lacerating the void he was made of. All the Awoken Ones poured their energy through me, enveloping his presence in a blinding light that devoured him.

We pushed forwards as he receded into the passage between reality and the malevolence of Nothing. When every vile particle left hell, I turned to Daniel, whose resolute gaze locked with mine.

'Yours is the time to bring the living into their future. Trust your soul, your own magic as I did. Let love drive your every move, every decision. As I now fulfil my destiny, you fulfil yours. May the power of love protect you all, forever.' And as I crossed the threshold of our reality, I thundered, 'Let go!'

The shell appeared in Daniel's hands, shining like a beacon of hope. As it opened, the diamond heart began to beat, its bright red light pulsing, expanding, and releasing countless strings of magic. Threads spread across the space, rocks, walls, and the large fracture I had just crossed, binding every atom, knitting everything together. Daniel pulled the artefact, tightening its magic, sealing every inch of Nothing's ancient gate.

He took Noah's hand, and they flew over the many stairs, the thousands of rooms, and the souls of the dead as everything crumbled into dust. Bookshelves, tomes, and black stones pulverized as they fled upwards. As they emerged on Crossing Island, the large fissure shrank in an instant, releasing a cloud of smoke and magic at its closure.

I travelled with the speed of an exploding cosmos, entering the link between hell and Nothing. Inside the enemy's matter, I roared, bringing him to the sudden realization of my actions.

'Take back your evil servants,' I thundered, gripping Death tightly. 'Face the fury of a power you will never understand!'

'How…' Nothing moaned as his dark matter contracted. Hovering like a gigantic black hole, he folded inwards, convulsing. 'How did you…'

My mother and my siblings expanded their magic beyond survival, invading his core, penetrating the depths of his void. As we found each other again, we merged, releasing a cataclysmic explosion.

Whatever happened then, when we sacrificed ourselves to protect our universe, it was final. In that moment, every connection to my true being went silent. The only piece of me surviving in Daniel's heart detached from the Gods, our eternal link severed.

I came to exist alone, a fragment of what I was, when I was Love, when I was him, and a part of Daniel who now carried me inside his heart, a fragment of a divine soul.

And I rose to my feet as Daniel stood back on his. Next to me, next to him, next to us, Noah's tears flowed freely, a torrent of emotions—joy and sorrow intertwined. His face was a mosaic of devastation and elation, and I joined him in his desperate disbelief. We hugged, pulling each other close as if trying to fuse our shattered hearts, our minds melding in a supreme understanding.

We had won the fight of many lifetimes.

My eyes drifted to Anita, whose inner despair echoed in my mind. Yet, happiness quickly followed as she approached us, her heart and arm broken but her spirit unyielding.

'You are alive,' she cried, her voice raw with emotion. 'You are alive!'

'I'm sorry,' I sighed. 'There was no other way. He is gone…gone with Love, with the Gods…'

Anita stood frozen, her silence cutting through the air like a knife. Her eyes, once bright with hope, now glistened with the raw, unfiltered pain of a heart-shattering understanding. Tears flowed down her cheeks, each drop a testament to the anguish ripping through her soul. Yet, despite the sorrow blinding her, she never broke her gaze, her eyes locked on to mine with the same determination she had always had.

In those agonizingly stretched seconds, an entire universe of emotions surged between us. The weight of unspoken words and shattered dreams bore down, suffocating in its intensity. And then, amidst the chaos of her breaking heart, she smiled—a fragile, heartbreaking smile that spoke of resilience and acceptance. Finally, she found her voice, trembling yet determined, and spoke.

'He saved me, he saved you, he loved us more than anything else. It's what he wanted,' she wept. 'It's all he existed for.'

The group moved around us, offering a comfort that felt undeserved. The Leonty's hands pressed on us, forming a circle of compassion, trust, and victory. Before I could ask, to see for myself if I had kept my promise, Trusk appeared on the horizon, carrying the love of my life with him.

A few moments later, I was at the shoreline, my hands on John's head as I pulled him close and kissed him. Behind me, the diamond heart appeared, glowing softly. It hovered above our heads for a few seconds, as if bestowing a blessing with the power Love had left within me, within us. And then it disappeared, dissolving right into my chest.

Surrounded by friends and allies, we gazed at the sky, the weight of our victory and the profound loss of what had been sacrificed ached deeply inside our hearts. We all stood there in silence for what felt like an eternity, looking at the serene blue world above, the dark presence of Nothing a long, distant memory. The bright new day was a testament to resilience and hope, a beacon of light in a world that had been dark for far too long.

And as the sun rose, painting the sky with hues of dawn, I looked at that gathering of indomitable warriors and I knew that we had not only won our greatest battle but had forged a future where love could flourish anew.

Chapter Twenty Four

Epilogue

∞

One by one, all the Leonty crossed the node, except for Revelia and Una. The latter hesitated, her eyes meeting Noah's, words struggling to surface. She had much to say, yet only smiled and whispered, 'Don't be away for too long. Runae needs its king.' With a final glance, she walked through the divine gates.

It was as if an invisible roll call had been made, and all the Leonty were summoned but one. Revelia moved instinctively, her eyes reflecting neither prophecy nor apprehension. She knew a better time had come and was certain we wouldn't be apart forever. She wrapped her arms around Anita and whispered, 'Take the time to heal.' After a pause, she added, 'It's just like you told me, once. We are not just friends or allies. We are family. I may no longer be bound to this world, but my heart lingers here. Please don't force me to look ahead, desperately craving to see you again.'

'We'll never be apart, ever,' Anita responded, her voice resolute.

'Daniel, I don't think anyone in this world or in Runae could ever repay you. We were blessed the day you walked into our lands and even more when you came back to save us. Thank you for making me believe anything is possible.'

With that, Revelia smiled, tears brimming, and disappeared inside the node. Almost like a shadow, Trusk followed her trail but, hesitant, he turned around and stopped. His face showed the clear desire to stay longer, perhaps forever.

'Daniel?' he said.

'Yes?'

'Don'f leave me again, please.'

'I won't,' I replied, kneeling and taking his hand.

'How's your wing?' Anita asked, joining us in a hug.

'If's fine, Anifa,' he said, and we smiled at the sound of her strange name. 'When fhe Harpy wenf, so did her spell.' He turned and stretched his wings. Moments later, he took off and flew through the portal.

There we stood, the four of us alone, as if replaying the night in Castlecross, when John had finally accepted the magic, and we opened our hearts to Siobhan's memories and fabricated the most terrifying conjectures. This time, we had reached the other end of the impossible journey, knowing where our relentless fight for truth, love, and justice had led us. With a simple movement of his hand, Noah made the clepsydra appear and, absorbing the portal's energy, shut it off.

'Where do we go from now?' John suddenly broke the silence. 'What life are we supposed to live? The one we had before or the one we have now?'

'Both,' Anita, Noah, and I said in unison. We had become one body, one mind, bound by magic, fate, and love. There was no other life we would live but the one that had all of us together.

My artefact briefly reappeared in the cold air of the rising morning and, after embracing us in its magic, transported us to Castlecross, by the house John and I had just moved into. As we appeared in the garden, John walked towards the front door and let us in.

Before we could follow suit, Anita gazed at the two of us and started to cry again. For the three of us there was no need to speak, nor to lay in the open the nature of our sorrow, her pain. Anita's emotions spoke loudly, the devastation of losing Eros mixing with the joy of be together again, alive and well. She took our hands as her eyes met ours. A brief smile appeared, and yet it was quickly engulfed by the darkness keeping her heart in hostage. A darkness made of a future without the one who had loved us and protected us. After a long silence, she spoke.

'Half of me wants to believe he never existed, that we never left the house, that night when we started to read your mother's journal… And yet, the other half can still feel him. I grew old with him… I raised you, Daniel, with him. He was with me when I thought I was going to die, standing there in front of Death…'

'Is there a chance?' Noah asked me. Anita's desperation broke his heart as it shattered mine.

'The Awokens are gone,' I replied, struggling to speak. 'They all entered Nothing's core through the gate to put an end to his evil's will. There is no coming back for any of them. Most of Love's essence is gone too. All is left is a tiny piece inside me, inside the artefact I was gifted with…'

'We left with so many questions,' Anita finally spoke again. 'And came back with so much…too much to handle. I honestly hope Creation knew I could keep her artefact in custody because, the way I feel now…well, I don't know where to find the strength.' And she moved her hands on her face, drying up her tears.

'We find it in each other,' I said, hugging her. A moment later, Noah joined us in a bigger hug, his eyes gazing at the small cottage.

'It's way smaller, but it looks pretty,' Noah said. 'Well, a lot older than the other one…'

'Thanks,' I replied smiling. 'It's definitely younger than you… The crown did cover all the grey hair,' I added, as we moved inside.

'I know! I can't believe I'm fifty-five…'

'Oh, please, I feel like I'm a hundred and fifty,' Anita moaned, and we finally let out a shy laugh.

In that moment, in the warmth of our laughter, we knew we had found our place—both in the world we left behind and the new one we had forged together.

'Stay still for a second. I can't just heal one part of your body,' Noah said, looking at Anita's shoulders. 'But I can do better than that.'

A soft light surged from within his chest. Green hues bounced and reflected on Anita's body as they moved inside a bubble of magic. Moments later, they re-emerged, astonishingly transformed into younger versions of themselves. It was as if Noah had erased the traces of years, the troubles, and worries etched deeply in their wrinkles. They looked exactly as they had the day they met in Noah's Bridge.

'I put on the kettle. We can have some t—' John's words broke off at the sight of the two, youthful once more. His jaw dropped in shock, and then he added, 'Well, whatever beauty product you're using, I want it too!'

'I'm not done,' Noah replied, a glimpse of happiness flashing in his eyes. 'Give me your hands.'

John moved closer, eyes fixed on the magic unfolding. This time, the clepsydra's reverting power did not aim at John directly. Instead, a small, ethereal sphere appeared and wobbled in John's arms. With eyes shut tight, Noah struggled to recreate what his heart desired. Eventually, the clear shape of Daisy appeared before our stunned eyes.

The joy in that single moment was so strong that John and I started to cry, while Daisy licked our faces, happy to see us, completely unaware of the time that had passed.

'Thank you,' John said to Noah.

'Now, I'll happily have that tea before I go…even if I don't want to really leave this place, any of you,' Noah sighed.

'Stay a little longer,' I said. 'Help me keep this one under control.' I smiled, pointing at Anita.

'Hey! May I remind you I'm your mother?' she pushed back, caught between fun and reprimand.

'No, not any more you're not,' I teased. 'You're too young to be my mother…' I moved into the kitchen, laughing.

'Can you believe it?' I heard her complaining. 'All these years, the madness you put me through, yes, both of you!' She continued all the way to the back garden, where the tea waited on a wooden table, hot and steamy.

It's peculiar how our lives turned out. The way our steps were counted, our destiny shaped even before we came to life. And yet we existed long before, living so many lifetimes we can't even recall. Noah, Anita, and I all shared our hearts and souls with the Gods that existed for millennia. We fought for them, we died for them, we came back and kept our promise to them.

Yet, all seemed like a pure flicker of imagination. As we sat at the table, I gazed at them, the loves of my life, and thought, *Did we ever leave Anita's home that day? We could simply pretend we imagined it all.*

But in my heart, I knew it wasn't possible. I shared my heart with a piece of Love's soul. Anita held the memories of everything that had happened. As if Cherish still lived through her, she was the beholder of everything that had been. And, lastly, Noah had moved from being a lonely boy, without a family of his own, to being the king of an entire planet, loved and supported by all the friends we had met along the way.

The tea was hot and soothing, the conversation warm and effortless. For a moment, we were just people, not bearers of divine destinies or heroes of ancient prophecies. We were friends, family, bound together by an unbreakable bond. As the morning sun rose higher, casting golden light on our gathering, I knew that was the true reward for all we had endured: the simple, profound joy of being together, of having each other, and of knowing that, no matter what came next, we would face it as one.

In the chatter and laughter we shared, sipping tea like it was any other normal day, I looked at John, my heart swelling with joy knowing he was still mine and I was still his. I glanced at Noah, a man who had entered my life through dreams, true prophecy, and magic, and had come to stay, like a brother, like a piece of my own soul. And I gazed at Anita, who had become more than a friend. She was the mother I never had, the faith I never believed in, and the trust in the impossible I couldn't hold on to.

'What if, next summer, you come here, Noah, and we all go together?' John's question interrupted my trail of thoughts.

'I'd love that,' Anita said. 'That place, that house holds so much love… Eros, Daniel, and I had an incredible time there.'

'Daniel?' Noah called, noticing my distraction.

'What is it?' Anita asked.

'Nothing.' I attempted a smile. 'I was thinking about Harry…and Shannon, Mark, damn, even Patrick. And my dad, Cherish, Iris… I know a piece of Love is still within me. I know I'll have to continue his work in keeping this world filled with magic. Like Noah for Runae, my duty lies here, mastering the power of love to keep this world safe…'

'You won't be alone,' John said. 'None of us will be…' He placed a hand on Anita's shoulder, triggering a smile from her.

And there, we sealed our promise. As we had been there for one another, so we always would be. Even with the Gods gone, we would continue our mission, their mission, carrying their responsibilities on our shoulders, counting on each other's support.

Two worlds had been saved from the emptiness of an endless dark night, and we would keep protecting them, protecting the people we loved, and honouring the memory of Love, Time, Health, Soul, and Creation.

In our hands lay a future that almost wasn't. In our hands lay the promise of supreme protection. We had forged our readiness in the darkest fights. We were ready because of it; we were ready because we had each other.

And together, shielded by the power of love, we would always be.

∞

The Power of Love

The Three

The Power of Love

The Three

R.J. Kinnaird

About the Author

Ross Joseph Kinnaird was born in a far land something like 1000 years ago. He moved to Italy as an infant and grew up in the deep south, shaped by the sun and the wildness of the sea. After moving to Ireland in 2010, he began collecting and organizing the many stories he had written. They all seemed to have one theme, one soul. With the Celtic magic that his new home brought to him, Ross finally saw his novel taking shape through the mystical eyes of his mind. And so, *"The Power of Love"* became the journey of a lifetime, perhaps spanning many lifetimes.

In the realm between reality and fantasy, he fused together the diverse ways life presented itself to him. Through a literary roller-coaster of emotions and feelings—sorrow, happiness, friendship, and love—Ross J. Kinnaird wrote the many stories we tell ourselves in our search for greater meaning.

"Art, feelings, music, emotions have always been the strongest part of me. I was only a young teenager when I started transferring my busy mind onto paper.
As the years passed, life and experiences enriched my soul to a point where The Power of Love finally took form.
With the strongest connection to what I saw life as, the story of Daniel, Noah and Anita became an extension of who I am, of who many of us are."

R. J. Kinnaird

ISBN: 978-1-7394634-6-5

For more info on The Power of Love Series

thepoweroflove series.com

I hope the adventures of Daniel, Noah and Anita have brought you joy, fun and love.

The Power of Love – The One
The Power of Love – The Two
The Power of Love – A Tale of Time
The Power of Love – The Three

Printed in Great Britain
by Amazon

46819233R00199